THE
POWERS
THAT BE

THE
POWERS
THAT BE

MIKE NICOL

THE ATLANTIC MONTHLY PRESS
NEW YORK

First published in Great Britain in 1989 by Bloomsbury Publishing Ltd.
First Atlantic Monthly Press edition, September 1989
Printed in the United States of America

Library of Congress Cataloging-in-Publication Data

Nicol, Mike, 1951–
    The powers that be / Mike Nicol.
    ISBN 0-87113-291-5
    I. Title.
  PR9369.3.N54P6   1989   89-31284   823—dc19

The Atlantic Monthly Press
19 Union Square West
New York, NY 10003

First printing

FOR JILL

CONTENTS

ONE

1

TERRIBLE THINGS

Every morning for the three years he terrorised the village, Captain Sylvester Nunes had his daughter, Frieda, shave him on the verandah. Even in winter, when the wind came off the sea like fish-knives, she brought out the bowl of steaming water, the strap, the lather and the cut-throats to perform the ritual while he watched for signs of rebellion in the streets.

First Frieda would sharpen the razor on a leather strop until the blade was so keen a fly could not have stood on it. Next she would lather his face using an old ivory-handled brush which had belonged to his father. She would begin shaving on the left side, passing down the sharp jaw to the chin, returning to scour the hollow of his cheek. All it took was four quick, sure strokes, with a deft turn of the wrist between each to flick foam into the bowl of water. The left side done, Nunes would tilt his head until he could see some of the villagers loitering outside the trader's store, and Frieda would mirror her actions. Always she had to be careful not to trim the thin moustache that set his mouth in a sneer. Finally, she would lather his throat, which reminded her of the skin of a plucked chicken, and, working from the Adam's apple to the jaw, quickly clean off the stubble.

Frieda had been shaving the captain for ten years, ever since the death of her mother.

'Ah-man, it doesn't matter if you are only eight,' her father had said. 'The men of this family have always been shaved by their women, so you will have to learn.'

Frieda could remember that as he said it he paused with a lump of ice in his hand to look at her, and kept staring for such a long time that water began to trickle between his fingers; then he smiled and went back to packing the ice around the body of his wife. In that heat her mother's corpse wouldn't stop perspiring and they used up all the ice in the fridge waiting for the doctor.

The next morning, as he showed his daughter how to angle the blade, the captain told her the story of a woman who had tried to slit her husband's throat.

'No man wants to die like that,' he said, 'and this man wasn't a fool. Although his eyes were closed he knew what she was thinking. So even before the thought was through her head, he had shot her with the pistol he kept in his pocket.'

In those days it was just another of his strange stories. It didn't occur to Frieda to ask why the woman wanted to kill her husband, or why he should so coldly shoot her. Nor did she say anything about the sudden death of her mother, although she would have found the sudden death of her father strange. He was not the sort of man to die like that, overnight, quickly, without any warning.

And so Frieda began shaving her father with increasing sureness and skill, until one day – admittedly by then she was much older – as she lathered his face, she thought: I am now my father's wife. And she hummed a tune she'd learnt years before from her mother.

'Do you love me as much as Mother?' she asked, lifting his chin to clean the bristles from his neck.

'Daughters are always loved more than wives,' he replied.

And they both laughed.

Nunes took immense delight in the morning ritual, more so, in fact, than when his wife had shaved him. Yet there had been a time, before Frieda was born, when it had been foreplay for their love-making. In those days he had been aroused by the touch of his wife's fingers, and by the risk of exposing to her that most vulnerable part of his neck. When she gently pushed his head back he would be overcome with an excitement that hardly allowed her to finish. The sight of him erect made her giggle and inevitably she cut him, which fired his lust even more. Then he would pull her head down and make her lick the blood to staunch it.

The birth of Frieda took away his desire. His wife was still willing, but he would not respond, only wanted her to finish so that he could get out of the house.

When Frieda began shaving him the emotions of his early married life were awakened. But this wasn't the same lust; it was tantalising, complicated, unnerving. She was more skilful than her mother, quicker to learn, more ready to please – after all, she was his daughter, and she idolised him. He never thought that it would be any other way.

Ah-man, how he hated this forgotten hole: the heat, the flies, the sand-fleas, the mosquitoes that bred in the saltpans and lagoon, the smell of death from the never-ending succession of seals that hauled up on the beach to die, the loathing of the people. And how they loathed him, despite their smiles he could see the hate in their eyes. But he endured all because he represented law and order and he knew that in this stinking port a great crime was being committed.

During the first year, the captain brought his boot down on the village's neck. And, as he'd done to so many helpless victims before, he kept it there while they choked in the heat and dust. It was one way, he'd always found, of getting to the little secrets of a person's life. Like what were the lights he saw once a month off the headland, and why did some conversations cease when he came within earshot? But no one would tell him, so he trod harder.

There would be no more dances, no more drinking in public, on Sundays after church everyone was to stay at home. The trader, Fagmie Jabaar, was given strict licensing orders: Monday to Friday between eight in the morning and six in the evening, Saturdays until one, closed on Sundays.

'But how can I make a living if people can't buy when they want to?' protested Fagmie Jabaar. 'And what of my café on a Saturday afternoon?'

'People must learn that there are times to shop and times to drink,' replied the captain, leaving Fagmie Jabaar to display the regulations, signed By Order.

Then he opened a register. Family by family, Nunes called in everyone, to find out names, surnames, history. Who was your father? Who was your mother? Who was your grandfather? Who was your grandmother? Painstakingly he recorded all the information in a ledger which was locked in his trunk each night.

'But what is it for? Why do you want this?' asked the fisherfolk.

'There must be records,' he said. 'There cannot be laws unless there are records. And without laws what chance is there of order!'

The people were unhappy. It was as if the captain had invaded their houses and demanded precious heirlooms. They felt that something had been taken away and imprisoned, they were no longer free.

Although no one liked what was going on, no one complained, until the captain began proclaiming his laws. Now the man had gone too far, thought Augustin Shoote. As the villagers' guardian angel, their reverend, the time had come to intervene.

The fisherfolk were never to forget the day he confronted Nunes.

3

It was the first time anyone had stood up to the captain, and it was to be the last. He showed them that he would not tolerate any interference in his affairs, even from the Church. What he decreed was law and not to be challenged. Although everybody was grateful for Augustin Shoote's concern, they were so alarmed by Nunes's temper, by the fire it seemed to ignite in him, that the incident frightened them even more.

It happened one midday. In his room at the back of the church sat Augustin Shoote preparing a sermon in the heat. He never found writing easy and would spend long minutes staring at the whitewashed wall, lost in thoughts that were far removed from his text. Gradually, he became aware of someone sobbing in the church. He found, on a pew in the vestibule, old Mrs Vygie Bond, the mother of Vygie Bond, the fisherman. Augustin Shoote took her to his room and poured the old lady a strong measure of the only brandy that remote settlement possessed. After two glasses, which left the bottle less than half full and brought a momentary frown to Augustin Shoote's forehead, she stopped crying.

That morning, Mrs Vygie Bond told him, she had been called by Frieda to see the captain who told her he had now finished classifying everybody according to the law, and that she, and her family, being of mixed blood, fell in the second class. Mrs Vygie Bond had no idea what he was talking about. So Nunes put it simply: it meant she was no longer allowed to sit at Fagmie Jabaar's tables and drink wine; that was now reserved for people in the first class. But, she protested, she always sat at Fagmie Jabaar's tables and drank wine, as did everyone else, why couldn't she do so any more? Because, replied the captain, becoming angry, that was the law and without law there was no order. By now he was not only shouting but banging his fist on the table and Mrs Vygie Bond had fled.

Augustin Shoote gave her a final tot of his precious brandy and sent the old lady home with the reassurance that he would go and see the captain.

'Bless you, Reverend,' said Mrs Vygie Bond. 'Praise the Lord.'

Augustin Shoote had no clear idea of how to accost Captain Nunes. As he stepped from the quiet dimness of the church into a whiteness that hurt his eyes, he felt the sand burning through the thin soles of his sandals and a sweat of heat and anxiety broke out in his armpits.

Augustin Shoote chose not to go straight down the street to the

4

captain's house. Instead he cut through the scrub to the lagoon so that Nunes, if he happened to look out his window, would see him approaching from the fisherpeople's cottages. It was a gesture, he thought, of solidarity. As he crossed the square, Fagmie Jabaar ran out of his store to stop him.

'Please to come and look, Reverend,' called Fagmie Jabaar. 'The captain, he has made a classification.'

There, pinned to a board outside the shop, was another of the captain's notices, signed By Order. Augustin Shoote couldn't believe what he read.

Nunes had divided the village into first- and second-class citizens, and prepared a list of laws by which each group was ruled. Augustin Shoote found his name in the first class. It meant he could swim from the beach but not in the lagoon. He was not to visit the fisherhuts without a permit authorised by Nunes, although people in the second class (most of the fishing families) could visit those in the first class provided they went in the back door. Fagmie Jabaar was to build a wall down the centre of his shop and to serve people in the first class from one side, and people in the second class from the other. As Mrs Vygie Bond had told him already, no one from the second class could order a drink at Fagmie Jabaar's tables. In families where marriage had paired a person from the first class with another from the second, they would be classified according to the lower status. And in future such marriages would not be allowed. Nor could the classes live among one another. The hill was reserved for those in the first class, the shores of the lagoon for those in the second. Finally, in church, all first-class citizens were to sit on the right-hand side, all second-class citizens on the left.

This is impossible, thought Augustin Shoote. The man is mad.

Some minutes later, Frieda showed him into the kitchen where the captain, in his vest and underpants, was eating lunch. On the table lay the revolver Nunes always wore strapped to his belt. The captain looked up and motioned with a fork for Augustin Shoote to sit.

'What is your problem, preacher?' he said between mouthfuls.

Augustin Shoote glanced round the kitchen trying to find some reassurance among the unwashed pots and pans. Yet even this room, the most homely in any house, was hostile.

'You can't do this,' he said at last. 'You can't come here and destroy a community.'

The captain stopped chewing. There was inside him a heat he

5

hadn't experienced for years, not since the night his wife had died. Ah-man. Ah-man.

'I can do anything the law says. And it says that people must be classified and live accordingly.'

He went back to his food.

'What you are doing is inhuman. They may be the laws but that does not make them right.'

Nunes finished his mouthful, picked a bone off the plate and sucked out the marrow.

'You make me very unhappy, preacher,' he said. 'In this heat you make me very unhappy.'

Their eyes met for the first time.

'What do you want me to do about it, huh! Do you want me to forget about the laws, to go away and pretend that there is not a great crime being committed here? Ah-man, you people cannot hide it from me for ever. I shall find out what is going on.'

Nunes picked another bone and sucked it. The first he threw into the back yard where a dog, chained to a tree, strained to get it.

Augustin Shoote looked up at Frieda who stood with bowed head in the doorway. What did she think of this? Or did she not question it? Disturbed by the preacher's expression she went to stand behind her father.

Augustin Shoote clenched his fists below the table. 'You have no right to do this,' he said. 'It makes no difference what the laws are, here they don't matter. Can't you see people struggle just to stay alive?'

Nunes stood up so violently his chair fell over. There were great drops of sweat on his forehead and cheeks, his lips were tight, swearing. Yet Augustin felt he was sitting in a most perfect silence while about him swirled a terrifying chaos. Then abruptly a smell of putrefaction, as though a dead rat lay beneath the floorboards, invaded the cocoon of his silence.

In the square, the villagers stood watching the captain's house. Despite the sun and the flies they waited, the women with babies or young children on their hips, the men on their haunches flicking stones. First they heard Nunes shouting, then a revolver shot. The children started to cry. For some moments their lives, too, seemed to be suspended in a silence unbroken even by the sea. But when the captain's front door was wrenched open and Augustin Shoote fell down the verandah stairs, they too smelt death. Nunes, ridiculous in his underwear, the revolver still in his hand, shouted at the knot of people to disperse. Slowly they edged away as Augustin Shoote got to his feet and limped off towards the church.

The next day Nunes summoned Mad Minnaar, the crone, and began the interrogations.

There was no particular reason why he chose Mad Minnaar; perhaps she was the first person he saw that morning while Frieda shaved him, or maybe he had a deep aversion to this strange prophet of doom. It is also possible he'd found out that she called him the goat and wished to teach her a lesson. Late in the evening, when Augustin Shoote heard that Mad Minnaar had still not been released, he began to suspect Nunes had deliberately chosen his victim. He must have seen her as all that was bad in the village: a woman enslaved by superstition, who saw signs and omens everywhere, who had committed, to the captain, the unforgivable sin of taking up with a man of the second class. If he could destroy her he could destroy every one of them.

All night a light burned in the captain's front room where he sat across the desk from Mad Minnaar asking question after question until all the answers became one answer: the apocrypha of a soothsayer. It is difficult to believe he learnt anything except a vast mumbo-jumbo that saw God's warnings in a comet and his retribution in a goat. Certainly, towards the second evening the captain's temper gave out, worn thin by the crone's fantastic mumblings. Which is hardly surprising because by then they'd been at it for thirty-six hours without a break. Those who'd been stationed in the street to ensure Mad Minnaar came to no harm said that one moment all was perfectly quiet and the next the captain was cracking his sjambok as if a pack of rabid dogs was at his heels. They heard him shouting at her to get out, saw their tussling silhouettes against the curtain and the next thing he had thrown her into the street. But strangely Mad Minnaar didn't run away, instead she tried to get back into the house. She was raving now, the way she sometimes did when she'd had too much dagga. The captain began beating her off, lashing her across the face with the quirt. Still she wouldn't go. It was the Brothers Kreef and Stevie who ran in beneath the whip and dragged her to safety.

The next day the captain took his morning shave on the verandah, morose and gaunt-eyed, the revolver strapped to his belt. Everyone who saw him noticed the gun and knew that what Mad Minnaar had always told them was coming true.

A week went by, then Nunes called in Fagmie Jabaar.

Most of the questions merely invited the trader to gossip about the villagers. Did he like Mondling? Was Baleen really the grandson of a Norwegian whaling captain? Where did Lady Sarah get all her beautiful silver and such expensive furniture? Harmless questions which were hardly the stuff of an interrogation.

Fagmie Jabaar answered as best he could, recounting the village stories, making up his own where his knowledge fell short. The captain laughed often because Fagmie Jabaar had a vivid imagination. In fact the shopkeeper put him in such a good mood he offered tea and biscuits, lunch, and a beer in the evening which they drank on the back stoep where it was cool.

Just before dark, the captain asked Fagmie Jabaar why his shelves were getting emptier and emptier.

'When we came here,' said Nunes, 'you sold beer, chocolates, sherbet, Coca-Cola, tins of everything. You were as well stocked as a town grocer. But now you have run out. And each time the coastal steamer comes in to take your order you shrug your shoulders and say nothing this month. What way is that to run a business?'

'I'm doing my utmost best, mister captain,' said Fagmie Jabaar, 'but these are poor people without money.'

'Yet not so long ago they must have had money to buy all the things in your shop. Is that not so?'

Fagmie Jabaar squirmed on the chair.

'Ah-man it is very strange, don't you think, Fagmie, how suddenly this village has got so poor?' Nunes finished his beer and with his arm resting lightly on the trader's shoulder ushered him through the house and out the front door.

Fagmie Jabaar slept fitfully that night and for many nights afterwards while across the square the interrogations got longer and longer.

No one was treated as cordially as Fagmie Jabaar; instead the tales of Nunes's black moods and temper grew until those who had not yet been confronted by the captain became sick with worry. Their imaginations festered on his leering face, spittle in the corners of his mouth, red eyes racing in their sockets, and the hand that banged the table, toyed with the gun hanging in a holster from the back of the chair. Would he use it? Everyone was convinced he would – after all, hadn't he almost shot the preacher? Yet they would not tell him what

8

he wanted to know: it was better to be eaten with fear, even to die, than to betray their only hope.

And so they prepared for the days and nights of torment. Some, like Jong Jan, with stoicism, others, like Vygie Bond, broke before Nunes had even raised his voice, or fouled themselves as the captain spun the gun on his index finger. But for all their terror, no one would tell him what he so desperately wanted to know. Nor was anyone ever declared innocent. To Nunes they were all guilty, conspirators in a great plot against law and order. Sometimes, weeks later, he would have Frieda summon a person he'd already interrogated and put them through the same questions, the same threatening, swearing performance until they wept. It was the thought that Nunes could come for them at any time which churned in their stomachs. He'd got some up in the early hours of morning, and snatched others from the street even on their way to church.

One such was Landed-Little Marsdon, the radio ham. He had to face the same questions again and again, night after night, week after week. How did you get this equipment? From a sailor and my long-dead father. Is it registered? No one ever told me it had to be. Who do you talk to out there? Passing merchants and the spirits of the dead. What do you mean, the spirits of the dead? On quiet nights dead captains raise their ships to sail again. Which would make Nunes slam the table with his fist and wave his revolver in Landed-Little Marsdon's serene face. 'Don't give me this chicken-shit,' he would bellow, 'the only souls on earth are clothed in flesh. I've had enough of your ghosts and spirits. What is that language you use?' and Landed-Little Marsdon would reply, 'It is the language of the dead.' Yet for some reason, the radio ham always escaped the violence which welled within Nunes. Perhaps because the captain was unsure how to treat that angelic face, especially when Landed-Little Marsdon summoned voices from the equipment when it was switched off.

As the months passed, Nunes became increasingly malevolent. The fire the preacher had rekindled in his stomach burnt fiercer, turning his nights into sheets of pain and his days into agony. He could feel the flames reaching into his chest, scorching the soft fabric of his lungs. In the darkness he could see sparks on his breath.

Ah-man, it is because of these people that the fires have started, he reasoned, they must put them out. And his only relief was to see suffering in others.

Not wanting to repeat the exhaustion of the Mad Minnaar session,

9

which had left him as burnt-out as his victim, he dragged a mattress into the interrogation room. When the hours felt like hot coals behind his eyes, he would stretch out on it and cat-nap. Although he never fell into a deep sleep, those snatched hours were enough to keep him going for days. Of course, his detainees weren't allowed that privilege. They were handcuffed to the chair and prodded awake by Frieda when their heads sagged. Quite possibly, Frieda did not enjoy this collaboration, but in those days she would have walked into hell for her father.

As if depriving people of sleep for days on end were not torture enough, Nunes also resorted to what he called the searchlight technique.

'In time, Frieda,' he said, attaching a lamp with a saucer-shaped shield behind the globe to his desk, 'this light will brighten all the dark corners.'

After that, interrogations were done mainly at night. He found that people hauled from bed and forced to stare into that blinding white circle, with his disembodied voice abusing them from the darkness, were soon as frightened as cornered animals. They told him nothing, but he was unconcerned, all he wanted was their fear.

Neither Mondling, who secretly sympathised with Nunes, nor the respectable Boatswain Baleen and his wife, nor Augustin Shoote, nor Lady Sarah escaped interrogation. They were not subjected to the same horrors as the other villagers, nor did he detain them for more than ten or twelve hours at a time, but Nunes had them there repeatedly as he searched for a truth in the fisherfolks' stories. The only people he let alone were Fagmie Jabaar and Montague Planke, the baker, something which Montague and the villagers found more and more sinister as the tyranny of Captain Sylvester Nunes tightened.

The interrogations were only part of Captain Nunes's oppressive regime. He had an almost missionary zeal to reform.

'How can you let these people drink?' he once demanded of Augustin Shoote. 'You who claim to be a preacher?'

'They do not have many other pleasures,' Augustin Shoote replied.

'Then I will act for God,' said Nunes.

He loathed the villagers' drunkenness, especially that of the old man called Jong Jan whom he would often find unconscious in the shade of a fishing boat, cradling his jug of wine.

'I am going to die soon, captain,' Jong Jan had told him, as he lay on the floor, his mouth bleeding from Nunes's punch. 'This means nothing to me.'

Nunes couldn't understand that, he wanted to hit the old fisherman every time he saw him.

But their drinking was not the worst of it, they also smoked the devil's weed, dagga. And they smoked it the way he smoked tobacco, openly in the streets, on their stoeps as if it wasn't a crime.

'Ring the bell, I must speak to everyone,' he had demanded of Augustin Shoote, one morning when the fishing boats had returned. And once they were in the church he had threatened to sjambok their bodies and have their souls committed to hell.

'Now go,' he said. 'Dig out the plants and burn them.'

What good had it done? He knew they were still growing the dagga somewhere. So it became another obsession to plague his nights. And when the fury in Nunes's head scorched his pillow because he had once again been thwarted by a simple man who would not reveal the secret at the heart of the village, he would turn his attention on their illicit crops. Almost gratefully, people would confess to a few dagga plants among their tomatoes rather than face his endless questions. Nunes knew it was no solution, but to see fear deepen in the eyes across the table took his mind off the terrible fires in his gut. Yet it was those very fires that eventually gave the villagers some reprieve.

Frieda could feel how they were consuming her father. There was a heat in his body that made a furnace of the bed even on the freshest nights, a heat that damp towels and icepacks couldn't cool.

'You are killing yourself,' she told him when the fever was at its worst and his body had erupted in boils. 'You must stop doing this.'

And surprisingly he listened. He stopped the interrogations. For days he stayed indoors, brooding, watching from the depths of his gloomy rooms the fisherfolk cleaning the nets, eating their salty bokoms, a dried fish that turned his stomach, or getting drunk on the sweet wine they made from melons. Gradually, under Frieda's constant attention, the fires died down.

When the captain imprisoned himself, appearing on his verandah only for the ritual morning shave, the villagers, far from being relieved, became more apprehensive. What did this new behaviour mean? At least when he was about, poking his nose into houses, searching through their possessions with his stick, at least then they knew where he was, what he was doing. Nobody liked it, but they came to live with it, as they came to live with the long sessions staring at his bright light, answering his questions with lies that got more and more complicated as the hours wore on. But this silence, this strangeness, made them uneasy. As the days turned into weeks they asked: Was he ill? Was he angry? What could they do to appease the brooding god? Some of them, despite the suffering he had brought, even left fresh eggs, fish, vegetables on the verandah where his daughter would find them. But their presents were ignored, or, worse, thrown in the street. And when Augustin Shoote went to visit the captain, on the pretext that all men were God's children, Frieda would not let him in the door.

'You must go away,' she said, 'my father will not see anyone.'

Yet every morning there Nunes sat on the verandah, reminding them that he was still watching, still planning to discover their secret.

For Frieda, those weeks were hell. Nunes would not talk to her, would not let her come near him except for the morning shave. All day he wandered listlessly from room to room staring out the windows at the bright streets as if expecting to see something he had never noticed before. At meals he ate begrudgingly, often leaving most of his food untouched.

'Ah-man, I can't get the taste of this hole out of my mouth,' he shouted one suppertime, hurling his plate to the floor. 'It is foul, rubbish for sealice and crabs, not for men.'

'But it came from the villagers,' said Frieda.

'What? It came from who? Stupid, don't you see they want to poison us? Get rid of it. Throw it in the streets, let their dogs die rather.'

So Frieda had to throw any food they received in the street while her father watched from the dark depths behind the windows.

Then he changed again. As suddenly as he had turned morose, so he regained his humour. The fires had gone out.

'Come, Frieda,' he said as she wiped the last traces of lather from his face and neck, 'we must dress for church.'

Not since her mother's funeral had Frieda set foot in a church. While the captain often saw himself as an agent of God, he was suspicious of churches and churchmen who would frequently invoke a God he didn't recognise. To keep his faith pure and his daughter out of the hands of lascivious priests who were known to take young supplicants as they knelt in prayer, he spurned the church. Until suddenly, one Sunday morning in September, he again felt the need to take his place on a pew among the common people. So what if he was shunned? So what if he and his daughter had to sit like jackals on a beach while the seals edged away? Wasn't he showing that they worshipped the same God, that like them he had to ask forgiveness for his sins?

In fact his presence caused more than a stir among the congregation. It was so unexpected, so welcome to Augustin Shoote that, in the spirit of the moment, he changed his sermon from heralding the promised Kingdom to proclaiming love of one's neighbour. Afterwards, he shook the captain's hand, and tried to find beneath the sunglasses that merely reflected his face some flicker of the emotion that had brought Nunes to pray with these sufferers.

The captain did more than go to church. He invited the old German, Mondling, to play draughts on his verandah in the late afternoon. Of course, it had to be Mondling, the fisherfolk whispered to one another, didn't hyenas always sniff out their own kind? And they were relieved that Mondling wasn't party to the secret, because they knew that in half an hour he would tell Nunes more than he had found out in a year. Even now, weren't they gloating together, laughing in the way of men who have the power to control the lives of others?

But whatever it was Mondling divulged, and it must have been substantial for he'd lived through the bad times and the good, the captain kept it to himself.

Then he did something else uncharacteristic. He went to visit Lady Sarah in her isolated house above Whale Beach. Normally, if he wanted to see anyone, he had Frieda summon them with a curt, 'You must come immediately, the captain wants you.' But this time he dressed in a tie and jacket, removed the revolver and its holster from his belt and took some flowers that Frieda had collected from the shores of the lagoon.

His first visit lasted less than fifteen minutes, and he returned carrying the flowers. The villagers sniggered to themselves. But two days later he went again. This time he stayed longer and came away without the flowers. Had he charmed Lady Sarah? the fisherfolk wondered. Surely not, Lady Sarah was nobody's fool. She understood men like the captain, she was wise to their tricks. Or was she? The next week he went again, three days in a row on visits that grew longer

13

and longer each time. And then it became a routine: on Monday, Wednesday and Friday mornings Captain Nunes would take tea with Lady Sarah.

What could they be talking about? people wondered. It wasn't the secret, that was as safe with Lady Sarah as it was with any of them. But as everything about Lady Sarah was a wonderful mystery, they soon stopped questioning further. If she could accept, or at least tolerate the captain, then they would be friendly but wary. Yet when she invited him to her dinners, occasions to which Mondling had never been asked, the villagers were confused. Did it mean he had become one of them?

What, indeed, to make of his new friendliness? Why this sudden interest in fishing that brought him down to the beach every midday when the boats came in? And the kindness towards Jong Jan, whom he'd punched and mistreated from the beginning? How could he now offer the old fisherman his foreign cigarettes and stand there talking with him about tides and shoals as if there had never been a time when he'd blackened his eyes at the merest excuse? Was he laughing at them? Trying to win their confidence by becoming one of them? Surely not. But although they didn't think so they were still wary.

The new Captain Nunes was a dark enigma. He sent blankets to the poorest when the weather turned cold; he gave the children sweets which they could no longer buy at the store; he even overlooked the spring crop of dagga and said nothing when it was harvested and left to dry on back stoeps. No one went so far as to smoke it openly, but he knew of their habits and chose to ignore them.

When the fires died down and the flames had cleared from his sight, Nunes looked at his daughter the way men look at wives who have betrayed them, with a longing for the time before. Not that Frieda had been unfaithful to him – on the contrary, she had cared for him, loved him, given herself to him in ways far beyond a daughter's duty. But in the captain's eyes she had already betrayed him.

During the morning shave he said, 'You must make friends here, Frieda. After all this time you are still a stranger to these people.'

'I'm happy with you,' she replied, testing the razor-blade against her thumb. 'I've no need to talk to others.'

'Maybe not,' he said, 'but you must get out more.'

The words almost sparked the fires again, the way a sudden wind can fan dying embers, but Frieda didn't know it, nor could she see his bunched fists beneath the towel.

Ah-man, he thought. Bastard. Bastard for doing this.

But it was not his idea. Wasn't it Lady Sarah who at tea the previous morning had said, 'Captain, it's not right for a young girl to be stuck in a house all day. Let her get out and become part of the village'?

No, that was impossible. She was his. And if she couldn't be his, then she would be nobody's. No. Impossible. Yet the thought persisted and the torment: Can I lose her to a fisherlout? To some mixed-blood moron? My little girl. The child of my sperm. My starlight. My wonder. My flower. Ah-man, what is there then for me? Neither woman nor daughter: I shall be alone. And what good is a man alone? I would kill her rather than have a slime around her neck. She is mine. Yet . . . and yet. I am the subject of gossip. It will not do. There must be respect for the office of law and order. So, I will do as she says, and hate the woman, the perfect Lady Sarah who keeps a bastard for her pleasure. Why does that not set tongues going? Especially as it is the greatest filth, condemned by God and man, worse even than fucking a goat. But go on, take my Frieda, make her one of yours. Yet . . . and yet. Must it go so far? Can't she still be mine, and my ears and eyes to the village gossip? Surely their secret is worth one kiss. Even . . . even, God help me, a fisherman's hand on her breast, or . . . up her . . . up her, ah-man, up her skirt, if that is the way to the secret. And what if that is not enough? What if he has her on the dunes, spreads her thighs once, twice, ten times. Fills her with so much seed she leaks for a week and smells of fish. A dead mackerel, rank with oil. Already the stench is in my nose, the stench that no carbolic will cleanse from her. Is that worth the secret? To have a daughter foul with dead fish in the house? Ah-man, I would have to kill them. I would get the secret and kill them. There is no choice. No father can have a spoiled girl for a daughter. If she loves me she would not do that. She would not open her legs and defy my love.

Such were the dark thoughts that soaked the captain's sheets in perspiration night after night until he feared the fires had started again. So he went to Lady Sarah for help.

'But who, Lady Sarah?' he asked.

'Why, the boy Stevie, of course,' she said.

Of course, the boy Stevie, already a seasoned fisherman with lines cut by sun and wind beginning to appear at the corners of his eyes and mouth, Jong Jan's grandson, but for all that a boy who could possibly be reclassified by virtue of a doubtful father and grandmother. It could have been worse. On the one hand, such a pity that the parents were dead, victims of a freak wave that had swept the couple from the rocks where they were picking mussels and drowned them in a fast current that lost its energy somewhere near the Equator. Just such a pity their bodies were never found, but, on the other hand, also a Godsend, for now who was to say the boy wasn't class one?

'They're the same age,' said Lady Sarah, heaping more sugar into his tea. 'They'll get on. He's a boy with a kind heart.'

Maybe, thought Nunes, but I have seen him peeing against the harbour wall and that was no boy's cock he held in his hand.

Yet, two days later, when the boats came in, Captain Nunes, in starched uniform and polished boots, despite the summer heat, went down to the beach to invite Stevie to lunch. From a distance he cut a slightly absurd figure, standing stiffly to attention while the men did a half-bent jig of greeting as they jumped ashore. He talked briefly to Jong Jan, then the boy Stevie approached and stood before him with bowed head. Even when the captain turned on his heel and marched off, Stevie did not move.

Frieda had learnt about her father's intentions only that morning, as she performed their daily ritual.

'Today,' he had said, 'I am going to ask someone to lunch.' There was a brief pause while he tried to gauge her reaction, but Frieda never wavered, deftly drawing the blade down his jaw and flicking scum into the basin of water. The captain cleared his throat. 'We shall have marrows and mutton and you are to wear the dress with the thin straps that belonged to your mother.' Again a pause as Frieda tipped back his head. The blade rested briefly on his Adam's apple as she adjusted the angle, then, with hardly a rasp, wiped off the lather to expose the chicken-flesh neck. 'It is time you met people,' Nunes explained when she had finished. 'I am going to invite the boy Stevie.'

Stevie was not unknown to Frieda; he had once almost made her laugh with his antics in the street as she watched him from the safety of her high verandah. She had wanted to giggle at his silliness, and would have but for the appearance of her father in the door of Fagmie

Jabaar's shop. She had gagged with confusion, knowing that he had been spying on her.

She was just as confused now. Since her mother's death no guest had set foot in their house. Those who crossed the threshold did so out of not friendship but fear. They came to whisper secrets to Nunes, secrets that would sometimes get them killed, or to go through the painful hours while he teased out plots and plans they had all but forgotten. Even for Frieda the house was more jail than castle, although in those days she couldn't see the barred windows or the heavy door that kept her from the outside world. Yet the captain's obsession and jealousy held her more securely captive than could handcuffs and chains.

Confused but obedient as ever, Frieda swept the house that was always clean despite the constant dust and sand brought in on the wind. To an extent the housework stilled her thoughts, but sometimes as she caught a glimpse of the white day beyond a window, she grew uneasy. What troubled her most was not that her father had invited a mere fisherboy from the second class to lunch, but that he'd done it for her sake. Hadn't he once said, 'You must never leave me, Frieda, or terrible things will happen'? And, during the fires, when his skin had almost turned to charcoal, she'd seen a terror cross his eyes as he realised he was alone, dying in the midst of a fire invisible but all consuming. Had his love for her died, as it died for her mother? Was that why on the past two mornings she had woken alone in the bed they had shared since her mother's death? Was that why he had taken to sleeping on the mattress in the interrogation room? She could not admit it. Perhaps it was the fires again, she thought. But she knew it wasn't, just as she knew terrible things would happen.

Which they did, for no matter how carefully she pressed the dress with a heavy iron heated on the stove she could not take out all the creases. Yet the captain's uniform ironed smooth under clouds of steam without any trouble at all.

Nor was she happy about wearing the dress for such an ordinary occasion. It was a dress that demanded an event, one of those garden parties she'd once glimpsed behind a high hedge when they lived in the town. Men wearing beige suits and women in cotton dresses like hers sitting on white furniture on the lawns and beneath the trees, eating scones and drinking tea. It was a dress for such an occasion, not for a lunch with a fisherboy who probably didn't know in which hand to hold a knife or fork.

All morning the captain sat in the interrogation room with his feet on the desk, staring at the wall, listening first to the sweep of the broom, and later to the hiss of the iron. When he heard Frieda preparing the marrows in the kitchen he got up, put on his uniform and then demanded to see her in the dress. While she changed, Nunes sat on the bed. For the first time Frieda felt uneasy before those coal-black eyes, so self-conscious that she turned from him to hide her naked breasts.

The dress emancipated the woman in Frieda; revealed a delicacy about the shoulders, a suggestion of breasts, soft, just swelling beneath the cotton fabric, a purity of skin, that Nunes had never noticed before. When she stood against the light he could see a curve of hips and long thighs starting from the shadow of her crotch. But most of all he was drawn to her hair. Especially he loved it in the sun when it flared auburn between his fingers, smooth as watergrass. It was the loveliest of heads, and he had run his fingers through the hair of many women, some to caress, some to get a grip on before he pulled out a fistful by the roots.

'I never noticed you were such a beautiful woman,' Nunes said as he left to go down to the beach.

In the instant before the vegetables burnt to a cinder and the mutton chops became as tough as dried meat, Stevie arrived, barefoot, but wearing an old suit, patched and darned, that had belonged to Boatswain Baleen's father in the days when he regularly sailed south to visit the brothels. His hair was slicked down with a squirt from a tube of hair oil, sold per squeeze by the enterprising Fagmie Jabaar.

Nunes didn't stand on ceremony. He showed the boy to his seat at the table in the kitchen and said grace even while Frieda was serving. The meal began and ended in silence. Stevie ate uncomfortably, never lifting his eyes from the plate. Frieda, too, kept her face shielded against her father's glare, escaping to the sink as soon as the meal was over. But he called her back.

'Ah-man,' he said, prodding at the remains on her plate. 'Haven't I told you to eat the bones? Hey! Hey! Now suck them clean.'

Stevie needed no reprimanding. Like the captain he picked and chewed at the chop bones until there was nothing but a taste left for the dog in the yard.

At the end of the meal the captain grew morose. He felt cheated. He had wasted good mutton chops: neither the boy nor his daughter had spoken a word to one another let alone exchanged glances. Yet hadn't he seen them fooling about? So what was the matter now, couldn't she behave like a hostess, couldn't she make the least effort to be civil, did she have to sit there with that long face that he wanted to hit until the cheeks were stinging red? Suddenly, he stood up and said to Stevie, 'It is time you went.' His face was black as it had been when the fires flared in his stomach. Frieda knew she would have to bear his anger.

'Bitch!' he yelled, when Stevie had gone, gripping her face and forcing her to look at him. 'Have I taught you no manners?'

All over the village they could hear the captain beating his daughter and her sobs in between his ravings. Poor Stevie ran into the dunes but her cries were everywhere. He knew she was being beaten because of him.

Captain Nunes sulked for a week. He would not take tea with Lady Sarah, nor invite Mondling round to play draughts, and the villagers hardly dared breathe in case the least noise exploded his wrath in another bout of violence. Frieda bore the beating and the moodiness with a stoicism inherited, although she didn't know it, from her mother. When she appeared on the stoep the next morning to give him the ritual shave, her face was swollen, her eyes discoloured, and her lower lip cracked and still congealed with blood. Yet, as ever, her hand was firm and deft. How could he beat his own daughter so savagely? the fisherfolk whispered to one another. And they couldn't see the weals on her back where he'd attacked her naked body with his belt. Never before had Nunes so much as lifted a finger to his daughter, but with the sure knowledge that in the end she would betray him, he'd raged against his own impotence and cunning.

Once again Lady Sarah broke the impasse. When Nunes eventually visited her she told him gently that really he shouldn't have expected anything more from the lunch, that young people needed less formal occasions, and why didn't he let the villagers hold a dance? After all, he'd allowed Fagmie Jabaar to stay open as long as he liked, and men from class one and class two could now drink together at the outside tables, and there were many other things he'd turned a blind eye to, without, you must admit, captain, the sky falling in, so why not let them have a dance? Why not, indeed? The more he thought about the idea, the more he liked it.

'All right,' he said as they parted. 'You organise it.'

Which Lady Sarah did. It was the first dance there'd been since the day the goats got out, heralding the arrival of Captain Sylvester Nunes, and, as with all things Lady Sarah did, it was a huge success.

The dance was held on the square in front of Fagmie Jabaar's store one warm and windless night in January. As Lady Sarah said, it was a night for love, and with the help of Mad Minnaar, who spent the entire morning scouring the backveld for plovers' eggs and leaves from tiny desert plants that bloomed once a week and died, that's how it turned out. With little more than a day's warning, the fisherfolk turned the square into a carnival as they had done in the times when their pockets were heavy with coins, when Fagmie Jabaar's shelves bowed beneath the weight of chocolate bars, tins of spices, fruit, spaghetti, jams, sherbet, blackballs. As they fastened paper streamers, dug out from some vast store that Lady Sarah kept in the cellars of her house, from one gable to another, or hollowed marrows for lanterns, or cooked enormous pots of fish-rice with herbs and chillies, or stood watching Fagmie Jabaar's giant still bubbling out enough melon wine to float a fishing boat, they forgot the horrors of the previous year, the way nightmares are forgotten in the morning, and were as happy as they'd been when Montague Planke first brought on the good times. Even the captain was caught up in the excitement.

'I must make a speech, Lady Sarah,' he commanded, 'to start the festivities.'

'But, captain,' she said, 'this is a dance not a rally.'

'Never mind that, I will make a speech,' was his retort, as he strutted off to supervise the arrangement of tables. 'See that Jong Jan and his men build a podium next to the flagpole.'

Of all the villagers, only Frieda kept out of the frenzied activity. Nor did she watch from behind the curtains, but stayed in the kitchen, staring through the open door at the dog panting in the shade of a thorn bush. These moments of distraction, when she stopped mending the straps that had been torn from the cotton dress, spread a dark foreboding through her until she again took up her furious stitching. Terrible things were going to happen and she had no power to stop them.

In her house of corrugated iron, pervaded with the grey smell of sex, Mad Minnaar was whipping crushed leaves of desert plants into the yolk of plovers' eggs and muttering what could have been mistaken for incantations but were actually nursery rhymes. Some hours later she took from her oven two brown scones, more powerful than a mixed bag of rhino horn, Spanish fly and peanuts, wrapped them in a strip of cloth torn from the end of her dress, and set out to find Lady Sarah.

Throughout the long afternoon the villagers kept to their cottages, ironing, darning, combing washed hair until, as the sun fell past the horizon, the band – Jong Jan on a mouth organ, Vygie Bond squeezing notes, cracked, sharp, sometimes melodious, from a concertina and Finella Baleen shaking a tambourine – began to play. Those first rousing tunes released from their excited homes a stream of fisherfolk that included even the ever complaining Mrs Beg-rip, Mondling, Augustin Shoote, and the last of the goatherds who lived on the other side of the lagoon. Fagmie Jabaar threw open his doors and wheeled out three great barrels of melon wine to be served free of charge as they'd been paid for by the captain that morning. From her house above Whale Beach swanned Lady Sarah on the arm of Samuel, who smiled for the first time since that fateful morning when he'd watched through his telescope the dust raised by Nunes's lorry as he drove nearer and nearer; beneath trays of doughnuts, freshly baked, staggered Montague Planke still beaded in sweat from the heat of his ovens, laughing at the children who swooped on him like gannets; out of the furthest fisher cottage, wearing the suit he'd worn once and once only and white shoes he'd taken from the feet of a dead sailor caught in the nets, came Stevie all brash and bravado eating a brown scone, the best he'd tasted in his life; but nobody turned heads more than the lovely Frieda in her cotton dress with its thin straps over her shoulders. Even the music stopped as she and the captain swept on to the dusty square already dancing the one, two, three waltz which he'd been taught by his mother on a gold mine in the north.

It was long after the captain's speech, although he still stood on the podium in his full uniform drinking from one of Lady Sarah's glasses and waving to the villagers as they danced beneath him – so long after that Fagmie Jabaar had just turned the tap on the third barrel of wine, and Montague Planke reappeared from another secret trip to the beach – that Frieda found herself dancing on the clumsy white shoes of the boy Stevie. How she'd got there she couldn't remember, there was so little to the night except the hot pressure of her father's hand in the small of her back.

'Don't they make a splendid couple,' Lady Sarah said to the captain.

'At least he sucks his bones,' said Nunes.

On the bright, beautiful morning after the dance Frieda shaved her father expertly but in a daze, cleaned the house and prepared lunch with no thought for what she was doing, stood on the verandah at midday to watch the little boats round the Head and felt relief in her heart when Stevie jumped ashore waving and blowing kisses as if they were alone in the world. She did not pause to wonder why it was that relief and not joy first filled her heart. For love is not only blind, it is careless as well.

From that afternoon on, the lovers lived in one another's arms. They went for walks round the shores of the lagoon as far as the goatherd's hut and beyond; or explored the northern beaches until a brown hyena turned them back. On the jetty Frieda first learnt to bait a hook; and on calm evenings they rowed round the Head to fish for squid. From Frieda, Stevie discovered a fantastic world peopled with giants and fairies, bandits, judges and poets when she told him stories, some invented, some half remembered from the days of her mother, and sang sad ballads of star-struck lovers. Like plovers they made a bed in the dune grass, but despite the power of Mad Minnaar's scones it was some weeks before they gave in to their bodies and unleashed a desire which drove them to that nest, despite the howls and shrieks of jackals and foxes, every night once the village lights were out.

Their coupling gave them pure moments when nothing existed except the deliciousness of their bodies. For Stevie, the hard daily ache of rowing to the fishing grounds and the endless boredom of waiting for a sharp tug at the line between his fingers disappeared as he lost himself in folds of velvet and long sensations that rippled his skin the way the lagoon rippled under the north-west wind; and Frieda knew, for the first time in her life, a stillness of mind untroubled by her father when she could gradually sink into deep, deep down. Afterwards they would sleep, curled together until a subtle change in the light brought an end to their embraces. In the months of their idyll, I was the only one to see them hurrying out of the dunes, but I kept their secret as the village kept a greater secret from the captain.

The last days of summer were as perfect for the villagers as they were for the lovers. Nunes had let almost all his regulations slip, although he would not tolerate women drinking at Fagmie Jabaar's tables. It was the first step to prostitution, he maintained, warning Fagmie that if he ever caught a woman consuming liquor on the premises he would tear up his licence faster than a gull ate a crab. Allah forbid, Fagmie Jabaar would exclaim in horror, and Nunes never knew whether it was the thought of having his licence shredded or the drinking women which troubled the trader most. But apart from that one stipulation, the captain was more relaxed. When he was not at Lady Sarah's he was on his verandah playing draughts with Mondling or, occasionally, he would fish from the end of the jetty with Jong Jan. The regular patrols that had struck fear into many an innocent heart stopped, and, although he still dressed in uniform, Nunes no longer carried the revolver in the leather holster on his belt.

And towards Frieda he was what Lady Sarah would have called 'a normal father', except for his insistence on the ritual morning shave.

'I do wish you'd stop that performance,' she once chided him, 'especially out on the stoep.'

But he only laughed and said, 'Ah-man, my good lady, what else are women for, if not to serve men?'

'Even their fathers?'

'Especially their fathers.' And he frowned, the way she had seen him frown during the days of the interrogations.

But the ritual was the only demand Nunes made on his daughter. For the rest, provided the house was clean and there was food at mealtimes, Frieda was left free to pursue her romance. In fact, Nunes encouraged it, even insisting now and then that she bring Stevie home for a meal, which was by no means a repeat of the first occasion, although he always had Frieda serve mutton chops. He took a strange pleasure in watching the boy suck bones the way he believed true men should.

'Men can't live on fish alone,' he told Stevie, as the two of them, stripped to their vests, ate lunch in the hot kitchen. 'Men have got to eat the red blood of beasts to stay men.'

After the meal he would cajole Stevie into an arm-wrestling contest while Frieda cleaned up.

'Let's see how tough you are, fisherman, let's see if that's not just jelly in your arms.'

Stevie was strong. Ten years in the boats had given him powerful shoulders and arms: he was also much younger than the sinewy captain across the table. But those thin arms held a strength he couldn't (or wouldn't) match, and time after time he fell beneath their power.

'You're still a boy,' Nunes would taunt him. 'There's no steel in your baby-fat.'

Stevie took the criticism in good part: wisely, he realised there was no point to upsetting the captain.

To Frieda, the arm-wrestling sessions were a sign that at least her father was at ease with Stevie, even if he still could not accept the two were lovers in all but deed. The omens, she felt, were on her side. And the day Nunes chased the roosting chickens off the lorry, cranked the great engine into life and drove Stevie out to the saltpans, Frieda saw nothing but good fortune in her stars. It was on that night, with the desire in her now an impossible ache, that she finally surrendered to the power of Mad Minnaar's scones.

It seemed that all the jealousies which had stacked up in Nunes's heart, and the thoughts of his daughter's betrayal which had driven him in torment to a separate bed, had been allayed. But perhaps this was wishful thinking, because the captain's mind was also occupied with other matters. The long hours he spent with Lady Sarah were not passed in idle chit-chat. On the contrary, since his change of heart she had been appointed to tell him the story of the village, in the hope that to know would be to understand. At three rowdy meetings shortly after the dance the villagers had decided, despite the regulations, the interrogations, the protestations of Mad Minnaar and Montague Planke, to reveal to the captain the secret they'd kept more closely than the most intimate details of their lives.

'You tell him, Lady Sarah,' they'd chorused, 'you tell him when the time is right.'

The three meetings, probably the only meetings Nunes never found out about, were held in Montague Planke's bakery as soon as twilight had drained from the sky. Certainly if Nunes had gone out on his stoep for a breath of fresh air he would have heard them arguing and arguing that the captain was not a bad sort now that he had settled down, and why did they have to continue suffering like this with no food in Fagmie Jabaar's shop, no beer, that awful melon wine, and having to scrounge for every bit of food, when they could be wealthy beyond their wildest dreams and eat like kings?

But he didn't, so he didn't hear Montague Planke's reply. 'Because,' argued the baker, looking from one weathered face to the next, 'I know this man.'

'But we can't go on like this,' said Boatswain Baleen. 'If the shoals don't come in this winter we'll die of hunger.' Yes, that was right, they all agreed, and turned to Lady Sarah because she knew the captain better than anyone.

'I think we should tell him,' she said. 'He's not such a bad sort.'

But still Montague Planke, Fagmie Jabaar and Mad Minnaar disagreed. Hadn't there been signs and portents? she said. Hadn't there been plagues of locusts and long-tailed stars in the sky? Hadn't the goats got out on the day he arrived? Hadn't she warned them, even before Fagmie Jabaar arrived and opened his shop, hadn't she warned them of what was going to happen?

On the third night it was only Montague Planke and Mad Minnaar who didn't want to tell Nunes. Fagmie Jabaar, who should have known better, had been won over.

'All we've got to do is sit it out a little longer. He'll go away. I know the man,' argued Montague Planke.

'But how much longer?' asked Lady Sarah. 'You've been saying that every month for the last two years. The captain's not going to go away. He likes it here. He's settled down.'

'He's even ordered a siren to welcome the boats when they round the Head,' said Finella. 'Surely that shows he's become one of us.'

'He'll never be one of us,' said Montague Planke sadly. 'I know him, he's police.'

'Maybe he's changed,' said Fagmie Jabaar.

'I think,' said Boatswain Baleen, 'we should let Lady Sarah tell him when she thinks the time is right.'

Which is when everyone chorused: 'You tell him, Lady Sarah. You tell him when the time is right.'

That was it. That was a wonderful idea. Why not trust to Lady Sarah's good judgement once more? Through tired eyes, Montague Planke surveyed the villagers. Once again, he thought, the powers that be are going to let me down.

It was a happy crowd of fisherfolk that slipped off one by one into the dark that night. Now that Lady Sarah was going to tell the captain, their poverty was almost at an end.

Of course, in the days to come Nunes listened avidly to Lady

Sarah's revelations, learning more in those two final summer months than he had done since setting foot in that Godforsaken village. At last, he felt, he was getting closer to the secret at the village's heart.

2

A BAD WIND OFF THE LAND

It was some days after the last of the three clandestine meetings before Captain Nunes had a chance to take tea with Lady Sarah. Suddenly, he was in demand: to be taken fishing, to meet the men at Fagmie Jabaar's for a drink in the evening, and, of course, to play draughts with Mondling. At last, he thought, I am getting to the heart of the matter.

And then, as if in answer to some silent prayer, Lady Sarah said as they sipped their tea, 'You know, captain, I've never told you the real story of how I came to live here.'

'Is there a real story?' asked Nunes, doubtfully looking at the treasures in that sun-filled room.

No one had ever satisfactorily explained how raw fisherfolk had built a double-storey house that looked like the work of master craftsmen, with its pillared entrance and the sweeping arches of its tall windows. The floors were reputed to be of ships' timbers and the beams of driftwood, the fireplaces of burnt brick from the dinosaur clays of the lagoon and the door handles carved from the ribs of a hundred southern right whales. And that was not to mention the elegance of her ornaments, of her furniture.

For her house was a museum of gracious treasures from the outside world: lace, brocade, fine bone china, silver teapots, jugs, bowls, candlesticks, brass boxes, bells, oddments, copper kettles, scuttles, crystals so fine they held a note into infinity, Persian carpets, flokati rugs, mohair mats, tables of yellow wood, cupboards of oak, chairs of walnut, mahogany beds, fine paintings by old masters, graceful sculptures by unknowns, sherries from distant vineyards, full-bodied reds from the choicest slopes, all the finery of a rich world.

To the villagers, how Lady Sarah had come by her possessions was as much a miracle as manna from heaven. It was something no one questioned. One day there were no curtains, the next the windows were adorned with stately drops. One day the floors were bare, the next they were covered with undreamed of wonders. For near on twenty years the luxuries of fine living found their way into Lady Sarah's home as if wherever she was they would be too. Beautiful objects were a part of her life in the same manner that her fingers and toes were a part of her body: useful appendages without which life would be difficult but not impossible. And probably because she was not overawed by wealth, nor even seemed to notice the magnificence of her dress and furnishings when all about her people made do with what the meagre earth and sea provided, probably because of that, everyone else accepted her riches as the way of things. Just as it is senseless to question the waxing and waning of the moon, or the full or ebbing tide, so to enquire about Lady Sarah's prosperity was naïve.

As Nunes well knew. To his questions, whether they were put during a strident interrogation or polite tea chat, she had always replied, 'They are just here, captain. What difference does it make how they got here? Surely all that is important is that they are pleasing to look at.'

So perhaps he had justification for raising a sceptical eyebrow at Lady Sarah's offer to tell her story. However, she merely laughed at him.

'Of course there's a real story, captain,' she said. 'All stories are real stories once they're told.

'Now, picture me, a much younger woman, you realise, standing with her husband of three days in the stern of an ocean liner on a frozen December afternoon watching the lights of a smogged-in city growing dimmer and dimmer. Imagine with what feelings of high hope and sadness they must have seen the last of the lights disappear as the fog walled in about them, vulnerable emigrants making their way in the world.

'Now picture them, days later, arm in arm about the deck, laughing at the captain's table, eating prawns in exotic ports when the liner stopped to re-fuel, crossing the Equator on a flat ocean, looking up at the changing constellations, and the Southern Cross rising higher and higher each night. See how she sheds coats for print frocks, and her cheeks catch the sun like peaches. Believe me she was happy, she had everything to live for.

'Do you know who else was on that ship, the ill-named *Southern Hope?*'

Lady Sarah glanced quickly at her guest who was stirring the sugar at the bottom of his teacup.

'I'll tell you. Two sisters called Minnow, fleeing the lusts of some guardian who'd had them in his care since their parents died. Timid girls. They kept to themselves: po-faced bystanders at Bingo, deck quoits, even the masked ball where men laid odds they'd be able to charm a smile to those tight lips. Not a chance. It took a freak wave in a wild night, and later the toss and tumble of boiling surf, to change those quiet girls into the Mad Minnaar and raving Mrs Beg-rip we know today.'

'That is impossible,' Nunes burst out. 'She told me herself she is the last of four generations to live at this place.'

Lady Sarah smiled. 'You have been told many things, captain, but, in truth, you know very little. Even with all your interrogations you've not scratched the surface of this place. Believe me.'

No, it is not possible, thought Nunes. That disgusting crone could not deceive me so convincingly, spin such a fantastic tissue of lies.

'Never mind,' comforted Lady Sarah, 'I shall make up for all the deceptions.' And she went on to describe the ball, and herself in her husband's arms waltzing past first one sister and then the next, while a freak wave was building in distant waters, rushing towards them until what had begun as a sea drizzle became a gale, and there it was, a wave as tall as the sky and bearing down. An hour later the ship was gone. All who survived, frightened, crying, tossed about in a lifeboat, were: Lady Sarah, her husband, the sisters Minnow, three sailors and a boy who shortly died. Come morning the sea went down, the sky cleared.

'It was then, captain, that Mad Minnaar sprang from the body of that quiet little girl. Wild-haired, red-eyed, rocking the boat, she stood firmly in the bow, lifted her arm to the horizon and said, "There it is." Of course, everyone looked, but there was only an empty sea. "Row," said Mad Minnaar. "It's not far."

'What else could be done but row? One direction is as good as another in an endless ocean. "More to port, stop drifting to starboard," she would call, as emphatically certain as one who could see not only land but a haven. And indeed, I believe, in a sense she could, if not with her eyes, then with her mind's eye because she said to her sister, and I remember this clearly, "I see your husband, Dorothea, laying his nets out to dry along the shore"; and then, with bitterness, "And mine, worthless sot, drunk again, collecting driftwood and bottles in the tide line."

'Night fell, how different to the one before when we'd all been in evening dress, dancing. True, we were still in evening dress, but salt-soaked now, smelling of sweat and fear, dreading long dark hours in an open boat. I suppose if one of the sailors had known how to guide by the stars he could have steered us in an approximate way according to the Southern Cross, but, on the other hand, who needed the stars when standing in the bows was a muttering woman cursing her sodden mate-to-be with a terrifying vehemence and calling port, starboard, starboard, port if the ocean drifts shifted our course?

'All through that night, next day and night we wore the skin off our hands at the oars until on the following morning there was land before us and a storm behind, which we had to out-row on empty stomachs, throats thick with thirst and our hands wrapped in bloody rags.

'First came the rain, so welcome a sailor died of it, head tilted back, mouth open, lurching from drop to drop until he fell with the rain into the sea and disappeared, just like that. Which left me, my barely conscious husband who'd broken his arm when the ship capsized, the two Minnows, apparently more concerned with marital thoughts than reality, and two sailors.

'The next moment the wind took us into the beach surf where timber-crushing waves made short work of the boat. How unbearably ironic, I thought, to have gone through so much only to drown now. The last thing I remember is hearing the soon-to-be Mad Minnaar shout to her sister, the future Mrs Beg-rip, "It's not the end of us, keep your head up and pretend you're a tiny fish." Sound enough advice in a swimming pool but that surf would get the better of a seal. As it did, it got the better of the sailors, and my poor husband.

'There I was battling to keep myself and my husband's head above water, when out of the dunes, where he'd been watching, shot young Samuel, only twelve years old but a powerful swimmer, and went through those waves with the grace of a dolphin. Next thing his small arms were around me, and not a moment too soon he got me to shore. But all I could gasp was, "My husband, please save my husband." Of course, it was much too late. I remember seeing my dear Gordon's hand flutter like a stunned seagull in the surf, then slip below the waves.'

Lady Sarah fell silent. Nunes watched her the way scientists watch insects: closely, piercingly, until the hardness of his gaze drove her to the window overlooking Whale Beach.

'Do you know what grief is, captain?' she asked.

He didn't answer.

'Grief to me was walking that beach, day after day. Sometimes I wanted to rush down the sand and into the waves. And then I would look up at this hill where these people were building my lovely house and feel ashamed, ungrateful. After all, what good is sorrow, captain? My husband was dead. I was very much alive. But all the same one cannot stop being sentimental. Oh God, I was sentimental. When the house was built I used to stand at this window and look out over a calm, calm sea and wonder, captain, how it could ever have been that rough to claim my poor, poor man. Sometimes, when the water was so clear you could see the lobsters scuttling from rock to rock I used to long to ask Marsdon Beg-rip, Landed-Little Marsdon's dead father, to row me out there so that I could peer down through a glass bowl and maybe see him lying gently on the bottom, swaying in the currents. Never, I vowed to the spot where I lost him, will I let another man lay a finger on me. Isn't that sentimental? Hopelessly romantic? And in the end I couldn't even keep that vow. That's how weak the flesh is, captain. No matter how strong the will, there is always the flesh.' She paused. 'But I don't have to tell you about the weaknesses of the body, do I, captain?'

Nunes shrugged. 'We are only human, Lady Sarah.'

'I suppose,' she said after a moment's hesitation, 'that it was inevitable my husband should die. He had never done anything wrong in his life, he was too good for this place.' Again she stopped, then sipped at her tea. 'No doubt someone has told you about that piece of local folklore, have they, captain? That only people with troubled pasts end up here?'

'Yes,' he replied, 'but it is an old wives' tale, Lady Sarah. Surely an intelligent woman like you doesn't believe in village superstition?'

'It would seem to be true.'

'Bah! It is a story made up by the crone. Tripe, nonsense.' Then a fire lit in his eyes. 'But if you believe it, Lady Sarah, then you, too, must have something dark in your past.'

She smiled. 'And captain, by the same token, so must you. What is more, you came from the land. At least I washed out of the sea. And you know what Mad Minnaar says: "There is always a bad wind off the land."'

'Then what about Samuel?' said Nunes smugly, hoping that he had cut close to the bone.

Lady Sarah sighed. 'Why is it, captain, that no one can accept Samuel? Neither you, a man of the town, nor the villagers, who are used to all sorts. I wish someone could explain it to me?'

Nunes laughed. 'He is very different from everyone else.'

'When I arrived here, captain,' said Lady Sarah, 'he was a young boy, barely twelve years old, forced to look after himself and sleep in the old blubber shack. In winter there wasn't an inch of dry space inside. It's a wonder he didn't die of exposure. So I took him in. Good, good, said the fishwives, the lady will need a servant. Shall we build on an outside room? asked the men. No, I said, he can sleep inside. The next thing I know, a pile of sacks arrives. What's this? I ask. It's for you to put down on the kitchen floor so's the boy's got something soft to sleep on.

'Unfortunately, I am too polite to lose my temper, but I did take them all upstairs to show them Samuel's bedroom. Which, as I'm sure you've been told, is next to mine. Another scandalous detail that has kept their tongues wagging ever since.

'Oh, I know what they thought, that my husband's death had been too much for me to bear, that when the black grief finally left me I'd send him down to his rightful place on the sacks in the kitchen. But I haven't and I never will: that room is his for as long as he wants it.'

She smiled. 'It might amuse you to know, captain, that Samuel had been expecting you for years. Every day, once in the morning, once in the evening, he would scan the horizon in case he had to warn the village of your approach. You see, captain, like Mad Minnaar, he knew about you. He expected a bad wind off the desert.'

Lady Sarah laughed to defuse her remark, and the captain had to smile, too.

'Ah-man, you have a way of putting things,' he said, and looked out on that perfect summer day: the sea seemingly scattered with diamonds, the smack of small waves on the sand, and a breeze just stirring the curtains in the room where they sat among the remains of their tea.

'I'm sure,' Lady Sarah said, 'that you've heard some version of Samuel's history, but, perhaps, as it is a day for recounting the truth, I should tell you about him.

'I don't know how much history you've read, captain,' she began, 'not that it would be much good because the lives of people like Samuel's parents never found their way into the official history books. After all, they are just ordinary people and what historian is concerned with ordinary people when he is writing about generals and statesmen?

'However, I'm sure you're well schooled in what have become known as the wars of independence, which to my mind were nothing more than an excuse for mayhem and plunder, but be that as it may. Towards the end of that gentlemanly war, all the farmlands, including those of the local tribes, had been burnt to a stubble by that mad Kitchener of Khartoum. All the natives were left with – and mind you they were completely disinterested spectators – was a fistful of IOUs and a promise from a grumpy queen, doubtless unaware that they had been issued in the first place, to honour them. But I suppose a bagful of IOUs is a small compensation when your mielie lands lie smouldering and your children whimper with hunger.

'To add to their troubles, these poor people were also put upon by rebellious Boer gentlemen hell bent on maintaining their beloved stocks of dried meat. Anything that vaguely resembled a cow had its throat slit, its best quarters carved into little strips and hung on a fence to dry. Yet more IOUs were dished out on behalf of a government that was in transit via Mozambique for Switzerland. I can tell you the wise man didn't build dreams on cashing in his chits for a fortune when peace was finally declared. The wise man got out of that part of the world and went in search of other pastures. Because the wise man (and the simple man for that matter) was not only beset by gentlemen but also by rogues.

'As you know, captain, nothing is loved by brigands and their ilk more than a war. Where else have they the freedom to do as they please, or the opportunity to lay the blame for their misdeeds on any one of half a dozen imperialist platoons, or roving guerrilla bands?

'So, Baster Jan, not to look a gift horse in the mouth, plundered up and down the Great River far and wide during those years until he had a mounted force that would have been the envy of Boer or Brit. But all the gentlemen warriors ever saw of those legendary beasts was a clean pair of heels. Yet you won't read about Baster Jan's doings in the history books. There's not a word about his rapes, murders, robberies and attacks, because historians are not concerned with the common man. They seem to place more emphasis on major battles than a single night of pillage that decimated an entire town. But I can tell you, Baster Jan's scorched earth policy made Kitchener's look like a picnic fire, and he had enough dried meat to keep the president happy in the Alps for twice his lifetime.

'There wasn't man or mongoose who didn't go to ground when the thunder of his distant hooves started shaking the candle on the table, even if you look in the official war records, you won't find so much as a footnote about this beast Baster Jan.

33

'Which brings me to Griqua Joseph and his wife Mary, honest God-fearing people of missionary learning, once crop planters and cattle minders on the outskirts of Old Dithakong, sufferers beneath the match of Crown authority, mourners of slaughtered kine, rape and assault victims of Baster Jan, left for dead at the sacking of the town. When they came to their senses they gazed around at smoking ruins, not a soul spared, not a fowl, not a half-eaten cob, just a bleating kid overlooked. In that nightmare, Griqua Joseph and his Mary collected what they could, tied a rope round the kid's neck, and prepared to walk to the ends of the earth if need be.

'Well, this place, as you know, is at one end of the earth, unsullied by official or unofficial plunders, tranquil, paradise amidst mayhem. At least that's what we like to think.

'The first the young couple saw of their future home was a twinkle of water and a scattering of houses in the distance. Nearer, they came across the cemetery with its haphazard arrangement of wooden crosses, and rejoiced that they had come among Christians. How overwhelming their joy must have been when, rounding the koppie, they saw the church with its gaping roof.

'But after all those favourable signs they were quite unprepared for the hostile reception that awaited them. From afar this place might have looked like paradise, but the natives were decidedly unfriendly. Some of them even carried long sticks, one a sjambok, and they wouldn't let Griqua Joseph and his Mary closer than twenty yards.

'You see, captain, as I told you, deep in the village's memory, there is a story about a man on a donkey who appeared one day from over the sand horizon, bringing with him an awful plague. Now, in his footsteps, came two people leading a young goat, which gave no one cause for celebration. The children were locked indoors, the women forbidden to so much as cast their eyes on the strangers. And yet, the villagers hesitated before throwing the first stone or lashing out with their staves. Perhaps they saw in the man and his wife a resigned expectation that this was the nature of life, and were appalled. Whatever it was, they followed Captain Hansen, their unappointed leader, and let Joseph speak.

'Now, when the occasion demanded, Joseph could persuade a rabid honeybadger to ignore a beehive and go on its way, so by the time he'd finished he was a teary blur to everyone confronting him.

'All the same, no welcoming arms were extended. Tears might have been shed, but all the hard-luck stories in the world weren't going to close those twenty yards. Instead, Captain Hansen made a suggestion. What if, he said, they were given a skiff and told to row out beyond Seal Rock before they could return to shore? It would be a symbolic gesture that would take away some of the bad luck they might have brought from inland. What if, when they returned, assuming they did return, the village gave them a piece of land well out along the beach and allowed them no closer until an agreed period of quarantine was over?

'So be it, all the villagers declared, which, in the light of future events, was the wisest decision they could have made. Although Griqua Joseph and Mary had never seen a boat before, let alone the sea, they and the young goat put out through the breakers with all the desperation of last-chance men. Mary cried, the goat bleated, Joseph looked at the land and bent his back. Not only did he go beyond Seal Rock, but he slipped below the horizon, returning the next day when everyone had given them up for drowned. Needless to say such bravery got them no closer to the village proper.

'Some two years later they were officially declared out of quarantine and life became less of a struggle. Joseph never ate another shellfish again, and Mary went off goat's milk completely. Although they were still treated with a little suspicion, in the main the couple were tolerated: she found work charring for the Beg-rips and the Hansens, while Joseph joined a fishing boat.

'They were both nearly sixty when Samuel was conceived, which caused many to wonder if it wasn't an immaculate conception. Mary gave birth as if she'd had a string of children to ease this one's passage into the world. Cynics said, easy come, easy go, but Samuel stayed alive against all odds.

'As you have doubtless discovered, the poor child shared only about a decade of his parents' lives, long enough to be told the dramatic tale of their deliverance from evil and acceptance, if not at the heart of this place, then, at least, beside it.'

'Ah-man,' said Nunes, 'and that you believe is the truth?'

'It is not what I believe is the truth, captain. It is what I know is the truth.'

'But I could tell you another story, Lady Sarah. I could tell you that he wandered here from a farm in the dry country after the drought had withered the crops.'

'I have heard that one, captain, but it is not the truth.'

'There is only his word for it.'

'Jong Jan will confirm what I've said. Go and ask him.'

Captain Nunes brushed shortbread crumbs from his lap and wished the revolver was strapped to his belt. He stood up, neat and crisp in the uniform Frieda had ironed not two hours previously.

'I am not a man to be trifled with, Lady Sarah,' he said. 'I have been sent here to keep law and order.'

'I am not trifling with you, captain. I have told you stories this morning you wouldn't have heard in a hundred years.'

'That is the point: why are you telling me these things now?'

'Because, captain,' said Lady Sarah, 'these are poor people living a hard life.'

'That is no reason.'

'It is every reason. When you understand that you will appreciate what it is like to live here. You will realise what you have done.'

'I have brought law and order.'

'No, captain. Sadly you have brought ruin. Ruin and despair. These people are not happy any more. They go hungry, they cannot dance and laugh, or get drunk at Fagmie Jabaar's on a Saturday afternoon. They are trapped, jailed, you have taken away all but their lives. That is why none of them will tell you the truth, because once they have done that they will be completely in your power.'

'And why is it suddenly all right to be completely in my power, as you put it?'

'It is hardly all right, captain. But I have convinced them that you are not a bad man. You have relaxed the regulations, you go to church, you have held a dance, your daughter is becoming part of the village. I have told them that the days before were a mistake, that they are over now and we must forgive and forget. The fisherfolk would like to, they would like you to be part of the village. Don't they welcome you into their homes, get you the best fish from the boats, go out of their way to greet you in the streets, even invite you to drink in Fagmie Jabaar's, surely a sign that they harbour no ill feelings? Can't you see they are trying to welcome you?'

'And for this, what do they expect?'

'Nothing. Your tolerance, perhaps.'

Captain Nunes lit one of the short, foreign cigarettes which he sometimes offered Jong Jan, and breathed the smoke, grey and foul, into the room.

'Perhaps I should tell you, Lady Sarah,' he said, 'that I came here

36

to investigate a great crime. I cannot suddenly stop my investigations, turn my back on deeds that are breaking the laws of the land.'

'Does that mean you will always be a policeman?'

'It means, Lady Sarah, that those who are not guilty have nothing to fear.'

'But that is what I am trying to show you, captain, that no one is guilty, that there is no great crime, that these are just poor people living their lives as best they can.'

She broke off and ran her finger down the piping on the chair. 'If I can make you see that, captain, it will save so much heartache and trouble. Come, sit down again, let me tell you about Mad Minnaar and her sister.'

Seemingly with reluctance, Captain Nunes seated himself in a chair and crossed his legs. From where he sat he could see a boat rising and falling on the ocean and the great brown heads of the kelp breaking the surface to watch the fishermen.

Lady Sarah's story began with Marsdon Beg-rip staggering from the tempest bearing the prone body of the younger Minnow in his arms on the day they were washed ashore. Whether she was unconscious, or in a swoon before the sun-tanned handsomeness of her rescuer, no one knows. But Mad Minnaar left off berating the drunken sot who fawned about her long enough to shout, 'Snap out of it, Dorothea, you're not fooling anybody. What's written is written, and there's nought to be gained in turning destiny into romance.' Dorothea, however, was having nothing of it, whether genuinely succumbed or indeed merely making the most of the circumstances.

Before nightfall on the day of their dramatic arrival, the younger Minnow was already betrothed to Marsdon Beg-rip, son of a dagga-smoking, melon-wine-imbibing, whaling skipper, now many years deceased. Admittedly Dorothea, through her sister's farsightedness, had known him two days longer than he had known her, but her haste in accepting his whalebone ring (with its beautiful sparkler which he had found on the beach and cut and polished over many nights in anticipation, as if he, too, knew that one day he would be delivered of a bride, just like that, out of the sea the way his nets were filled with shoals of mackerel) might have been called indecent, and probably was by Mad Minnaar, who was never offered a ring and consequently never married, in the legal religious sense, the drunken sot who had stumbled towards her across the tideline.

But whether the haste was indecent or not, gallant Marsdon Beg-rip, who had never seen a woman with such fair skin (although it had taken a punishing in the open boat), behaved like a love stricken fool, swept his twenty-four-hours-later bride-to-be off her feet and rushed her, still spitting out sea water, home to his wrinkled mother peeling squashes in the kitchen. She, it is reputed, didn't look up from her vegetables and until the day she died never cast eyes on her daughter-in-law. Nothing daunted, the Younger Minnow set about creating order in a home that had known only chaos since the day the deceased Captain Beg-rip had staggered, melon-wine-drunk, through its crooked portals.

At least, though, she had the good grace to wait until the massive sparkler was on her finger before she started calling the shots. Not that she had long to wait. No matter how irregular the preacher said it was – after all, the banns should have been read out on three consecutive Sundays, and there should have been a proper courtship, and such haste could only lead to disaster – Marsdon Beg-rip had the stubbornness of his parents, who had also defied all to be married, and coerced the poor preacher, who was one of his crew when he wasn't fishing for souls, into agreeing that the very next afternoon at five o'clock would be a good time to say the nuptials. And that's the way it was.

As soon as Marsdon set the time and date the whole village knew. What excitement! One day three ship-wrecked wash-ups, the next day a wedding, and as there hadn't been a wedding inside ten years it was an occasion which no amount of indecent haste would dampen.

'Dumb, dumb,' breathed Mad Minnaar to her sister.

'Green heart,' snorted the bride, pulling the veil over her face.

The villagers had one regret: with only twenty-four hours' notice there was not much that could be done in the way of new dresses. Candles burnt all night, fingers stitched and sewed, darned and patched while in the boatshed Marsdon Beg-rip threw his stag party.

'Now don't you go getting drunk,' said the blushing bride-to-be.

'Don't worry about me. Have a nice evening with Mother,' replied the groom, kissing his loved one on the forehead.

In the kitchen, Mother continued peeling squashes, her eyes cast down.

At dawn the boats were still pulled up the beach, the mackerel off the headland swam northwards, and one by one the numb-fingered women dragged their men from the shed.

'How could you, Marsdon? On our wedding day,' chided the imminent Mrs Beg-rip.

But Marsdon heard nothing, felt nothing until an hour before the ceremony when, with the bride in tears, Mad Minnaar dashed a bucket of salt water in his face, then went off to do the same for the preacher.

A miracle later the church was full, the congregation rose, and from the communion rail Marsdon gazed up the aisle at his radiant almost-wife sweeping towards him on the arm of her sister.

Some I-do's later, and under a shower of daisy petals, the couple emerged to the last rays of a winter sun, breaking through the clouds like swords.

'Praise the Lord,' said the preacher as if this was divine sanction.

'Praise the Lord,' said Mad Minnaar, 'I thought the sun had got lost.'

'Praise the Lord all you want,' grunted Mondling, 'though I'm damned if he hears a word of it.'

So the honeymoon began in the boatshed with Marsdon's melon wine to set their boat afloat, dagga smoke to fill their sails, and lobsters, crabs, prawns, mussels and smoked snoek sufficient to bloat every stomach for three days. There wasn't a man, woman or child who could walk a straight line by midnight, and by morning neither a crowing cock nor a weak sun could raise the revellers.

The thing that took the wind out of Marsdon's sails was the brevity of the honeymoon. No sooner was that one blissful night finished than married life came down on his unsuspecting head with the solidness of a saucepan. Wham! The world reeled, for an instant all went black, tears of pain filled his eyes and he turned to see his wife of one day glaring at him, a saucepan clutched across her breast.

'Don't you ever set foot in here again, Marsdon Beg-rip, with those sandy boots and that foul smell of fish about you,' warned the now Mrs Beg-rip. 'I don't spend all day cleaning this house so that you can waft in like the lord of the manor.'

'And where am I supposed to get washed?' challenged Marsdon.

'There's a basin outside and I'll pass you hot water through the window,' said his wife, giving her mother-in-law two more squashes to peel.

The village offered cold comfort. 'Put a ring on a woman's finger and kiss your arse goodbye,' said Mondling. 'It's no use you come crying to me,' said Mad Minnaar. 'If you were too love-blind to see

39

her true conniving self, and the Lord knows she showed her colours, then you deserve all that's in store for you, brother-in-law Marsdon.'

Now Marsdon was a fisherman and used to coming and going according to the seasons, tides and shoals. But suddenly here was his little woman demanding that he sit down to a proper breakfast of salted mackerel, two eggs and coffee before he so much as put on his boots. And she put a stop to his coming in after dark.

'There will always be fish in the sea,' she said, 'but the day might come when there's no longer high tea upon your table. So just make sure you're there to appreciate it.'

And worst of all she gated him. 'No going down to the boatshed every night,' she commanded, 'you've got other commitments now.' But she wasn't entirely unfair; on Friday evening Marsdon was allowed out until half past ten.

'I'm not standing for this,' he told Jong Jan and the Brothers Kreef after the first week. 'The woman's got to learn her place.'

He said it again seven days later.

At the end of week three he stormed, 'I will put my foot down more firmly!'

Come the last day of the month he said, 'Well maybe I've been a bit hasty, because it was difficult adjusting to marriage and as she's going to give me a son perhaps I should be more patient – after all she is from another country and doesn't yet know how things are done round here.'

At that Jong Jan whistled tunelessly and the Brothers Kreef looked into the depths and agreed what a wonderful thing it was to be a father.

Without doubt the pregnancy was hell. Never before has a woman been pregnant, Mad Minnaar said to herself as she made potions to settle her sister's stomach in the morning, or cleaned her house during the day, or boiled the family's vegetables in the evening, because the swelling Mrs Beg-rip couldn't stand the smell of cooking, was going to be sick, was going to vomit in the pot.

Five months of listening to gripes and groans, and Marsdon's mother, who had kept her eyes down and not said a word all this time, quietly died.

'Oh Lord,' cried Mrs Beg-rip, 'a death on top of a pregnancy, it's all too much. I just can't cope. And black makes me look twice as huge.'

Marsdon took his grief with fortitude: went out to the cemetery and dug the hole, nailed together some planks that had washed ashore, laid the frail remains of his mother inside and tacked a piece of canvas across the top.

His wife was scandalised. 'You can't bury your mother in that leaky box, just think of the worms and the maggots getting in. It's not right. It's not fair. She deserves better. You can't send your own mother to a pauper's grave.'

And for once Marsdon didn't whine an excuse. 'That's the way people get buried here,' he said, and gently pushed her aside so that he, Jong Jan and the Brothers Kreef could take the coffin off to the cemetery.

Graciously Mrs Beg-rip caught up with the pallbearers, because that was her rightful place now that she was family, and sniffled her way through the village past the church and behind the koppie to the graveyard. There she burst into a flood of tears at the sight of the shallow pit.

'It's not even six feet deep, Marsdon, how could you?' she wailed.

Marsdon gave her the look he'd given her only once before and again didn't whine an excuse. 'This ground's too hard to go any deeper,' he said.

'Oh oh oh,' she sobbed and was inconsolable for weeks.

'I always thought she was a strange woman,' said Lady Sarah, 'even stranger than her sister, but at least Mad Minnaar had good sound common sense, even if she did pay more attention to stars or tea leaves than the real world, whereas that Mrs Beg-rip, right from the moment she climbed into the lifeboat, seemed weird to say the least, and I think her mother-in-law's funeral gave her mind a last twist. Undoubtedly. You should have seen her, captain, bawling her eyes out, and we all knew damn well there was no love lost between them. No, she was lamenting the fate which had married her to a poor man's grave, and sometimes I can't help wondering if what happened to Marsdon wasn't God's way of relieving his earthly burden because, let's face it, the only one who could deal with that woman was their son.'

The birth, like the pregnancy, was wildly hysterical. Her screams woke the village in the early hours of morning.

'Get my sister. Call my sister, don't just lie there, Marsdon. Oh heavens what pain,' cried Mrs Beg-rip between groans, 'I'm sure I'm going to die.'

In her hut, Mad Minnaar heaved the drunken sot's body from her and before Marsdon could pull on his boots she was shouting at the door – 'Shut that noise, Dorothea, you'll drag the dead from their sleep' – and for the next ten hours the village lived from contraction to contraction. One every twenty minutes, and the screams went through them like ice.

When the gap went down to ten minutes and closing, the screams rose to one shrill note which only the head-first arrival of little Marsdon brought to a tender climax with the touching words, 'My baby.'

'Praise the Lord,' said Mad Minnaar, scraping the bee's wax out of her ears. 'There's a good girl, Dorothea, give the youngster a tit, he's bound to be thirsty after all the hard work.'

Outside, the village toasted the birth with a glass or more of melon wine, while Mad Minnaar went down to the rocks to scrub herself clean and throw bits of afterbirth to the gulls, praying all the time, 'Lord, give this child a way out of here,' a prayer which, who'll deny it, was to be answered before little Marsdon was twenty-five years old.

'My son, you're going to be a great fisherman,' said Marsdon-father, smiling down at wife and child.

Nor did Marsdon-father ever moan about his dominating wife again.

As Jong Jan said, 'It's amazing what a boy child can do.'

Amazing not only for what he did to the father but also for what he did to the mother, because just one peep out of him and she was there, rocking the cot, thrusting first one breast then the other into the baby's face until Mad Minnaar said, 'Whokaai, Dorothea, enough is enough, he's got a stomach like a Bushman already.' And later when little Marsdon was toddling she took him down to play with the children in the fisher cottages and once even carried him on her back to the goatkeeper's hut because 'he's going to grow up to be a man of the world and he may as well know right now that this place isn't the centre of the universe no matter what you might think', as she said to Marsdon-father when, in horror, he gasped, 'What! You walked all that way, alone, don't you know there are hyenas with jaws strong enough to crack elephant bones just waiting in the scrublands?'

But nevertheless she went a few times after that, challenging him on each occasion to stop her. 'Please,' begged Marsdon-father, 'don't.' And that is when little Marsdon came to the rescue, just as he and his mother were about to set off one day, with the halting words, 'No, Mama.' Flabbergasted, Mama Beg-rip ran around the cottages shouting, 'Little Marsdon can talk already and he's not yet twelve months old. The boy's a genius.'

Perhaps she was closer to the truth than mother's pride could ever have imagined.

Before he was five years old he had stripped a generator that hadn't worked for many years and, more to the point, repaired it. So in future if anything went wrong with the boat engines there was no waiting for the monthly tug to put in, little Marsdon could probably fix it.

'Where he gets it from, I don't know,' said Marsdon-father, 'but the boy understands engines, and that's more than can be said for many a mechanic.'

Although little Marsdon had more calls to fix engines than anything else, it was radios that really fascinated him. Radios made the air talk. When he first heard the hissing crackling loud soft voice speaking from the battered box in the tug captain's wheelhouse, little Marsdon was filled with wonder; he couldn't take his eyes off it (or his hands), yes, such was his fascination that he, normally a placid child, screamed and performed when it was time for the tug to leave.

'Never mind, little Marsdon,' said the tug captain, 'I'll be back in a month and then you can listen to the air again.'

For the in-between time all little Marsdon could think of were the millions of inaudible conversations brushing his ears. Then came the tug blowing a loud hooter with engines churning round the Head and the captain waving from the wheelhouse, his face bigger and redder and more wrinkled than ever, to put an end to little Marsdon's waiting every morning on the jetty.

'Hey, little Marsdon, look what I've got for you, a radio, which doesn't work, but I'm sure you can fix it,' and he held up that much prized possession.

Of course, little Marsdon fixed the radio and his ham days began.

'You shouldn't be talking to those strange people and at all hours of the night,' nagged his mother, 'it's not right for a boy your age. Why don't you stop him, Marsdon-father? he's your son, too, you know.'

But Marsdon-father did nothing to discourage his boy, rather the opposite. He closeted with him in the small room made smaller by the growing banks of receivers, transmitters, amplifiers, so that he could speak with men passing far out to sea.

'It's as bad as my sister talking with the dead,' Mrs Beg-rip complained. 'There are things in this world we are not meant to tamper with and voices that come from nowhere are one of them. For heaven's sake, Marsdon-father, send the child to bed.'

Nag, nag, nag and more nag, he thought, before crouching again next to the spluttering box that spoke in a language neither of them could understand – although eventually little Marsdon would – about the immensity of the night sky and an ocean as dark as a whale's back.

'Men at sea talk a lot,' was all little Marsdon commented when the monologue finally came to an end.

'Faced with the universe and an empty water, you have to talk or disappear,' replied Marsdon-father as he tucked the little body of his son into bed.

So while Stevie and the other children larked day long about the beach and jetty catching shrimps, chasing birds, cutting off lizard tails, little Marsdon listened to the passing world – over – to sailors telling of wonderful cities and wonderful women who waited for them in dockyard hotels – over – to captains who named him Sonny Jim and promised to call him when they were back in the southern hemisphere – over. 'What's the southern hemisphere, over?' he asked. 'The bottom of the world,' they laughed. 'Goodbye, over and out, Sonny Jim.'

How could shrimps, dead birds or tailless lizards be as exciting as a lonely radio man steaming wherever with the likeness of his beloved tattooed over his heart?

'Can little Marsdon come out to play, Mrs Beg-rip?'

'Of course, Stevie-lad, I'll call him. Little Marsdon, don't you want to go out and play with Stevie and them? Go on, boy, it'll do you good to get out in the fresh air.'

'Ah, Ma, not now. I'm busy with the master of the watch. I'll go out this afternoon.'

But this afternoon never came. Always there was an excuse, a ship he expected, a message he had to send.

'About what?' demanded his mother.

'About low pressures, high pressures, gale warnings, fog banks, goodwill,' he answered.

And that would be the end of it. She would take to her bed as she had done after the death and birth for hours, sometimes days, sometimes weeks, once for a whole month at a time moaning about a pauper's grave. 'Such an awful poverty for dying, oh my oh my what a hard death for old bones.'

'What is your mother moaning about now?' (Marsdon-father to little Marsdon.)

44

'Never mind,' said little Marsdon, 'see what I've built. A set for your boat so that we can talk when you're out fishing.'

'Come in, Skipper Marsdon, come in, this is Landed-Little Marsdon on the air, over.

'Hullo, Landed-Little Marsdon, this is Skipper Marsdon, reading you loud and clear, over.'

This happiness lasted perhaps twelve or fifteen months until the day Marsdon-father took the boat out by himself long before anyone was up and about or there was even a hint of dawn in the east.

Towards sunrise the sky was not merely touched with crimson but seemed to be burning, which caused Jong Jan, the Brothers Kreef, the rest and Vygie Bond to pull out their pipes and sit along the jetty smoking rather than go to sea. Aloud they wondered why Marsdon-father had gone out fishing because even before the red sky in the morning there must have been other signs like the gulls on the sand or the glassy water unwrinkled by wind, or the ache of one's piles.

In their hearts they knew what had made that normally placid man blind to the warnings of the changing weather, and sympathised. Who wouldn't have done what he'd done, and probably a lot worse besides many months ago, if his wife had taken permanently to bed lamenting morning, noon and night the hard ground of a poor grave?

'What's stony ground when you're dead,' mused Vygie Bond, 'as long as there's enough earth to keep jackals from your leftovers?'

'Ja,' confirmed Jong Jan spitting tobacco at a sandpiper, 'bones don't ache when you're dead whether they lie on silk or canvas.'

Most of the morning the fishermen sat on the jetty blowing smoke over the shallows, thinking about Marsdon-father and the wind that was somewhere below the horizon howling towards them as surely as the sun was shortening their shadows.

'It must have been a terrible thing that made him go out there,' said Vygie Bond, ''cos Marsdon-father's the last one to weigh his life against a couple of pounds of steenbras.'

The Brothers Kreef nodded, but Jong Jan sucked hard and said, 'Maybe, but it's more likely something very small because don't all gales start from a light breeze?' A light breeze like the one that was right then giving them the chills and turning the water the grey colour of trouble.

So they got up and went round the side of Marsdon-father's house and Jong Jan tapped on the window with the stem of his pipe where they knew little Marsdon would be talking on the radio.

Little Marsdon had tears in his eyes and he asked Jong Jan to come in and help him raise Skipper Marsdon. 'My father just won't answer. What's the matter with him, Jong Jan?'

Jong Jan could hear Mrs Beg-rip ranting in the bedroom about the sanctity of mortal remains and respect for the temple of the body even in the kingdom of death but he managed to close his mind to the penetrating voice and, holding the microphone in his shaking hand, said, 'Skipper, this is Jong Jan, please come in, over.' While he was talking he felt as if he was calling up the already dead and before he had finished there were tears in his eyes too.

'Skipper, this is Jong Jan, please come in, over. Skipper, this is Jong Jan, please come in, over.'

They waited, Jong Jan with his arm about the boy, and all the fishermen crowded at the window sad-faced, tears in some eyes, but there was just the empty hiss of atmospherics . . . until softly a weary Marsdon-father said, 'Hullo, Jong Jan.'

'What you doing out there, skipper?' said Jong Jan. 'Out there's no place for a soul when the morning's red, there's birds on the sand and an ache in my piles. You can't be catching fish because they've all gone deeper than our longest lines, so why don't you come back and we'll drink hot wine and smoke a pipe in the boatshed?'

They waited a long time to hear the words. 'All right, Jong Jan.'

Such joy, such hugging and dancing and smiles and flashing gums, it was like a party. Jong Jan was shouting, 'Vygie-yous-all go'n get the wood, wine and Mrs Bond's special brown cookies with jam; and little Marsdon you stay here and talk to your pa and make sure he comes in faster than wind.'

Yet, when he shut the door on Mrs Beg-rip's lamentations, it went through his mind: what a home-coming poor man, don't know if I'd come back to that, but then maybe he'll kick her out or move in with little Marsdon somewhere else – that's if he gets back, with the wind now whipping up stronger and stronger and the black clouds jammed from horizon to horizon and thickening.

And so the storm came up until Mondling, Lady Sarah, Mad Minnaar, Jong Jan, or whoever stopped at the window to find out what progress, were crowded in the Beg-rip kitchen making tea and trying to ignore Dorothea Beg-rip's wails (not even Mad Minnaar could get her to shut up now) while little Marsdon listened to a storm at sea with his father's tiny voice below the gale.

'. . . I can see land, I can see the Head, when the rain clears I can see your lights . . .'

'Praise the Lord,' whispered Mad Minnaar.

'If he can see us then we can see him,' said Mondling, struggling into his oilskins and going out to stand in that tempest on the very end of the jetty.

Then the radio went as silent as the moment after a great grief and little Marsdon said, 'He's gone. My father's gone.'

Through the rain and the coming darkness Lady Sarah supported by Samuel, Mondling alone, Mad Minnaar and her drunken sot, Jong Jan, Vygie Bond, the Brothers Kreef and the rest went home with that heaviness that surrounds the heart when you've lost someone dear. And little Marsdon? Little Marsdon sat in his radio room until grief put him to sleep. And his mother? She muttered and mumbled about going to a hard grave at the foot of a stony koppie.

In this night of sad loss let's follow Mad Minnaar and the man I've called (rather harshly you might think) the drunken sot home across the sand and the patches of vygies, flowering purple and red between the clumps of spiky dune grass which get up Mad Minnaar's dress and prick her legs, although tonight she doesn't notice the discomfort, to their shack (which can't be described otherwise because it is a corrugated-iron affair with neither brick nor mortar nor even clay and sticks and is slowly being consumed by the voracious eater rust) opposite the fisher cottages and behind the small sand dune that hides Mondling's secrets.

Let's go in through the door that Mad Minnaar opens with a bump of her shoulder into the dark room which smells of a hundred musky years of people breathing garlic and onion, sweating the odours of armpits and sour feet, farting bad cabbage and old fish, releasing the grey vapours of sex into a volume of air that hasn't been changed in all that time and try not to be overcome by the stench while she fumbles with a match at the paraffin lamp.

In the weak light see the chaos of unmade bed (coats and sacks and canvas for blankets, stuffed bags of wool and grass for pillows), the lovely ship's table stained with rings of wine, grimed with food; cold and congealed the last meal in the buckled pewter plates, underfoot a hairless zebra skin, clothes, rags, trunks, boxes; and bottles, hundreds of green-sea-scoured bottles stacked, piled, discarded everywhere. And, in a corner where the light ends, glimpse the big movement of a rat.

Hardly the most salubrious quarters for a woman used to the ordinary luxuries of middle-class life despite her guardian's extraordinary ways; nor does it quite fit with the Mad Minnaar who mollycoddled her younger sister through marriage, pregnancy and birth, although it does fit with the latter Minnaar – the Minnaar she became – who by then had certainly justified the appellation, mad. Which just goes to show what a strange force love is, because didn't Mad Minnaar let this very same drunken sot take her home from where she had been beached, and didn't he make love to her with his liquor breath until her body was consumed again and again and again with the most wonderful sensations that made it all worth while and, yes, more and more please kind whoever you are?

So there's the secret, sustained not once, not twice, but three times nightly, and once during the day if they got the chance praise the Lord oh it was lovely.

But surely love does not thrive on sex alone? No matter that she called him a drunken sot, there was more between them than a mere passion of the body. For like fire, passion eventually consumes itself; yet Mad Minnaar and her drunken sot seemed the eternal couple.

One must not forget either that no secrets were hidden from Mad Minnaar. She knew everything: thoughts at five miles were as clear to her as words spoken at five paces. So unlike Dorothea, who had to take Marsdon Beg-rip at face value, Mad Minnaar had direct access to the dark chambers of her lover's mind, and maybe she found there something, some deep hurt, which he had buried from the world. Who this man was, no one knew: his origins were as obscure as evening cloud. He was just a man who had been discovered one day asleep on the vlei grass as one day there had appeared a body in the lagoon – events which were one as inexplicable as the other.

'Heaven knows, captain,' said Lady Sarah, 'he was a troubled man, with more, a whole lot more, than just the drink eating him up, and I think Mad Minnaar knew that long before she ever clapped eyes on him, which is maybe some of the reason she was as she was towards him. Do you know that once on the beach, in those early awful days when I was given to sad walks, I came upon him, although for a time he didn't seem to notice me, so engrossed was he in raving at the sky?

'And you know, captain, if he hadn't been obsessed with the chances of finding a message in every bottle that washed up on these shores we would never have known you would be coming here?'

She smiled triumphantly.

Captain Nunes glanced from the eyes that mocked him out of the window at an empty sea. The boat had long since gone and the kelp heads were drowned in the rising tide. On the beach next to the jetty the fishermen would be cleaning the day's catch. He wished he was there, standing, as he usually did, slightly to one side of the silvery bodies, so that those with some life left did not flick sand on his uniform. There was, he found, a satisfaction in their death throes. Ah-man.

Reluctantly, Nunes brought his thoughts back to Lady Sarah. 'What do you mean?' he asked.

'I mean,' said Lady Sarah, 'that one day shortly after the bodies, Mad Minnaar's man found a bottle in the tideline with a note which unfortunately got torn to pieces in the excitement. But Finella, who, as you know, spends her days making jigsaw puzzles, pieced the scraps of paper together to form your name. There are some things, captain, which none of us can escape.'

3

THE WORST OF SORTS

Every eye in the village followed Captain Nunes from Lady Sarah's gate, down the sandy path into the smell of lamb chops and fried eggs, his lunch. He walked unhurriedly, inscrutable behind dark glasses, the badge on his cap glinting a random semaphore, his spider hands hardly moving at his sides.

But did he walk differently? Was there more spring to his stork-like step? Did he now look at the village with understanding? Would Fagmie Jabaar's soon be stocked with chocolate, sherbet, jams, tins of spaghetti in tomato sauce, town beer, black balls? Could they at last stop hoarding their wealth beneath the floor, the richest poor people on earth, and once again enjoy the good life? Could they? Could they?

Every woman peering through the chink in her kitchen curtain, every grandmother leaning on her stable door, every fisherman paused in the scaling of fish, every one of them from Augustin Shoote in the shadow of the church doorway, to Boatswain Baleen and his lovely Finella linking hands to say grace, wondered if their lives would change, wondered what was going on in the captain's mind.

Every day there were minor signs of change, an ordinance relaxed, a regulation amended, but the moment they waited for never came. Nothing in the captain's demeanour changed at all. He was neither less friendly nor more friendly, he still played draughts with Mondling in the morning, went down to watch the boats come in at midday, rested inside during the afternoon, stepped out on his customary patrol in the early evening before supper. But nothing changed.

On the third day the fisherfolk decided Jong Jan should speak to Lady Sarah.

'Why me?' he protested, 'I'm no good with words.'

'Someone's got to,' said Vygie Bond, 'we must bring this pimple to a head. And you're the senior man.'

Of course, it was not pleasing information Jong Jan brought back. The fisherfolk were outraged.

Why not? Why did she spend four hours talking to the captain without telling him the most important thing? Hey, Jong Jan! What does she think she's doing keeping us in poverty and misery? It's fine for her living in the lap of luxury, but if she had to sleep just one night in our houses she'd quickly tell him. Go again Jong Jan and let her know we're unhappy.

'Don't you see, Jong Jan,' said Lady Sarah, 'that I can't simply blurt out our secret? We've told him so many stories he doesn't know fact from fantasy. He's got to learn the truth about us, Jong Jan, and only then, when I judge the time is right, will I tell him. You entrusted me, everyone entrusted me, and I won't let you down. You go and tell them that. I'm sure we can all bear our hardships a little longer. I'm sure another month or two won't be the end of the world.'

'All right, Jong Jan,' said Vygie Bond, 'we'll give her a month. But you tell her that's it, that's the end, if she hasn't told him by then I'm going to tell him myself.'

So Jong Jan shuffled messages between the cottages on the lagoon and the mansion above Whale Beach, not quite understanding why he was suddenly the bad dog.

Nunes never noticed the comings and goings of Jong Jan; his mind was occupied with other matters. He was deeply suspicious of Lady Sarah's motives and still unsure about whether or not to believe her.

In this life, he sighed to the dog tied up in the yard, a man must either believe everything or nothing. It's when you try picking out the truth in this garbage heap that nothing makes sense. It falls apart. Rotten to the core with maggots and deception. Ah-man. Look at me, dog, look. An officer of law and order, a man who lives in black and white, wrong and right, good and bad, confused. Confused. Utterly confused. Ah-man. Who am I to believe? Would these insects lie to me when I could have squashed them beneath my thumb? Haven't you heard harder men squawk like starlings when I've put on the squeeze – huh! huh! – yet now I'm supposed to believe these mixed-bloods were so cunning and scheming as to lie. I can't believe it. Ah-man, I can't believe it. And yet, what has Lady Sarah to gain by these stories? Huh, dog, what has she to gain? That's my problem, dog. Ah-man, ah-man. I must go in there and say, 'OK, my gracious lady, what's this you're scheming?'

Despite this resolution, Nunes let a week lapse and then fourteen days before he went to see Lady Sarah again. That week tortured the hearts of the fisherfolk as they saw more and more precious time being lost in the endless rounds of draughts the captain played with Mondling.

But if their hearts were tortured, so was the captain's, because he lost game after game.

'You are not in your usual form, Herr kaptein,' said Mondling, as, yet again, he wiped Nunes from the board. 'You are letting me have it too easy. Come, we will play again, ja . . .' and he set up the pieces.

In that game, too, Nunes was demolished. Every move he made brought a cluck of disapproval from Mondling, who would then show the power of his play and leave a trail of devastation across the board. Nunes grew angry. Not so much with his companion as with a hot thickness in his head that prevented him from seeing even the simplest moves. When Mondling triumphantly captured his last piece on the board, the captain hit the table in frustration.

'Enough, that is enough!' he shouted.

Mondling calmly picked up the pieces from the floor.

'Ja, kaptein,' he said, 'it is enough. You are not, as you say, part of yourself today.' He got up. 'Perhaps it would be better for you alone.'

Nunes put out a hand to restrain the old man.

'Stay,' he said, 'we can talk. You can tell me about the revolts.'

'I can tell you all sorts of things, Herr kaptein, but is it not you who should be talking?'

'No, no, we all have our problems.'

'Men who have daughters always have problems, kaptein.'

Nunes dismissed Mondling's comment with a shrug.

'I have been told things,' he said unexpectedly, 'by Lady Sarah, and who is to say if they are true?' Then suddenly he realised that if anyone could corroborate her story it was the strange man on the opposite side of the table. The heat in his head seemed to ease. 'You have been here a long time, Herr Mondling,' he said. 'You were here when Lady Sarah came, were you not?'

Mondling nodded. 'Ja, I was on the beach.'

'So the shipwreck is true.'

'Ja. But if you will tell me what else I will find the lies.'

Nunes recounted what he knew and at the end Mondling could find no lies.

'It is the truth,' he admitted, 'but you must watch out for that woman, Herr kaptein, she is conniving.

'Me, for instance, I will have nothing to do with the so-called Lady Sarah. She is not what you or these people think – but it is not for me to give her the bad mouth, as you say, each one to his own.'

Mondling picked at something between his teeth, grunting with satisfaction when a brown sliver of food came away on his fingernail.

'You are another man, Herr kaptein, not like these around here,' he continued. 'Myself and you, we are strangers here, we have seen the world, we know about things. Yet you and I, kaptein, have never had a proper talk man to man about the world, about ourselves. You are unknown to me as I am unknown to you. Which is gut, ja.

'Good but not so good, it means we can never be friends, there is always this distance of the past between us. I would like us to be friends, kaptein, but that means we have to get rid of the past which is not an easy thing, especially as you and me we have moments of which we would rather others did not know. Is that not so, ja? But there can be no friendships unless there is trust and there can be no trust without openness, do you not agree? So, I would like to say something about myself if you will listen.'

Nunes waved his arm in a gesture of acquiescence.

'Ja. Gut. This thing, the revolts, that I will say you have probably read about in the history books but they do not have it the way it was. Always they have a bias, the bias of someone with a point to make; but I have no point to make, I simply tell you about the things I saw and felt.

'So, to begin. There was a man called Samuel Maharero, the leader of the Herero tribes which had been causing much trouble in Deutsche-Südwest-Afrika killing the German settlers, raping their women and daughters, cutting off the privates of the men, and many such horrible deeds.

'After making all this chaos this Samuel Maharero takes his men, women, children, goats, cattle, dogs, the sick, the old, the whole nation in to the Onjati Hills before the schutztruppe can teach them a lesson. This, of course, makes for a good deal of mutterings and mumblings among the heerenvolk because this is not good enough. They are sick up to the back molars with this shambles and all the talk, talk, talk with the chiefs because where does it get them? Nowhere. These schweinhunds still cause pillage and mayhem. So what is the use of talk they want to know?

'These mutterings they get all the way back to the Kaiser's ear and suddenly there comes a change in German policy. I think it is time we taught these black devils a lesson, says Kaiser Wilhelm. And the teacher who must give this lesson is General Lothar von Trotha, a fine man, a fine upstanding man with strong Christian principles.

'That was a man. That was a soldier. He knew what he was doing. You could see it from the moment he took command. None of this accommodate talk, none of this business we must all learn to live together, none of that nonsense: instead we must teach them a lesson and if they won't learn then we will exterminate the rubbish.

'That is the sort of talk the Kaiser and the settlers wanted to hear. They wanted to know that the great general of the troops had their welfare at his heart. So when he said to the natives, no more of this murder and stealing and cutting off of noses, the settlers said, that is right Lothar, you tell them, useless hotnot schweinhunds. So Lothar said, all you swart donders must leave the land, you have heard what the white people want, you have heard what I ordered, now go, or else I will run you out with the big guns. And the women and children mustn't come crying to me about their bad husbands and fathers who want to make war and bring misery on everybody's heads because I am not interested in snivelmakers: they will be shot or we will sjambok them into the desert. That is what I have decided for the black people.

'When I heard of it I said, "This man is for me – just show me where I can join the schutztruppe." Let me tell you, Herr kaptein, I was familiar with the Herero, that is why I knew the general was right, for these were not nice people, but cheats, liars, cattle-thieves, kaffirs without any fear of God, the worst of sorts.

'So I was there under Major Estorff with his five hundred men along the Omuramba-u-Omataka river course when we gave them the divine punishment. To get there we march south for many days through this thick thorn bushes, which is strong as the barbed wire of sheep-farmers, until the men were scratched and bleeding like we have already fought a battle. That only brought our blood up more. Eventually we can see the dust clouds above the Okambukauandja mountains and we know that Samuel Maharero is still there. The sun goes down and the day's sweat becomes like ice. Major Estorff says, "You men" – meaning the platoon in which I am – "go closer and find out what is going on."

'Off we go although we are dropping with the tiredness but there is so much anger in our hearts that we find the strength to push on until Gott-in-hemel there are as many stars in the bush around us as there are in the sky. One man climbs a tree to look about, and donderwette if we haven't walked among the enemy. Already the faint light is starting in the east and everywhere around there are voices and cooking fires. Surely if we are to be caught we would be eating our genitals for breakfast.

'But then a thought struck, because as I have said, those people were familiar to me. You see, mein herr, they had a deep fear of the ghosts and so they would not leave the fires until all the shadows from the night have vamooshed. Nothing to worry about I tell the men, we just walk right through like ghosts. Sure the men are not very happy, but what can we do, except be ghosts with our finger on the trigger?

'Ja, it makes me laugh to think about it. There we are right in the midst of Samuel Maharero's peoples and not one man would lift his assegai. If we had been five hundred men we could have wiped them out just like that, pfhut. But if we had been anything other than ghosts they would have pulled out our stomachs.

'And then, just when we are about to reach a hill of thick cactus which is beyond their camp, I see this bunch coming towards us. Leading them is a kaffir which I have known before when I was shooting elephants. In those days he was not a bad kaffir and could stop the sleeping sickness.

'"That is quite close enough, kaffir," I whisper below my breath, "you and me have a pact and this is not the time to call up the debts." To my commander I suggest, "Let me go and talk with the kaffir, we know each other from the swamps." But before I have advanced ten paces the kaffir has lifted this tall hat he wears and gives me a large grin. The next thing his party they turn around and go off into the thorn bush. The commander is very much surprised and says one day I must tell him how I know this kaffir. As the world goes I never get that chance because three weeks later in the thick of the fighting we find him dead: all blue in the face with his balls in his cheeks. His penis, too, it is missing.

'You have heard the saying about how war is mostly long card games while you wait for something to happen and then when something does happen the rest is fear? Ja! Well this was like this. For three weeks we sat with the cards until they were so dirty we could hardly tell the hearts from the spades. All the time we can see the enemy on the hill looking after their cattle, smoking their pipes in the sun and drinking beer as if there is nothing wrong in the world. Many a time I ask myself why doesn't von Trotha attack now, then it will all be over. But no, he waits and waits and waits until three weeks have gone by. And then one glorious morning from a far hill to the north the heliographs wink at us that the time has come.

55

'All day and all night the cannons fire so that when we get to the camp the next morning everywhere there is destruction, carnage, the dead, the mutilated, the dying, men with no heads, a woman's breast here, a fat buttock there, everywhere carnage and destruction. Never have I seen such a sight, never have I heard such cries.

'Yet, Herr kaptein, this was not the worst. Oh no. You must remember we have been spoiling for blood, we have debts to repay: rapes, murders, thefts, tortures; and now we smelt that blood.'

In the long silence that ended Mondling's revelations, Nunes looked at the strange old man with envy. Ah, to have lived in those times when the divides were simple, when there were Europeans, kaffirs and a savage land. Ah-man. How much easier.

Aloud he said, 'You are a fortunate man, Herr Mondling, those were heroic times. You have led a good life.'

The sound of Nunes's voice jerked the old man back to the verandah. For a moment a dread glistened in his eyes through their milky film, but it died almost as suddenly as it had lived.

'As I am sure you know, mein kaptein,' he said wearily, 'there is nothing in this world that does not have its price. And for this good life of which you speak I have had to show the colour of my money.'

With that he stood up, still a big man although stooped now, and with a nod at the captain went down the verandah stairs one at a time, grimacing with rheumatic pain. Captain Nunes watched Mondling hobble up the dusty street to the house with its tall fence where neither he nor any villager had set foot since an earlier generation had built it.

By all accounts, Mondling had arrived at the settlement many, many years before in the early hours when even the dogs were asleep. One morning there he was at the end of the jetty, arms folded, feet astride, a revolver of some sort stuck into his belt, bellowing into a loudhailer. Tied to a bollard was a thirty-foot vessel, the like of which no one had ever seen before, and many marvelled how it managed to stay afloat, let alone sail, it looked so top heavy, with a wheelhouse smack in the centre and portholes starboard and port on to a large cargo area. But the portholes were blacked out, and when some of the children tried to scratch off the tar on the salty glass to settle everyone's curiosity they were chased away with such ferocity, such a waving of arms as if he carried swords that they fled in terror, some of them even jumped into the lagoon to escape the madman's wrath, only stopping when they were well behind their mothers' aprons. While they hadn't seen very much, one had seen enough to start the oddest gossip.

Within minutes of that foreign accent bringing everyone out of their beds in alarm, Captain Baleen (father of Boatswain) was, as village elder, being pressed into selling the bear-like newcomer a plot of land. Never once did Mondling give a moment's thought to the possibility that he might not be welcome. After all, this was a free country, a man could settle where he wanted to. As Mondling was not given to wasting words the good Captain Baleen was soon placed under no misapprehension that what the buyer wanted was not only a piece of land but also a house built on the site he would choose during the course of the morning. For this service Mondling was prepared to pay with a coin the like of which Captain Baleen had never seen before.

'Good money,' said Mondling. 'All right?'

'Well,' hesitated Captain Baleen glancing over his shoulder to indicate it was only proper he consult the fisherfolk.

'Gut,' said Mondling. 'Now will you please excuse me? It has been a long voyage.' With that he disappeared into the hold of his vessel.

Needless to say the boats did not put out that morning; instead, everyone gathered at the end of the jetty speculating about the dark arrival who, some said, could only have been guided by the Devil. How else would he have found his way through the Head's rocky teeth? And Lord have mercy on us sinners, they crossed themselves, if the Devil held a candle for this man then maybe he, too, was a fallen angel going about the evil work of capturing poor souls. Which, to an all-ears little boy who'd seen more than he should have through a crusty porthole, brought to mind the steel cages the goatherds used to trap aardvarks and jackals. If cages were used to capture bad animals then maybe they were also used to capture poor souls. Hadn't that been what he'd seen? And if it was, shouldn't he tell? Yes, he should, he decided. But for the words he whispered in his mother's ear all he received was a terrified look and a sharp slap across the cheek.

However, his story went about the group quicker than a shark through a forty-pound cob. And there wasn't a heart that didn't feel a sudden chill because they were all of them sinners of one sort or another, all of them guilty of some indiscretion. Jong Jan, who was very young then, a mere teenager, thought of what he'd done to the goatherds' goats; Young Mrs Bond remembered a time with middle-aged Matie Kreef when they'd both had too much dagga and crawled among the nets one night; and Matie Kreef thought of the widowed Mrs Beg-rip bathing, the steaming water running down her fine breasts and the rivulets of soap slipping through her bush the way the tide fingered vlei grass; and Mrs Beg-rip thought of the candle she kept secreted among her underwear; and Captain Baleen remembered how he'd cheated on his wife; and all of them recalled things they had stolen or coveted, while some went quickly home to smash the idols they called on when the rains didn't come or fish were scarce.

Just when some were drifting off to cook lunch the wheelhouse door banged open and the stranger leapt on to the jetty.

'Don't any of you come snooping around or you'll feel the size of my fist and a length of sjambok across your bums, ja,' he shouted, shaking fist and whip; then charged down the boards with the look of an angry honeybadger so that the fisherfolk scattered like gulls.

'Where's the captain? Fetch me Captain Baleen, hotnot kaffir,' he yelled at Joseph. And poor Joseph, who had sat with his Mary to one side, jumped up in fright and fell and stumbled as he ran for Captain Baleen.

Together, Mondling and Captain Baleen tramped all over the village, down towards the beach where later Lady Sarah's house was built, then past the cottages and along the edge of the lagoon almost halfway to the goatherds; next he was pacing out ground below the koppie and, finally, he chose a spot among the sand dunes where he was hidden from everyone but no one was hidden from him.

'This is gut,' he said. 'You can tell your labourers they can build it here,' and he stuck four red flags in the sand.

And that is where the men toiled for many days, while Mondling, to them the devil incarnate (because hadn't they heard the gnashing of teeth in his cabin? wasn't it the thumps and poundings of a soul in torment they listened to on quiet nights when nothing could be muffled?), sat on the dune, ever vigilant.

Save our souls, prayed the villagers morning noon and night inside the church and out; and watched what came and went from his boat with eyes sharper than a snake eagle, for souls don't eat or shit. In all that time he never took on board more than one man's food, nor did the pail he emptied in the lagoon each morning have more turds than one man can excrete. Yet as surely as Almighty God they had heard the thumps and the poundings, the gnashing of teeth, and sometimes a howl more lonely than a jackal before dawn, more wounded than a dying penguin, which sent the chills up and down their spines and made sleeping babies cry.

Lord have mercy on us, they prayed, we have allowed a serpent into our midst.

Yet still they laboured dawn to dusk at his house, although their hearts were not in it, with but one thought: to finish, to have done with it even though each brick they laid was the devil's work.

And when it was done it was nothing to be proud of: a plain house of small windows, dark rooms, a deep cellar with grille doors and a head-high fence round the yard – but then no one wanted to leave his mark on that house.

Mondling must have moved his bags and chattels into the house on a night as dark as the one that brought him. Nobody heard him lugging trunks and cases from boat to house although some later swore to hearing the clink of chains and loud panting. When the village awoke there were curtains drawn at the house's every window, and the crusty portholes gave light on to an empty hold.

Timidly at first, but then, when there was no sign of his stirring, with quick courage, some of the fishermen went below and found holes where the cage had been bolted fast, and scratch marks on the boards that could only have been made by a desperate soul. And everywhere a smell, as strong as when drunk men sleep in the boathouse, a smell full of sweat and foul breath and the bad stench of loose bowels.

That was all they found before he came in shouting, 'Out donder scum, schweinhund und plague-locusts, out blitzen, vamoose, out, out, out, ja!'

A few moments later the massive engines thundered into life churning the boat towards the middle of the lagoon, where Mondling threw over the anchor, pulled all the stopcocks and sank it before the astonished eyes of the whole village. Still today, on the low tide, part of the wheelhouse provides a roost for cormorants and gulls.

Like a good captain, Mondling didn't abandon ship until it had settled in the mud; then he swam slowly to shore.

Try as they might the fisherfolk were unable to settle down with Mondling on their outskirts. The shrieks, howls, screams, cries, moans, lamentations, grindings, weepings and wailings that went on at all hours of the night were enough to keep even the dead from sleep. But no one was prepared to investigate. Except the children.

Terrified, but overcome by curiosity, they moled under the fence one night to see for themselves what the damned one looked like. Not for them the parents' descriptions of a naked body tormented by demons with red-hot knives and forks, descriptions which nevertheless became the stuff of nightmares – oh no, they wanted the real thing. Which, without reservations, they got.

In part, their nightmares were vindicated because when the first boy broke through the crust of Mondling's back yard and held up a lantern he came face to face with a naked girl covered in hair, her gums snarling over wolf teeth, four nipples on her chest, claws for nails, who moved like an animal and stank worse than jackals.

That was it, that was enough to send the moles back to the right side of sanity, shovelling sand into the hole quicker than they'd shovelled it out to prevent at all costs that monster escaping. Of course, nobody believed them. At least not until the men were in their cups after a hard day pulling mackerel, and the children had cried themselves to sleep after a sound spanking, and the woman had prayed to God Almighty what manner of man is it who chains up a girlwolf in his yard before her soul goes to hell, oh what shall we do? what shall we do? And Jong Jan's father, Old Jan, who always took the lead in times of trouble, said, 'We'll go at first light and look for ourselves and then decide what, if anything, is to be done.'

In the first light of the next dawn she wasn't there, but clearly Mondling kept an animal of some sort: why else the bones and the half-filled basin of blood? So they went again that night and there she was emerging on an all-fours lope from the cellar, manacled to a length of chain.

God have mercy on us what's this that isn't a woman or beast with enough tits to succour a litter and hair like a goat's, by the great beard of Moses what's happening with the world?

So it was true, there in his back yard, in the village's back yard so to speak, Mondling was keeping a strange specimen, neither one thing nor the other, and what, what was to be done? For days, weeks, they sat mumbling until Captain Baleen heard about it.

'What's this? I can't believe it.'

'But you have to, captain, four of us saw it, a girlwolf large as life chained to a stake.'

With a spark nobody had seen in the seadog since his wife had died, he rushed off to confront Mondling. What a shindy, a fur-flying rumpus that resolved nothing. Mondling was adamant.

'That girl she is an animal, the devil's practical joke, she can rot out there. I shall not lift a finger to do anything more than throw her bones in the evening.'

Which wasn't good enough for Captain Baleen.

'No human being, not even the worst raving lunatic deserves to be treated that way, and if you think we're going to turn a blind eye to your brutality you've got another think coming, Herr Mondling. We'll . . . we'll run you out.'

'Bah! Kaptein, you and which of the Queen's army, I suppose. What nonsense you suggest. But come, come and look at the little beauty to which you show such philanthropy and then see what a to do all-you are raging.'

So outside they went and the philanthropic Captain Baleen changed his tune at first sight of the creature, fear in its eyes, trapped in the middle of the yard.

Now the story of how that poor girl came into this world is a story of love, cuckoldry, betrayal, and finally, of course, death.

Some time after the revolts it seems Mondling fell in love wonderfully, irrevocably, increasingly besotted with each breath he took. The much cherished object of this infatuation was a young, seventeen-year-old orphan who stayed with her grandmother in the posthouse of the harbour town where he was the one and only arm of the law.

The not so young policeman – although how old is old in Mondling's life? – who had scorned women and love suddenly found himself out of his depth, floundering among emotions which terrified as much as they thrilled. That he could have had a daughter as young as the cause of his emotional turmoil never occurred to him; he just knew, each time she came to his house to collect the laundry, or whenever he saw her, skirts furled above an expanse of smooth thigh, collecting black mussels among the rocks, that he was gripped by a strong desire to have this girl, to possess her body and soul.

So, in his own clumsy fashion, he set about the courting of Meisie Koekemoer, which for the first three tedious months meant long hours ingratiating himself with Granny Koekemoer, while his heart-throb ran free along the beach and, confound it, among the sand dunes where, as he well knew, flowers that weren't vygies were regularly plucked.

However. As is so often the way of things, long before Mondling could bring himself to reveal his honourable intentions, Granny

Koekemoer's impatience for what she foresaw could be the good life, sat the two of them down on the sofa after dinner, lit a candle and stomped out of the room advising Mondling that when the flame went out he should be on the other side of the front door. One hundred and twenty-three candles later Mondling proposed, Granny Koekemoer, as legal guardian, accepted and three banns later Meisie became a wife.

Quite what Meisie thought of this arrangement it's impossible to say, although her later actions presume that she took up the bonds of holy matrimony with some reluctance. Nothing was ever said in so many words but clearly the grandmother considered she'd won a great victory in getting the child off her hands. Which seems to imply that Meisie was a spirited lass, who'd probably never set much store on keeping intact the thin membrane Mondling thought it had been his honour to pierce.

Much about what was to happen is explained if these assumptions are correct: high spirits on the one hand pitted against extreme jealousy on the other does not lend itself to marital bliss, so it is hardly any wonder that within six months Meisie was a prisoner in her own house, to the delighted approval of Granny.

Gated, forbidden social intercourse, especially with males, the wan face of Meisie Mondling, née Koekemoer, appeared for hours each day at the small front window with its view of the street and distant harbour. It must have been from that very same window that Meisie, three years after the marriage, and still without a child, one day saw the man who was to do to her heart strings what she had done to Mondling's.

If Mondling had not seen himself as a cut above those he policed, it is likely that Meisie's love would have been for ever unrequited. But no, her lord and master wanted a garden, even though there was no soil, only beach sand, even though nothing but the hardiest succulents and scrub managed a tenuous survival against the elements. And who should he engage as gardener but a no-good layabout who was to become the man of Meisie's dream? A man he'd had to throw into jail on not a few occasions for drunkenly disturbing the peace, the whitest kaffir he'd ever come across. Besides, this white kaffir had talked a hole in Mondling's head. 'Yes boss, I've got the greenest fingers in the desert, just bursting with tomatoes, pumpkins and flowers of every type.'

And so Mondling acquired a gardener and Meisie shifted from

window to window as she followed his progress through the sandy surrounds to the house. Perhaps, when he straightened up to wipe the sweat from his brow, he caught her staring and smiled, maybe even laughed when she drew the curtains on his brashness. Because all the time he must have known that through a chink in the curtains she was watching him, the young missus who never went outside. Perhaps then he decided to entice her, little guessing she would be a pushover from the start. However he did it, within days they were friendly. First he was knocking on the back door to beg a mug of water or a slice of bread and jam. The next day Meisie gave him tea and lunch, and he ended the following afternoon on one of her husband's thick wines. Which would have been scandal enough had she been found out, but of course she wasn't, and inevitably one dangerous thing led to another, even though Mondling could have dropped by at any moment to discuss the beans, which got longer each day, or the pumpkins growing fatter by the hour, or the petunias on either side of the front path in a show that was pure miracle to the inhabitants of that flowerless region.

To appreciate fully what happened between Meisie and her gardener, consider that the town had no more than thirty people classified white and ninety-four classified Bondelswart-cum-Afrikaner-cum-what-have-you, so there wasn't much anyone could do without it being known in one quarter or the other. Yet for a whole season, or more precisely three bean crops, two dozen pumpkins, endless bunches of carrots, continual vases of flowers and seven baskets of tomatoes, Meisie's love affair, blossoming in all likelihood on the conjugal bed, went undiscovered until she missed a period, oh my, just to prove she wasn't the sterile one.

The sight of her swelling stomach put Mondling in the clouds: so he was at last to be a father, his darling was forgiven, wasn't the world the most beautiful place. Meisie must have known the gardener had sown seeds in her as wonderfully as he had in the barren sands, yet she chose to sit out the nine months knowing that at their end all would be revealed. Either she wistfully hoped for a miracle or, more likely, the devil in her wanted to shatter the man who had made her life a nightmare.

Shatter him it didn't, not when he snatched the newborn babe from Granny Koekemoer's arms, not when he rocked the child to sleep in the weeks and months that followed, not when he took the six-, seven-, eight-, nine-, ten-, eleven-, twelve-month-old toddler down to the

63

beach to play on the sand, not until one day he got it into his head that his daughter didn't look anything like him, looked only vaguely like her mother but had the unmistakably generous nose and mouth of his gardener. This cute child, he realised, was no throwback from some distant union of contrasting skins, no surprise from a genetic stew, this was the product of illicit, adulterous, wicked, totally unforgivable whoremongering, in his own house what's more. As dawn is first a red glow whitening just before the sun rises, so his anger spread through his body as the dim realisation turned into absolute certainty.

The dawn was fiery, a fisherman's warning, when he entered the bedroom after a troubled night pacing the kitchen, lifted his formerly dear wife from between the sheets and threw her against the wall again and again until her bones were crushed to pulp and there was nothing left of her but a bloodied bag of flesh.

Then he went after the gardener. But the gardener was nowhere to be found. Although he searched through the Bondelswart-cum-Afrikaner-cum-what-have-you quarter, in every hut, under every bed, in every cart, every boat; although he rode for tens of miles out into the desert in every direction, he could not find the man who had so thoroughly destroyed his world. No one had seen him go, no one had any idea where he might be.

That night, the baby girl, a mere one year old, the apple of Mondling's eye, was thrown out to sleep in the orchard so lovingly cared for up to the previous day by the green-fingered gardener, her father. From that day until the day she died the child never again set foot in Mondling's house, never learnt to talk, forgot how to cry, became an animal dependent on the scraps thrown to her from the back door or over the fence and the bowl of water, filled every second day.

4

THE FOURTEENTH DAY

Although Mondling's account of the Herero revolts and his hints and allusions left Captain Nunes with much to ponder over, he was to learn nothing more about the secretive Südwester, because just fourteen days later events came rushing at him inevitably, destructively, finally. And no one, with the possible exception of Frieda, was expecting it.

That fourteenth day emerged from darkness into a cold grey, and the night's rain did not cease. Nevertheless, as was his custom, Nunes had Frieda shave him on the stoep. Today he did not notice the cold; he sat in shirtsleeves while Frieda shivered in a coat she'd cut from blankets.

Had anyone been watching Nunes and his daughter closely, they would have noticed that, of late, perhaps over the last thirteen days, the easy grace with which Frieda performed the morning ritual had been replaced by a stiffness bordering on fear. Undoubtedly her skill was as deft, her strokes as sure, but she seemed to recoil when her fingers touched his skin. This morning was no different: she took a long time preparing the razor and lather, steeling herself for the task.

What happened between Nunes and Frieda in those thirteen days happened without words; it just grew (a seed sprouting, an ember flaring) inside them, ordained, powerful, divorcing father from daughter until in his brutal way Nunes tried to regain the daughter he'd had and burnt himself in the heat of the moment.

Perhaps it was what Mondling said about daughters being nothing but trouble that set Nunes brooding. Perhaps it was simply one of those deep chemical changes in the body which can so radically alter the way one eyes the world. But suddenly he started seeing his daughter draped around the neck of a village lout and it brought anger to his stomach. Anger and jealousy. He remembered how she had been after the death of his wife, her tiny body curled against him in the night, and then, later, the softly growing woman still seeking his warmth. For how long now had she been out of his bed, a mere

65

presence in the house, slipping on bare feet about the rooms, seeing to his meals but less company than a servant, offering nothing of a daughter, while he, blind fool, ingratiated himself with the villagers and listened to the nonsense of that pretentious lady. All for what? Ah-man, the cunning of women. Those wily, loveless bitches out for nothing but their own pleasure, fickle-hearted sluts, even this one, his daughter, cavorting with mixed-bloods in the dunes. And what had it got him? Nothing. Not a clue to the villagers' secret, nothing but dried bokoms and toothless smiles. And at what cost? The loss of a daughter. It was time to call a halt, to pull the secret from Lady Sarah, to lock the girl in, to send the lout packing, to knock the villagers into line, to make the necessary arrests. They would see. They would all see that Captain Nunes was not to be trifled with. He had played their games for too long, it was time to bring back law and order, starting with his daughter.

For thirteen days he brooded about the village, acknowledged greetings with a mere nod of the head, no longer went down to watch the boats come in, no longer showed interest in the life about him. Even Mondling, who had most claim to being a companion, was turned away at the door by Frieda.

'My father is not in the mood,' she told him and the old man shuffled back up the street, moving closer to the edge of his life with every step.

Had he been shown in he would have found the captain, in undershorts and vest despite the winter damp and cold, curled on a mattress in the room where so many villagers had trembled in fear at his questions. And he would have been alarmed to see this powerful man foetus-like, rank with a sweat that oozed from every pore, so vulnerable. But Mondling's image of the captain was never thrown so dispassionately at his feet, nor was it shattered for the fisherfolk. Instead they watched Nunes patrolling the streets, because that was a duty he could not neglect for fear law and order would deteriorate, and kept out of his way. Well they remembered a time when he had morosely ruled their lives, and feared the return of such a regime.

'Lady Sarah has failed us,' lamented Vygie Bond. 'What chance is there now?'

'Maybe he's ill,' suggested Jong Jan hopefully. But everybody knew he wasn't; they'd seen the signs before.

So they went through the days with sullen defeat, heads bowed, smiles banished from mouths and eyes, quick to let their tempers flare at the least excuse. And behind them dragged snot-nosed children, whining, aware that something was wrong, that their world had become nightmare.

Only Mad Minnaar, stalking across the hours like a marabou, had a grin, insane, exposing the perfect teeth that were the only relic of her other life, laughing at the downfall she had so constantly foretold.

'You should have listened,' she shrilled. 'How many times did I not point to the signs and omens? But Mad Minnaar is crazy you said, and shut your ears. And look what has happened now. Now you are playing with fire.'

'We must pray,' intoned Augustin Shoote to those of his congregation who still gathered in his leaking church.

'I have indeed failed them,' said Lady Sarah to Samuel. 'I should have told him straight away. But what gets into the man? He is less predictable than the weather.'

Samuel offered no comment. He moved about the house like a ghost and kept the curtains drawn.

'What are the villagers saying?' she wanted to know. 'Are they blaming me?'

He looked down on a white face at the bottom of the stairs, sunken eyes, features drawn with worry, and would not tell her.

'I have no ears for gossip,' he said, disappearing into his bedroom to stare through the telescope that had witnessed so many human failings, had first seen the arrival of Nunes, and was now trained on the captain's house. In his evasion Lady Sarah knew she had failed to save the fisherfolk. It was then, in the solitude of the outcast, she longed for her dead husband and, drawing open the curtain on Whale Beach, cried slow tears like water seeping out from underground.

'Oh what is to be done?' she sighed.

Not far from her house, in the general dealer's store, another was asking the same question.

'What is now to be done, Mister Montague?' Fagmie Jagbaar wanted to know of the baker when he came in for a cup of coffee. 'You can see there is nothing left on my shelves, not even a day's dust, because what else has Sheemina to do, but dusting? Beneath the floor I have enough money to purchase a hundred houses, yet I cannot buy one bar of chocolate to sell to these people. What are we going to do, you and I? We cannot go back to the town, to jail for Sheemina and me and the orphan's home for Little One. What am I to do, Mister Montague?'

What indeed? During those thirteen days, Mister Montague knew less than anyone what to do. It was no good saying, 'I told you so, there is no hope with a man like this.' So he continued baking bread, trying to suppress the old, unmistakable instinct that all hell was about to break loose and the best thing would be to run now while there was still a chance. But where to? Miles of sea stretched before him, miles of desert behind. To one as inexperienced as he, both meant death in the end. Perhaps he could get out on the monthly tug, which, as luck would have it, was due that afternoon. Perhaps.

Ironically, the love-blind Stevie was the least affected by the change in Nunes. Of everyone, with the exception of his beloved Frieda, who had to bear scowls, angry words, even the occasional hand that lashed out as she passed her father in the passage, he should have seen what was going on. After all, he was there every day for lunch. But he didn't, and Frieda kept her fears to herself. Of course, he heard the mutterings of Vygie Bond, the Brothers Kreef and Jong Jan, but they did not rate in a world given solely to his youthful lust and love for the gentle Frieda. So the first time he saw the face of fear was on the fourteenth day when out of the rain came Frieda, barefoot, drenched to the skin, to warn him off.

'You must not come today,' she panted. 'My father is ill.'

'But tonight . . .' smiled the ever-optimistic Stevie for whom the powers that be had never dealt a bad card. 'Tonight in our nest . . .'

Ah, when he held the tender Frieda could anything be wrong with the world? Yet how she shivered.

'No,' whispered a voice that wasn't Frieda's. 'Never again.' And she was gone, running into the rain that was her tears too, leaving a poor fisherboy who couldn't believe his ears.

It was only in the darkness, way beyond the usual hour of their meeting, that Stevie finally realised what his dear dear Frieda had said. 'No. Never again.' But there had to be reasons, nothing came to an end like that, especially not a love affair which just the previous night had been filled with all the passion of their hearts. Which is why, through the wind and rain, he went in search of his Frieda, and how he came to see, framed in the misty glass of a kitchen window, the terrible violence that knocked his Frieda black and blue that night.

For some time, possibly for thirteen days, Frieda had expected her father's decree much as she had expected the beating. In fact, as soon as she saw the first flush of red in his cheeks, and the widening crescents of sweat in his armpits, she knew the days of laughter were over.

She lived in those days like a phantom, partly of this world, partly of another, sadder place: aware of a quickening heart when Nunes's boots mounted the steps; and of a relief when the door closed behind him. Every day she expected to hear his dreadful order that would loosen the inevitable way of things. Every morning she took the steaming bowl of water, the razors and the lather to the stoep wondering if this day was different from the rest.

On the fourteenth morning, grey and wet, she had lathered his face and prepared the razors. Nothing moved in the street: here and there lighted windows showed that women were in their kitchens.

'Are the boats out?' Nunes demanded as she turned up the wick on the paraffin lamp and began stropping the razor.

'Yes,' she answered, 'an hour ago.'

'They are desperate,' he laughed almost gladly.

'They are hungry,' she whispered more to herself than her father.

She did not pause from flicking the blade across the leather, but there seemed to be a tone of condemnation in her voice.

Nunes looked up at his daughter but she avoided his eyes, concentrated on working the soap into a lather, a difficult task in that hard, brack water.

The irritation in Nunes tightened across his chest like indigestion. So now even she was turning against him. Ah-man, how he hated this place, this place with its wet, mangy dogs digging through bins for scraps, this dismal, arsehole settlement, cold and bleak, desolate and forgotten with dripping rags of washing on the lines and its tight, inextricable secret more cherished than happiness.

'You have failed me, Frieda,' he shouted.

Failed to get from that fisherscum about her neck, whose thick lips had slobbered on hers, whose hands had crushed her breasts, who had probably lain between her thighs, the secret for which he'd sacrificed her. Ah-man, and that's the truth. But hadn't he been led on by Lady Sarah? Wasn't it she who had told him to let her go? Wasn't it she who had to be reckoned with?

Nunes spat. 'Women should stay in the house. You have no business in the world.'

His acid spittle flicked about Frieda's face. It burnt her, and the blade turned on his chin opening a tiny mouth of boiling blood.

As she watched the thin line curve down her father's flesh until it disappeared into his shirt, Frieda remembered the story of the woman who had been shot for the single, delicious thought of slitting her husband's throat. From her father's eyes, she saw he recalled it too, and maybe, under the cloth, his hand was on the revolver he once again wore strapped to his belt.

'Fool,' he said as she dabbed at the blood, but there was no anger in his voice, rather a triumph that this was all she was capable of doing. Even when he was at his most vulnerable, he still held the power of life and death, he was in charge.

And then he told her to stop seeing the boy.

'Tonight,' he said, 'you will sleep in my bed.'

It was a triumphant Captain Nunes who stood up from the chair when Frieda wiped the last of the lather from his face. Once more he was in control, once again he could bring law and order to this miserable place, these scumdogs, who deserved no sympathy. Now, no matter what it took, he would learn their secret, he would have them tell him, each one of them, he would have them all confess the dark sin they kept close to their hearts.

That morning, for the first time in fourteen days, Nunes had Frieda call Mondling. Despite the cold, and the rain that was sometimes blown on to the stoep, the two men played draughts, Mondling wrapped in a great coat, a blanket wound about his knees, the captain still in his shirtsleeves, but now wearing a cap, the symbol of his authority.

They were wild games that brought a laughter from Nunes which Mondling had heard only once many years before. Then he had been delivering a message to von Trotha, and while he waited outside the tent he heard the great man guffaw with the madness men have before they perpetrate the atrocities that lie scattered in history. Frieda, too, heard it and dreaded the coming of night. And those who were fetching their bread heard it and were alarmed.

'The time has come,' said Montague Planke, but no one was concerned with his prophecy, 'and now anything can happen.'

Stooped over a boiling kettle in her shack that smelt of sex and a hundred lives, Mad Minnaar heard it and said, 'Praise the Lord, the end is near.'

In the trading store, Sheemina heard it and put her hands over her child's ears. Even Boatswain Baleen heard it and looked at the lovely Finella, whom he had brought to this hell-hole.

But on the captain's stoep the games continued with Nunes riding the power of his play against a man who fought but couldn't win.

'Ja, mein kaptein,' said Mondling, 'this is more like it.' And although he lost repeatedly, he responded to the challenge with fervour.

Until, in a moment when there was neither rain nor wind, nor the bark of a dog, nor any human sound, Mondling felt a shiver start at the base of his neck and slip down from vertebra to vertebra setting his whole body in a dance with St Vitus. And he was cold, a cold that comes when the blood withdraws deep into the body turning the skin marble white. He looked up, and saw what he had expected to see standing at his gate. Involuntarily, he lifted his hand in acknowledgement.

'I must go, Herr kaptein,' Mondling rasped. 'I have an appointment.'

Nunes shrugged. 'If you must go, you must go.' He twisted in his seat to see who had caught the Südwester's attention. There was no one on the road.

'Tomorrow, Mondling,' he shouted at the stooped figure. 'Tomorrow we shall play again.'

Nunes left the draughts scattered about the table and went inside to dress in the uniform Frieda had ironed. He checked his revolver, clipped it into the holster on his belt, then, pulling on oilskins, went out. Frieda heard the front door slam closed and five minutes later ran into the rain.

Nunes did not go far. He took the path to the house overlooking Whale Beach where the curtains were drawn as if no one was home. Before he could knock, Samuel opened the door.

'Where is the Lady Sarah?' Nunes demanded.

Samuel nodded in the direction of the stairs.

'Call her,' said Nunes. 'She must come down immediately.'

Samuel had no need to submit to the captain's orders. From the top of the stairs Lady Sarah said, 'It is a long time since you have been here, captain. It would seem you would rather play draughts than learn about the village.'

Nunes looked up at this apparition in a house-gown which stared at him from purple eyes.

'And now it is all too late,' she added.

The captain rested his hand on the revolver butt.

'What I would rather do is my own business,' he said, 'and I have not come now to listen to more of your claptrap about the people of this place.' Nunes stripped off the oilskins and flung them on the hall carpet. 'I do not care about these people, I do not care whether they all die of red-tide, I do not care where they have come from or where they are going to, what I care about is what they are doing. What law they are breaking. And I will have that answer from you.'

Into the stillness at the end of his words broke the distant cry of gulls fighting over the intestines of gutted mackerel. And among them, on the shores of the lagoon, stood Frieda and her Stevie in one another's arms for the last time. Suddenly they parted; and, step by step, Lady Sarah descended until she stood a head higher than Nunes.

'And who is to say they are breaking the law, captain? What evidence have you?'

Like torch beams, Nunes's eyes searched the dark sockets of the face above him but found there no betrayal of fear, no glint of anger. He pointed at his stomach.

'Here' – spittle arched from his mouth – 'here in my gut is the evidence that you are all committing a great crime.' He stepped back, away from the figure on the stairs. 'There are criminals here. Criminals who have fled from the law, and these are people who cannot live without doing wrong. They are anarchists. Subversives. Everything they do is to destroy law and order.'

Lady Sarah snorted.

'And who are these people, captain?'

'In time you will find out.'

'But why do you not arrest them, if they are so guilty? Arrest them, captain, bring them to trial.'

She brushed past him into the drawing-room. Nunes followed and behind him Samuel moved closer. The room was greyer than the hall but Lady Sarah did not open the curtains.

'That is naïve,' he roared. 'I could arrest them within this hour, but that would not stop the crime, because they have spread their corruption among the villagers. Even if they are in jail their crime will go on.'

Lady Sarah rounded on him. 'What crime, captain?' she cried. 'For the love of God, what is this crime?'

Nunes folded his arms.

'That is classified information.'

'It is only classified, captain,' said Lady Sarah softly, 'because you don't know what it is. Like all your type, you imagine a conspiracy.'

'Insolence,' Nunes yelled. 'Insolence!' His collar tightened into a tourniquet, making him dizzy with anger. 'You' – he stabbed a finger at the V of skin visible between the lapels of her house-gown – 'you are to blame for this.'

'For what, captain?' retorted Lady Sarah. 'For your perversities? For your power-mongering? You destroy people, Captain Nunes. You squash them like ants. Even your own daughter. And all because you are weak and afraid.'

'Shut up, woman, shut up. I will not stand for this.' Nunes smashed a vase from its stand.

But Lady Sarah stood undaunted.

'I told you, Captain Nunes, that if you listened to all I had to say about the village, I would eventually tell you what this supposedly great crime is. I thought that as your daughter was in love with a fisherboy, a good boy, captain, who would make sure she was cared for, and because you seemed to have had a change of heart, I thought that we could welcome you here. But you are right; I am naïve. You are not interested in these people. You have not had a change of heart, you were just playing a game with me, a stupid game. And all these innocent people, even your daughter, were just pieces. Perhaps you hoped your daughter would find out about this great crime and tell you. But she hasn't found out, she hasn't even wanted to find out, all she is interested in is a boy who is warm and loving to her, a boy who is not like her father. Now you can see, captain, why you are alone, why you will never be truly loved – it is because you are suspicious, because you always believe people are about to do you down. It is you who are the criminal, captain, you who betray and terrify.'

Again, in the distance, the cries of gulls squabbling. Ah-man, that there should be such types in the world, such snakes, such low-life ... and Captain Nunes took the revolver out of its holster. He fired six bullets into a cabinet of silverware, reloaded and fired again into the furniture. Then he turned to Lady Sarah.

'The games are over now. You have one final chance. Either you tell me and save yourself and the villagers a lot of trouble or you must all face the consequences.'

He stood in the centre of the room beneath clouds of his own breath, khaki shirt damp with sweat, right hand twirling the lanyard that looped from a clip on the butt of his revolver to his belt.

'I have got nothing more to say to you, captain,' said Lady Sarah eventually. 'You are an evil man. For you there is no redemption.'

Nunes advanced on her. 'I am not interested in your sermons, woman,' he said.

Lady Sarah smelt the captain's breath, worse than the stench of dead seals rotting, but she did not flinch.

'You must come with me,' he ordered, taking her by the arm.

Despite the howling wind and the cries of the gulls, everyone, with the possible exception of Mondling, heard the shots and ran to the square in front of Fagmie Jabaar's, convinced that Lady Sarah and Samuel were dead. There they stopped short, brought up by the sight of the woman in house-gown and slippers, her wrists handcuffed, being marched through the wind and rain to imprisonment in the cellar beneath the captain's house. They saw her pushed, still manacled, not yet feeling the cold that clamped about her body, into the ages of dust where mice and birds had died. They heard Nunes shout, 'Let this be a lesson to you all.'

Behind them the birds massacred their fish, thrusting and tearing at the flesh; before them stood a man with his revolver drawn, steam rising from his clothes. The man pointed the gun over their heads and ordered, 'Meetings are forbidden. You must disperse. You must disperse.'

But they didn't. They were numb; no one moved. One of them thought of throwing a stone, another clenched the fish-knife in his hand. Yet even as the stone thrower bent down to scratch his weapon from the mud, and the knifeman crouched, the revolver went off. And now they were running, dragging children, tripping over their own fear, wondering who had been shot.

No one was shot. Although Nunes fired three more times, low enough for them to hear the air being torn above their heads, no one was shot.

Behind the counter in his shop, Fagmie Jabaar whispered to Montague Planke so that Sheemina couldn't hear, 'Now we are truly done for, mister. So please, tell me how we are to get out of this one.'

Which was a question Montague Planke couldn't answer although a scheme was clearing in his head. But before he could say anything Fagmie Jabaar added, 'For my opinion, Mister Montague, we should be out of here chop-chop.'

'Listen, Fagmie,' said Montague Planke, 'we can't go now. We just need one more transaction. One more and we've made our fortune.' He looked at the storekeeper's troubled face. 'Just two more days, that's all.'

'That's all,' mused Fagmie Jabaar sadly. 'By that time, mister, we could all be in the cellar with the Lady Sarah. You know how it is when he goes mad.'

Montague Planke smiled. 'He wants to catch us, Fagmie. All of us. For him it's not enough just knowing what we're up to, he's got to have proof.'

Fagmie Jabaar sighed. 'There is one thing I should have done. I should have left you with the good Doctor Taj.'

Outside it was quiet now, except for the gulls still plundering the day's catch. Fagmie Jabaar and Montague Planke came out from behind the counter and Sheemina served them tea. It occurred to Montague Planke that if Captain Nunes walked in he would arrest them both on the spot. Complicity. Conspiring to subvert law and order. And he wondered why the captain kept up the pretence of not knowing them.

'That time,' he said to Fagmie Jabaar, 'that time Nunes had you in there all day . . . do you still think he didn't recognise you?'

Fagmie Jabaar shook his head. 'Oh no, mister, to that captain one bearded Muslim is the same as another. If he knew us, you and me both wouldn't be drinking this tea now.'

Maybe, thought Montague Planke, maybe. But Nunes was a wily man who would bide his time. Although time, judging by the captain's display of arms, was no longer in great supply.

'What we've got to do,' said Montague Planke, 'is keep to our arrangements. It's when you start chopping and changing that plans go awry. As we well know.'

He looked pointedly at Fagmie Jabaar who was staring at the dregs in his teacup. Then the storekeeper's face brightened.

'Ah, but Mister Montague,' he said, 'if it were not for those long ago plans fouling up, we would not be such rich men today.'

'Bah!' said Montague Planke. 'You almost got me killed.'

'And you made me jump from such a height it could have killed me.'

The conspirators glared at one another while Sheemina cleared away the cups.

'All right,' said Montague Planke eventually, 'all right. That's enough of that. What we've got to do now is get ourselves out of this.'

The plan he outlined to Fagmie Jabaar on that wet afternoon, while the villagers trembled in their cottages and the captain fuelled the fires in his belly with mutton chops, simply involved asking Namaqua Drift, the tug captain, to pick them up in a week's time about a mile

75

off-shore. It was merely completing a cycle, explained the baker, pure symmetry. Hadn't they outwitted that sphincter, Captain Nunes, in just such a way before?

Fagmie Jabaar shook his head. 'If you were hearing me, mister, we would be getting out now and not in a week's time.'

But Montague Planke wasn't interested in listening to him, and, as it turned out, Fagmie Jabaar didn't heed his own good advice either.

That afternoon, beneath patchy skies, Namaqua Drift brought in the monthly supply tug. As always the fisherfolk lined the jetty to greet him, but this time there was no laughter, no fuss; instead they stood sullenly to one side cast in their troubles. Even the children were hushed. Perhaps they were thinking of the days when crates and boxes were unloaded for Fagmie Jabaar, and his shelves creaked beneath the wonders of tinned food. Of how they would peer through his windows while the boxes were unpacked and the goods put out in pyramids and rows, all impatient, all craving for a taste of sherbet, all dying for the moment when the doors opened. Perhaps, bitterly, that is what they remembered. Because, this afternoon, as on all the afternoons since Nunes's arrival, Namaqua Drift had nothing for the settlement, nothing except a small official box stamped Government Stores and addressed to Captain Nunes, which he swung on to the jetty, but which no one, not even Stevie, who would have jumped at any other excuse to visit his Frieda, considered humping to the policeman's house, or even telling him about. Instead they left it to Namaqua Drift to cart up to the captain.

'Don't blame them,' Montague Planke said to Drift, by way of explanation, some time later in Fagmie Jabaar's, 'they've got plenty of worries of their own.' And he went on to explain to the skipper the plan that had emerged like mist being burnt away by the sun to reveal a beautiful coast.

Not far from where Montague Planke and Namaqua Drift sat huddled over schemes of fortune and daring, the captain began assembling the siren he had ordered many months before. Once he had installed it on the stoep railing, he dusted his hands, gripped the handle and wound it until the siren shrieked across the settlement: hens let loose their eggs in alarm, dogs fled and seagulls dropped at Mad Minnaar's feet.

'More omens,' she muttered, plugging her ears with rags.

In the prison cellar, Lady Sarah remembered the last siren she'd heard, on a ship that was about to sink. Now we are lost, she thought.

76

Nunes laughed, and the more the children cried or the anguished faces of their parents begged him to stop the faster he wound the handle.

'Let this be a lesson to you,' he shouted, driving the siren to an even greater pitch.

'He must stop it soon,' Mad Minnaar comforted her man, who writhed with memories of camps and sirens, and solitary confinement in a metal box. 'He must stop it soon or the sky will tear.'

Gradually, the way melon wine pushes pain into the dim distance, the noise receded.

'This is just the beginning,' shouted Nunes into the stillness. 'There will be new regulations.'

Half an hour later he pinned those regulations to the noticeboard where Fagmie Jabaar had once advertised the good times. 'As from tonight,' read Montague Planke to the circle of fisherfolk, 'a curfew has been imposed on this place from the siren at sunset to the siren at sunrise. Anyone breaking this decree will be shot on sight. By order.'

'Not shot,' exclaimed Finella Baleen. 'Surely not shot dead?'

'Didn't he shoot at us this afternoon?' said Vygie Bond. 'Hasn't he left bullets in the walls and furniture of Lady Sarah's house? Hasn't he got her now in his cellar?'

'Things will get worse,' predicted Montague Planke, but his words were lost beneath the siren and the triumphant figure of Captain Nunes waving a revolver at the sky.

Nunes stood there for some minutes watching the deserted streets, aware that behind many windows others, with loathing, were watching him. But what did it matter? They were scum and criminals, drunkards and half-breeds, fit for nothing other than scrounge life. Ah-man. Yet where was justice that it cast him into such places, that it brought up such fires in his stomach? Justice. He spat to get the sulphur from his mouth: justice was only for the powerful. 'Only for the powerful, Lady Sarah,' he shouted suddenly, leaning over the railing. 'Do you hear me down there? There is justice only for the powerful. What do you say about that, heh? Heh! Now you see that sometimes even the rich cannot buy their justice.' And he laughed.

'Well can you laugh,' muttered Boatswain Baleen peering from his shed window as the captain put his pistol in its holster and went inside. 'Well, you can laugh until the day.'

Curfew or no curfew, many were about that night. The first was

Montague Planke, who spoke briefly with Landed-Little Marsdon at his window, then, despite drizzle and blustering wind, went down to stand on Whale Beach for more than two hours, occasionally flashing a torch out to sea. No sooner had he, as men of the night do, melted into the darkness, than a quick rectangle of light glimmered in the waters of the lagoon as Stevie opened his cottage door and slipped out. Much, much later, after a third and unknown figure had stepped into the streets and disappeared, Augustin Shoote left by the vestry door and met Montague Planke at Fagmie Jabaar's. Most of this escaped Captain Nunes although he, too, was out in the storm.

Planke's vigil on the beach was cold and fruitless but considering the high seas and the wind he had expected no less; his meeting later with Augustin Shoote, at Shoote's instigation, was merely to discuss developments, although it did end up with Augustin baring more of his soul than he might have done under less dramatic circumstances.

They sat before a dying fire, wind shaking the windows, and Shoote, his eyes gaunt from sleepless nights, hands knotted in tension, asked the questions which have troubled all deep believers.

'Montague,' he said, 'when I have reached a point where my faith, faith in God, in his goodness, in his purpose for mankind, seems clear and strong, when I feel fulfilled, always then the vision crumbles and I am knocked to my knees in exasperation to pray for insight, to beg for some meaning yet to be shown nothing but misery. That is not God's will, Montague, he did not want us to suffer, and yet we suffer more than rejoice. Tell me why is Nunes here? Why does he beat old women? Why does he lock up someone who has done no wrong? What have we done, what horrible sin lies buried in this village that these poor people must be made to live in such mortal terror? It is enough to make me stop believing. Here is no Sodom, no Gomorrah, no Babylon. This is an ordinary village with ordinary people. They deserve to be left alone to live out a life that is hard enough. But no, one must endure tyranny. I would stop believing, Montague, if I were a stronger man, I would stop believing. Yet I can't. Even when the bodies washed ashore I tried to renounce my God, but I could not, even in this adversity he demands my faith.'

Montague Planke stood up. 'Don't question, Augustin,' he advised. 'The others need you. That's enough. They need your strength.'

'But how can I give it when I lack strength myself? How can I explain that God is good when the very image of evil sits in our midst imposing his will? Then I look at them, these fisherfolk, and I see faith, the simplicity of belief which I cannot share. How can they accept these things without screaming at the sky, without shaking their fists, without crying with rage? Why is it so easy for them, so difficult for me? If I could only believe like them, Montague, I would find some peace. I cannot accept this . . . this sorrow. We are meant to live in God's grace: but he demands more than man can give.'

With those words Augustin Shoote and Montague Planke ventured out again into the night and quickly disappeared.

Earlier, Stevie, instead of cutting through the village as he usually did, had made a wide arc into the scrub, passing at the bottom of Mondling's house where no lights shone, at the far side of the church where Augustin Shoote sat over his meagre supper, and then behind the goat camp and Captain Nunes's house to the nest in the dunes. There he waited: a foolish lover, hoping against hope that Frieda would give the lie to her words which had saddened him all afternoon.

About the same time that Montague Planke gave up the senseless signalling, Stevie decided he had to speak to his Frieda. In the dark and rain the two men passed within yards of one another, although Stevie was too deep in thought to notice the figure of Montague Planke suddenly crouch into the scrub as he came over the skyline. Perhaps if there had been less on Stevie's mind things would not have gone the way they did. At least, that was the opinion of Montague Planke many months later when he remembered how he'd sighed when the youngster had taken the path towards the captain's house.

Stevie crept close to the misty kitchen window, close enough to see Captain Nunes beating his daughter with a belt. Nunes was furious, uncontrollable, lashing out at the girl, and in his violence overturning table and chairs, smashing crockery, hitting anything that came within the sweep of his blows, until Frieda lay huddled on the floor. Even then he reached down, shook his daughter until her eyes rolled in their sockets, all the time shouting insult after insult.

'You slept with a mixed-blood. You have shamed me, bitch, I shall be the laughing stock of this miserable hole.'

Somehow, through lips already swollen, she sobbed a defiant, 'I love him,' only to unleash another barrage of blows.

'Don't talk to me of love,' shouted Nunes. 'I shall cut the balls off that bastard.' He stood over the crumpled body of his daughter. 'Tomorrow,' he panted, 'tomorrow you will call Mad Minnaar and we will put an end to this matter once and for ever.'

It all happened so quickly that Stevie never had a chance to intervene. By the time he started hammering on the back door Nunes had already slammed out the front. Which is just as well, for he would have shot the gallant lover dead right there and then, as Frieda well knew. And although she wanted nothing more than to be taken into those protective arms, to have his lips kiss the hurt and bruises on her body while the warmth of him gave her back some strength, she could only look into his eyes with a new horror.

'Go,' she sobbed against the door. 'Before he finds you, please just go.'

And in the end Stevie went, an ache in his chest because he didn't understand what was happening or why she would not let him comfort her.

For all the pain in his heart, Stevie had sense enough to return home along the path that took him past the church and Mondling's house, but, as Montague Planke had noticed, he was sunk too deep in thought really to be aware of what was going on around him. Or maybe, as he emerged from the shadows of Mondling's fence, he no longer cared if anyone saw him or not. Of course, at the opposite end of the street stood Captain Nunes, and, of course, Nunes shot him, or rather shot at him, without so much as a who goes there. The sting of the bullet knocked Stevie to the ground, but in the same instant he was up and running, leaping the scrub, dodging between buildings, gone before Nunes was halfway down the road. Nobody seemed to have heard the shot, certainly it didn't interrupt Augustin Shoote and Montague Planke, but then it was a loud night, with wind banging shutters and tearing loose roof tiles, let alone the occasional stroke of thunder overhead. Nunes gave up the chase the moment he saw his quarry bounding away. Ah Stevie, he panted with satisfaction, for Stevie was small game who could be dealt with in the morning, unlike his daughter who was again going to know his wrath within the hour.

And so into the uneasy night: in the church Augustin Shoote wrestling with his soul, as was the mysterious Mondling on his kitchen floor, Lady Sarah beginning to die her death of cold with Samuel crouched like a dog at the cellar grille, many a villager gripped by nightmares, Montague Planke nursing a head sore from too much wine; and Stevie bandaging his sore head scored by a bullet but with nothing to soothe his aching heart. It was a night on which not even Nunes slept easily. Although he had forced Frieda into his bed he could take no comfort there: in fact he was more restless because of her rigid body beside him. Long before dawn, he was up, pacing the house until Lady Sarah felt his boots were pressing on her skull. Eventually anger overcame him. What right had this daughter, a violated woman carrying the child of a mixed-blood, to lie between his sheets, what rights had she, now little better than a common fishertype, even to be his daughter? The fires flared in his stomach and he hauled Frieda from the bed and left her curled and sobbing on the floor.

'Get up,' was all he said, 'it is time for my shave.'

On the stoep Nunes sounded the curfew's end and waited for Frieda to attend him. He watched the first boats pull round the jetty into the chop and spume at the estuary's mouth, imagining Stevie among them, his head aching from the bullet wound, but his heart undoubtedly singing with insurrection. Well, let him sing; the tune would change soon enough when the boats returned. Hadn't he said curfew breakers would be shot? Didn't he especially need to teach this bastard the lesson of his life? Ah-man, there would be law and order again, a proper time and a proper place for everything. No more loitering, as they were now, outside the coolie store, no more of their treasonable meetings in the streets; because wasn't it true that whenever more than two were gathered together subversion and anarchy would only spread and fester? I shall give them discipline, he almost shouted. I shall teach you, miserable half-breeds, the lessons of goodness, I shall be your saviour from this mire of indolence – but his words were muffled in the hot towel Frieda wrapped about his face.

Despite the bruises that shot pain to the very core of her being, Frieda performed the ritual as deftly as she had done on that first morning before the marvelling eyes of the fisherfolk. Then she had played to the crowd, trying to show in each caress of the blade a love that was more than a mere daughter's. Now it was a duty, empty of emotion, dry, unfeeling, dead. She might shave as close as ever without nicking the chicken-flesh of his neck, but his skin's heat against her fingertips only quickened the anxiety within, making each stroke more difficult, more skilful than the last. Finally, when she closed the cut-throat and wiped the last traces of soap from his face, Frieda allowed herself to glance at the tiny boats rounding the headland. Although they were almost invisible in the swell and salt mist, she could see her Stevie, the bandage showing beneath his cap, grimacing as he pulled on the oar.

Nunes, threading the belt with its holster and revolver through the loops on his pants, noticed the direction of her glance. He scowled; perhaps women never had the sense beaten into them.

'When I get back,' he said, 'it must be over. Hear me' – he forced her to look at him – 'over. Cleaned out. Virginal.' Nunes laughed. 'Tell her I want to feel a new hymen.' He thrust her away and went down the verandah stairs.

At the grille to his cellar crouched Samuel, poor dog, soaked to the skin, clutching a strip of canvas across his shoulders. Nunes put a hand on the revolver butt, slowed his approach. With his boot he pushed the faithful follower to one side, hissing, 'Get dog, get.'

Samuel sprang away, knife in hand.

'Ah,' snorted Captain Nunes, 'the hero awakes.' Deliberately, with his hands behind his back like a preacher, he walked up to Samuel until the knife-point pricked his chest and became the centre of a small circle of blood. It would have been so easy for Samuel to stick the blade in deeper and deeper until it found that one vital organ beating less than three inches away. But he didn't. Instead he stood mesmerised by the small blood he had drawn, neither resisting when Nunes took the knife from his hand and threw it in the road, nor defending himself from the blow that stunned his face.

'Useless turd,' Nunes spat as if clearing a foul taste from his mouth. 'If you weren't anything but a lapdog I would shoot you now.'

From the cellar he dragged a coughing, wheezing Lady Sarah, her hair turned grey overnight, the dung of bats and rats staining her silk négligé, the cold that would never be cured streaming from her eyes and nose.

'Your power has gone, lady,' said Nunes to the figure at his feet, 'you are nothing now. A nobody which not even all the riches in your house can change.'

Those were the last words Captain Nunes ever said to Lady Sarah. He turned his back on the pathetic couple – Samuel wrapping the canvas round his mistress, gently lifting her from the gravel – and set off on the patrol which took him first to Stevie's cottage, where he told the fisherman's bedridden mother that her son would be arrested for insurrection the moment he returned with the morning catch, and then, via the street with its tell-tale blood where the previous night he'd shot the curfew breaker, to the house of his friend Mondling, with its garden gate unlatched, and, even more peculiarly, the front door half open, which led him into a house colder than the wells of charity, the hairs rising on the back of his neck as each step took him deeper into the iciness until, in the kitchen, he found Mondling's body, twisted, deformed, terror still fastened in his eyes, a rope of entrails disgorged from his mouth, a death that was not of this world.

The fear which Mondling, choking on his intestines, could never express found its voice in Captain Nunes. His scream, heard even in the fisherboats beyond the Head, caused the men to up anchor and put their backs into rowing faster than smugglers – all save Stevie, who began suddenly to moan with pain – and brought the rest of the villagers, except Mad Minnaar and Frieda, to Mondling's house.

From the church opposite came Augustin Shoote clutching a Bible to pull down the shutters on the torment of the soul with an 'Our Father who art in Heaven': then Montague Planke: 'Hallowed be thy name'; Boatswain Baleen: 'Thy Kingdom come'; Finella: 'Thy will be done'; Fagmie Jabaar: 'Allah be merciful'; Landed-Little Marsdon: 'On earth'; Mrs Beg-rip and the fisherwomen with their children, who had only once before set foot on Mondling's property, clustered at the gate: 'As it is in heaven.'

'This is murder,' roared Captain Nunes above the prayers, but no one heard him until he'd said it again and again. 'This is murder, I tell you . . . murder.' In the silence that came when everybody looked up from the tormented face of Mondling to the grim face of Nunes, realising for the first time what he was saying, into that quiet he dropped his accusation. 'The murderer is Stevie.'

His words were heard as clearly by Stevie's bedridden mother in the cottage alongside the lagoon as they were by Mad Minnaar and the suffering Frieda in the shack on the hill, and they set up a wail that began on one side of the village, was echoed from the other and taken up by the women and children at the gate. It drove Nunes wild.

'Shut them up. Shut them up,' he yelled drawing his revolver, but nobody tried, nor could they have stopped the lament. Instead it rose to a cacophony demanding evidence, pleading for mercy, crying for justice, dancing about the grotesque and forgotten corpse of Mondling, until Nunes ran outside shouting that he would show them murderer Stevie's blood on the street. And it was only when the villagers saw the rusty stain in the dust that they quietened in despair.

'That blood,' said Nunes, 'comes from a bullet wound. It was Stevie I shot. He is the murderer.'

Rousing himself against these sureties, Augustin Shoote challenged him to 'Prove it when the boats came in, captain, but even then it doesn't make him a murderer.' Before Nunes could reply, he and his flock ran to the beach, more concerned now with the living than the dead.

The boats were rounding the jetty as the panting horde splashed into the shallows, expecting to see Stevie's strong back leading in the first boat as he always did. But he was not among the members of either crew and the worried look on Jong Jan's face, twisted round to judge how much further they had to go, brought a groan from the crowd. In their midst, his immaculate boots just beyond the reach of the tiny ripples at the water's edge, stood Captain Nunes, triumphant, with folded arms.

Before Jong Jan could run his boat up the beach, Vygie Bond and the Brothers Kreef had lifted Stevie from the slops and placed him on a dry patch of sand. Someone covered him with a blanket, someone else held melon wine to his lips, Augustin Shoote bent down to listen to the racing heart that could surely not last another minute, watching the muscles convulsed and bulging, jerking Stevie the way children jerked their puppets.

'Please help him,' chorused the women.

'Call Mad Minnaar,' yelled Augustin Shoote.

'Stand back,' said Nunes. 'I must arrest the murderer.'

No one moved. Instead the knot tightened about the now vomiting Stevie.

'You can see the wound,' shouted Nunes. 'I order you all, stand back.'

'Where's Mad Minnaar?' pleaded a desperate Augustin Shoote cradling the young fisherman in his arms. 'Someone get Mad Minnaar.'

But Mad Minnaar couldn't help. At that very moment, tears streaming down her face, she wrenched Stevie and Frieda's baby from its mother's womb, and on the sand the father spat blood and died.

From the moment Mad Minnaar had opened her door to Frieda earlier that morning, the tears started, never to cease.

'This is the way things are,' she said, wiping her eyes, as the young girl, tearless, neither shaking nor with quivering lips, entered the greyness that was Mad Minnaar's home. 'And there is no escaping that.'

All morning the two women sat embroidering birds and flowers in bright startling colours on the only white cloth Mad Minnaar possessed, an enormous quilt which she fed from a box a yard at a time.

Frieda created yellow forests with red hornbills looping through the trees and carpets of delicate blue flowers that would have been crushed by the lightest footfall. From her tropics to Mad Minnaar's fantastic peacock, tail spread in full magnificence, there arched a rainbow, sharper, cleaner than any Frieda had ever seen. Before the forests were half grown or the peacock had lifted its tail, Mad Minnaar poured two cups of a tea made from bucchu leaves that had dried all summer. At the same time she put on to boil the crushed roots and hairy flowers of milkwort, stirring in, teaspoon by teaspoon, a pigweed's red mulch. If there was any smell at all from the steaming mixture it was a slight sweetening in the air, but so subtle only an outsider would have noticed. Nor did the concoction, which Frieda drank like soup, taste of anything other than potatoes and beetroot. When she'd finished, Frieda handed up the bowl without a word. The two women, one clear-eyed, the other weeping, continued their embroidery, but now Mad Minnaar watched for that first flicker of pain across Frieda's face, and when it came she gave the girl a cup of camomile. Her tea and the embroidery finished, Frieda lay down to dream the nightmare which not even the strongest herb could stop.

And in the dream she saw Stevie fishing with Jong Jan, Vygie Bond and the Brothers Kreef on an ocean that caught the sun like a pane of glass. In the bottom of the boat mackerel, kabeljou and seventy-four kicked against their legs, a good haul that would mean days of wine and food. Then suddenly, although no cloud obscured the sun, the day went dull and Stevie, her Stevie, collapsed among the fish, thrashing like them, every instant he was down there becoming more fishlike, sprouting scales and fins until Frieda couldn't tell him from a mackerel. No matter how much she shouted in desperation from the shore, neither Jong Jan, Vygie Bond nor the Brothers Kreef noticed what had happened to their companion, just as no one noticed that once again the sun shone brightly in an endless sky.

Through tears that welled constantly in her eyes, flooding now at the sight of Frieda in pain, Mad Minnaar went about her strange and dangerous business. Although only once, many years before, had she performed it, her hands sailed over the slightly rounded stomach, coaxing the child within to break away, to give up its short life for the sake of its own happiness and that of the villagers. Because, said Mad Minnaar, if you don't you will bring with you only suffering and grief for yourself, your mother, us all, until the very day the captain dies. What she didn't know, until Vygie Bond burst into her shack pleading,

'Come quickly, quickly, he's dying, Stevie's dying,' was that as she washed out the gaping wound between her patient's legs with bread and butter plant leaves, she washed out the life not of one but of two, and that a third, Frieda, may as well have died because she was left nothing more than a husk.

Vygie Bond stood in the doorway while Mad Minnaar finished attending her charge. The white quilt with its forest and peacock shone brilliantly in the greyness. On the stove simmered milkwort and pigweed, giving off a faint sweetness that Vygie Bond would never forget. He thought of Stevie and the death that had started in this shack.

'Was there no other way?' he kept asking himself until Mad Minnaar shook her head, and he noticed how wet her black dress was from the tears streaming down her cheeks.

Eventually, when Frieda was asleep, she stood up and handed Vygie Bond something soft and damp, wrapped in a towel.

'Bury this with him,' she said.

All afternoon, the men dug graves in the hard ground of the cemetery behind the hill. Mondling's was next to his daughter, and on his cross Nunes had Augustin Shoote inscribe: 'In memory of a proud soldier and patriot.' But he gave orders that Stevie was to be buried well away from his family, in a corner against the fence. And on the cross Augustin Shoote was told to write: 'Stevie, murderer.'

'But there is no proof,' protested the preacher.

'All the proof you need is that wound in his head,' replied Nunes.

Once again Augustin Shoote found himself searching for signs of humanity behind the dark glasses. But all he saw was his own reflection.

He sighed. 'There has been no trial.'

'I am the judge,' retorted Nunes. To the men muttering as they dug, he shouted, 'Do you hear that? I am the judge.'

No one ever believed Stevie was guilty, especially Jong Jan who told Montague Planke at Fagmie Jabaar's in the hour before the funerals began that he was sure he'd seen a strange man in the village the previous morning when he sat in the sun nursing his hand that rheumatism had stiffened like a claw.

'Ah,' said Fagmie Jabaar, 'but if I am not being mistaken you were also nursing melon wine,' which made Montague Planke laugh although he didn't feel like laughing.

'No,' said Jong Jan. 'It's true. He was there, I saw him slip between the cottages of Vygie Bond and the Brothers Kreef towards Mondling's place.'

'So why didn't you chase him?' Fagmie Jabaar wanted to know.

'What chance has an old man?' replied Jong Jan sadly.

'Forget it, Jong Jan,' said Montague Planke. 'This place is too small to hide a stranger. And we have troubles enough without imagining strange men.'

'OK, OK,' said Jong Jan getting up from the table, 'maybe an old man's eyes do play tricks on him when he's in the sun drinking wine, but these eyes have never played tricks before.'

'Do you think it's possible?' asked Fagmie Jabaar, when the door closed behind the old fisherman.

'No,' said Montague Planke. 'However Mondling died it wasn't at the hand of another man.' He leant across the table. 'Now tell me what Landed-Little Marsdon heard.'

'Tonight,' whispered Fagmie Jabaar, although Sheemina was in the kitchen. 'They were telling him they're coming in tonight. But not to Whale Beach. This time, mister, to the jetty.'

'The jetty! Are they mad?' exclaimed Montague Planke, getting up to pace the room. 'It's much too dangerous, the captain's house looks on to the jetty. We must tell Landed-Little Marsdon to put them off.'

'Too late, Mister Montague,' grinned Fagmie Jabaar, taking some delight in his co-conspirator's alarm, 'the plans they are laid.'

At the church, Augustin Shoote started tolling the bells.

From her bed, where she lay in the weakness of pneumonia, Lady Sarah called to Samuel, 'Why are the bells ringing?'

'Because of the deaths,' replied Samuel without telling her who had died; nor did she seem interested to know.

'There will be others,' was her only response.

From her bed, on the floor of Mad Minnaar's shack, Frieda shouted Stevie's name until the weeping woman gave her more camomile tea and soothed her to sleep.

From her bed in the last cottage on the shore of the lagoon, Stevie's mother was carried on a stretcher by Boatswain Baleen, Vygie Bond and the Brothers Kreef to the church.

The service was short. 'More about Mondling than Stevie,' Nunes had warned Augustin Shoote. 'And nothing subversive or I'll close you down quicker than a second-hand sale.' Because there had been no time to make coffins, the bodies were sewn into canvas sacks by Finella, and these the men carried from the church to the two shallow pits in the rocky ground. Only Augustin Shoote and Captain Nunes stood beside Mondling's grave, saying the last rites, sprinkling grit until the Brothers Kreef came forward to fill in the hole. The rest of the villagers wept over Stevie's solitary grave.

'That's enough,' said Nunes before Augustin Shoote could pray for Stevie. 'Murderers don't need prayers. Cover him up.'

But the preacher didn't listen, and Nunes, realising this was not the time to force his will, stood to one side, feeding the fires in his belly with hate. One by one the fisherfolk filed past the grave, some dropping dried flowers from the previous spring, others the scales of fish Stevie might once have caught. Although Captain Nunes watched the mourners closely, at every moment expecting insurrection, he didn't see Vygie Bond bend down and gently lay something soft and damp wrapped in a towel, beside its father in the grave. No one questioned it; everyone knew. The Brothers Kreef covered up their sorrow.

As the fisherfolk began to disperse, Captain Nunes shouldered his way through to where Fagmie Jabaar, Sheemina and Little One still lingered by the grave.

'That's enough,' he hissed, 'you've no right to be praying here for Christian sinners,' and, taking Fagmie Jabaar by the arm, said loudly so that everyone could hear, 'You're under arrest.'

'What for?' screamed Sheemina, clutching her husband. 'He's done nothing.'

But her protests and the wails of the bewildered Little One didn't stop Nunes from marching his captive off, handcuffed, at pistol point.

The only one in that crowd of angry faces who knew what was going on was Montague Planke, even now edging, as inconspicuously as he could, to the furthest side of the cemetery, ready to leap the fence, take his chance with the captain's aim and make off round the side of the hill if there was any sign that Nunes might be after him too. But the purposeful way Nunes propelled Fagmie Jabaar toward the village reassured him that, at least for the time being, he was free. Why it should be so he couldn't understand. Nor could he figure out why the captain was still playing games. What could he hope to get out of Fagmie Jabaar that was anything better than jibberish? Or was it all some elaborate foil to force him, Montague Planke, into making a mistake?

As it turned out, Nunes didn't put a single question to Fagmie Jabaar, although he beat him into a constant pain before throwing him out into the street long after curfew. By that time nobody had seen Montague Planke for some hours and the next morning he was still missing.

TWO

5

THE WAY OF THINGS

There is a revelation, told by Mad Minnaar, of how that place, the settlement, came to be. A revelation told once only, when she was in a rage at Fagmie Jabaar, which made little sense to anyone who heard it, except that it contained a profound message of doom. For Mad Minnaar, in the heart of the settlement, there nestled, like a seed waiting to germinate, the time of its own destruction. It was always there, inescapable, waiting for the right moment.

Looking back to a time when elephants foraged in the river above the lagoon, when crocodiles lay like old trees on the banks and hippos snorted and yawned in the middle water, it is easy to see what happened as a chain of events, of coincidences, chance shipwrecks, chance meetings that now can be seen as a pattern, an order even when there was chaos, that led inexorably up to the death of Mondling, the death of Stevie, the disappearance of Montague Planke and what happened afterwards. The danger, when looking at that pattern, is to impose, with Mad Minnaar, a moral judgement. What happened, happened. The world is as it is. There is no meaning in good or bad, there is meaning only in that it happened. Everything else is a story.

At the mouth of the lagoon a band of strandlopers, men, women and children, completely naked, scavenge the rocks for shellfish. They live in the caves of the Head but are not permanent residents, preferring to drift up and down the coast when the pickings thin out. Yet inevitably they return to the cliff caves and even today those caves are littered with the shells of their many meals.

It is a clear morning with an unseen low pressure system sweeping up from the Antarctic south getting hourly closer. By mid-afternoon the strandlopers can see cloud on the horizon and feel the first gusts of the dreaded north-wester. With great bundles of brushwood they huddle for warmth in their caves, as gales and thick rain come in. Not the sort of night to be at sea.

93

But there are some men, and sheep and goats and a cock and two hens, at sea in a small wooden sailing ship that is floundering badly with its sails in tatters. Poor Portuguese discoverers who have braved heat, calm, scurvy, savages, other storms in their intrepid voyage down Africa only to come to grief against a stubborn rock, later called Seal Rock, in a wide bay. Perhaps, between the torrents of rain, they see the flickering fires in the cliffs and pray for a safe deliverance from tempest and cannibals. Most of them have their prayers answered, as do some of the livestock they carry, the sheep, the goats, the cock and one of the hens. More than likely, if they have any control left of their vessel and supposing they have seen the fires, the captain might have deliberately decided to run aground. But he reckoned without Seal Rock which, lost in the surf and spray, pulverised the *Ave Maria* and hurled all souls to the mercy of the furies. God knows how the poultry made it across two hundred yards of impossible seas to shore, or, for that matter, the sheep, goats and men, but they did, and the strandlopers looked kindly on them all.

Some days later, when the low pressure system had moved off across the dry interior bringing snow to the higher mountains, the weather cleared enough for the sailors to take stock of their miserable misfortune. The people they had landed among, especially the females, looked more beautiful than the women they had left behind; and as each tide washed provisions ashore from the wreck their spirits began to rise. Things could have been worse.

They took wives, built shacks, tended their flocks and planted the seeds of pumpkins, marrows, tomatoes, and a melon that the sea had graciously scooped out of the *Ave Maria*'s broken hull. The seeds of that melon were to be the source of much merriment and drunkenness in the years to come.

Under the tender loving care of born vegetable gardeners, a small strip of desert bloomed for what might have been as much as two fruitful seasons. Then, out of the desert and into this paradise, came a sick man on a donkey claiming to be an ivory trader after a small stock of elephant tusks rumoured to be stored at the settlement. What he'd heard was correct, although there were no more than twenty tusks of indifferent size. When he offered to sell the tusks on behalf of the villagers, hospitality turned to suspicion. Simultaneously his illness took a turn for the worse and it was soon obvious that he was about to undertake a journey he had not anticipated. During his last night on earth he succumbed to a high temperature, but not before he feverishly revealed himself to be a run-away slave who had done someone to death to get the donkey.

A few days after the mysterious man died a child went down with a raging temperature and great pus-filled pimples. Then an old woman, two boys, a man in his prime; one by one the dreaded disease got them all. They were horrified to see their skins boiling with pustules, and their families dying where they lay. No one was spared the pox, bar two brothers and a young girl thought to be the ancestors of the goatherds who lived down the lagoon. Too weak to bury all the bodies, the brothers turned the little village into an enormous funeral pyre.

Their community destroyed, the two brothers and their common wife moved away from the beach to the farther end of the lagoon with their goats, sheep and poultry and built a stone cottage. The vegetable patch was abandoned but the vegetables and the melons refused to die. Not many years later there were new hands to tend them.

The next bunch of émigrés arrived at that forsaken place not by accident but by design. And their designs were on whales: those swimming factories of blubber, liver oil, sperm oil, spermaceti and whalebone which could be turned into soap, paints, lubricants, cooking fats, glycerine, cosmetics, drugs, dyes, fertiliser, corsets and, lastly, if circumstances were absolutely desperate, meat.

One whale in particular attracted northern men below the Tropic of Capricorn, where the sea could be as treacherous as any government, yet abounded in untold herds of profit. The name of that whale was the southern right.

With a draw card like that the southern oceans were soon awash with blood. On the beaches great cauldrons bubbled and languages that had never been heard before were spoken in remote settlements.

Those who came first were Norwegian, as yet not armed with that revolutionary harpoon gun, which was, in fact, undergoing tests in a countryman's back yard.

At the wheel of the *Whistling Virgin* was Captain Knut Hansen, who sailed blithely into the mouth of the lagoon as if it were a minor version of one of his homeland's fiords. Fortunately his confidence in the depth of the waterway was rewarded, thanks to heavy winter rains which brought the river down in flood and flushed out the mouth. Close behind him was Captain Beg-rip in the *High Spirit*, blowing great clouds from his short pipe and wetting his lips from a hip-flask of rum. Tied to port and starboard of both vessels were four deceased baleens, already partly plundered by sharks. Way up the lagoon the two brothers and their common wife must have heard the commotion of arrival and decided to stay put, venturing out to extend the hand of hospitality only on the third day.

When they did go down, they were probably surprised to see an encampment of four white tents and three enormous fires under three blackened cauldrons heaped with a blubbery flesh that smelt foully. It was a smell they would get to know. Such was its power that it hung on every on-shore wind for miles inland, signalling to jackals and shaggy hyenas alike that there was offal to be had. Not far from the fires were four flensed carcasses, their giant bones already sinking into the sand, as would do hundreds after them.

Captain Hansen came forward to greet the locals. Although neither could understand a word the other said, they must have conveyed enough to give him a history of events leading up to the funeral fire. As it happens, they were standing among the charred remains (Hansen notes in his log that one of the brothers actually dislodged a skull while they were standing there, then idly kicked it aside) when Captain Beg-rip discovered the melons. He let out a loud whoop and went staggering down to the camp clutching the fruit. Three days later the sailors tasted the potent spirits of that place, a secret brew that went from father to son and finally became the property of everybody. That night the company got roaring drunk and lost most of their provisions to the jackals. Next morning no one was well enough to care. Among the merrymakers were the two brothers and their wife. A little bartering must have taken place, as Captain Hansen mentions securing the girl's favours in exchange for some knives.

In his log, under the date 2 November, Captain Hansen writes:

Both Beg-rip and I liked the spot so much that we have left a small contingent there to tend the vegetable patch. Some natives of mixed blood have sold us sheep, goats and poultry. We intend to return in three months with wives and children to set up a permanent station. No one is whaling these waters, yet it is only three days' sailing from the Cape and a ready market.

By Easter of the following year the Norwegians had returned, although their captain was now Knut Hansen junior. Knut Hansen senior lay beneath the cold Atlantic waters, into which he had been dragged by a belligerent sperm whale, with three harpoons sticking in its valuable head. In the depths, beneath a baleful one-eyed stare, the captain drowned, his body never to be recovered.

On the return voyage Knut Hansen junior threw a wreath and his father's favourite sextant into the grey ocean at the spot where the tragedy had occurred. Other than that he showed no emotion but set his face into the wind, squinting hard to keep his eyes from watering. His wife also stood at the rail looking out to sea, grateful that Knut Hansen senior was no longer around to pester her with his loose hands. Possibly, though, she might have wondered why she had followed her husband to this godforsaken stretch of the world, a thought which must have persisted when she first saw the barren lengths of coastline and the rather desolate spot that had captured her husband's heart. But she was a woman who did right by her spouse, although the reverse did not always apply.

However, enough of the Hansens. Not half a mile behind them was the rum-tooting, pipe-smoking Beg-rip, without his wife because she had refused to move from the village where her parents and her parents' parents and probably her parents' parents' parents had lived. Maybe she told him that what was good enough for them was good enough for her. Perhaps Beg-rip shrugged, took his sou'wester off the peg behind the front door and sailed out of her life for the last time. As for his children, they had already gone their separate ways, and, as they had never seen much of their father, could hardly have been of a mind suddenly to loyally follow him to the ends of the earth.

So came the Hansens and Beg-rip to an inhospitable bay on an equally inhospitable stretch of coast.

For five and a half years the vegetables flourished, the great iron blubber pots were seldom empty, the stack of whalebones increased enormously, Captain Beg-rip's supply of rum gave out but the melons came into their own, two sailors drowned at sea, which, considering all the whales slaughtered, was not a bad accident rate, another sailor drowned blind drunk in the lagoon shallows and was buried at sea, and in the fifth year, Mrs Hansen gave birth to a daughter, Beatrice.

She was attended at the birth by the company carpenter who doubled as a doctor. He'd earned his medical reputation after amputating a sailor's leg with his fretsaw. Against all odds the man lived, and as a gesture of his other skill the doctor fashioned his patient a wooden stump.

For the indulgent Captain Beg-rip, who thought he had experienced everything life had to offer, there was a second revelation which he might even have ranked higher than his discovery of melons. The source of the revelation was none other than the goatherds, whose passion for his melon wine was surpassed only by their passion for smoking the leaves of a spiky plant.

Why Captain Beg-rip had chosen to take a jug of melon wine out to the goatherds, Mrs Hansen (for she is the often bitter recorder of those years) does not say. She does, however, have a lot to say about his condition when he returned. Clearly then, while he was imbibing his precious spirits with the two brothers, they must have repaid the compliment by filling his pipe with their magic tobacco. Captain Beg-rip was probably hooked from the moment he realised he could see the sound a bee was making as it tripped among the wild daisies.

Such results were well recorded by Mrs Hansen:

About three o'clock in the afternoon I was disturbed from my rest by my alarmed husband who said Beg-rip had taken leave of his senses. I followed Knut into the harsh sunlight and on the beach found Beg-rip, his arm around one of those stinking goatherds, dancing around a cauldron. They were so drunk they could hardly stand, and frequently collapsed into the fire, which had no marked effect on them, except to make them laugh. Naturally, many of the sailors enjoyed the spectacle, encouraging the sots to further acts of stupidity. Even my husband seemed to be most amused.

When Beg-rip's hair caught alight all he could do was shriek with laughter. Fortunately two sailors had the presence of mind to douse him in the lagoon, but it only made him laugh all the harder. I lost my temper and screamed at him to shut up. For a moment he did, then ran up and down the beach until he tripped over a rib-bone and fell flat on his face. Never have I seen a drunk, let alone Beg-rip, and I have seen him drunk many times, behave in such an extraordinary fashion. After that exhibition my husband had him tied to his bed. When I looked in on him that evening he kept saying the bees make a yellow sound, except when they are angry then it is white. I told Knut we would have to watch Beg-rip as the drink had addled his brain.

There is no record of when the first dagga seeds were sown in the vegetable patch but it must have dated from around this time. Mrs Hansen notes that the men had started growing a local tobacco, adding that it seemed to make them even more lazy. She complains about the thick smell of the tobacco which made her giddy. Even a good airing didn't seem to freshen her house, and she mentions disapprovingly her husband's liking for an occasional pipe in the evening.

It was during these years, too, that Captain Hansen acquired another name. His wife, ironically, welcomed the nickname and even used it herself, which must have caused the sailors some mirth. She thought it referred to his prowess as a whaler. She was partly right. It referred to his prowess, but not as a whaler.

With so many whales ending up in the melting pots, Captain Hansen found that he had to sail south to the Cape at least once every two months. His wife, despite her protests of loneliness and boredom, was never allowed to accompany him. The reason was obvious: he didn't want his pleasure interfered with. At the Cape there were plenty of women whose corsets his dexterous fingers untied, earning him the name of Baleen. If women didn't regret the passing of that restricting fashion, then Knut Hansen did. He felt something had gone out of his romantic interludes without the preliminary fondle of lace and whalebone.

So passed five and a half years, until in a howling July storm a new group of settlers came to the Bay.

No one witnessed their arrival, and it was only when one of their number knocked politely on Captain Beg-rip's door that the villagers knew they had visitors. Because the captain was stoned or drunk or both, the knocker had little joy. However, he was overheard by an irritable Mrs Hansen trying to coax her five-week-old baby to sleep. (At the time Captain Hansen was away.) She, mistaking the stranger for one of the goatherds, flung open a window and shouted at him to be quiet. Apologising with a deep bow, the drenched man demurely asked, 'Madam, may we please take shelter on your stoep?' 'Certainly not,' she replied and indignantly slammed the window shut. Fortunately others took pity on the stranded company.

The strangers were a group of Filipino fishermen and their families. They had gone fishing in waters too far from the Cape when the storm had snatched them out to sea, beaten them northwards, then hurled them back at the land again. In one sense they were more fortunate than the Portuguese but less fortunate than the elder Captain Hansen. Their craft might have missed Seal Rock, but it did not find the sheltered waters of the lagoon. Instead it was beached on the high tide-line as if of no more consequence than driftwood. Shaken but unhurt, the occupants clambered out clutching their few possessions and were relieved to find themselves in a remote outpost of civilisation.

While God did not feature greatly in the lives of the whalers, except when they were out on the blue oceans searching for those misty fountains, He was an ever-present force to the Catholic newcomers. Every Sunday they would hold a service of thanksgiving for their salvation from the hostile elements. It soon became clear, much to the annoyance of Mrs Hansen, but to the gratitude of Captain Beg-rip, that none of them had any desire to return to the Cape, but they did pester Captain Hansen to buy all the relics of their religion. In the mean time they set to work on a church.

Such industry had never been witnessed at that place before. Not only did the Filipinos build a church, they also built a row of cottages along the shore of the lagoon. Within a month the number of houses had more than trebled. All that was lacking was a complete roof for the church, as the congregation had neither tiles nor the wherewithal to buy them. Fortunately Captain Hansen was as generous a man with his money as he was with his body and always returned from his visits to the Cape with a small stock of roof tiles. In those prosperous days nobody realised the whaling industry would collapse long before all the tiles had been purchased. So for more than two decades the vestry gaped at the heavens.

Praises to the Lord, bells on Sunday, midnight masses, blessed melon wine – it all got up Mrs Hansen's nose. She complained of the bells which woke her baby, she complained of the singing which disturbed her rest, but most of all she complained that using melon wine for communion was a blasphemy. And that from a lady who hadn't set foot inside a church since the day she walked up the aisle as a blushing bride. When her anger erupted her husband went out after whales, or stuffed dagga into his pipe and listened to the sound of borer beetles in the floorboards. Like the rest of the settlement he was content. Catholics or Buddhists made no difference to him: new blood meant new opportunities.

Religion, houses and marital bliss weren't all the Filipinos had to offer. From the depths of the sea they harvested galjoen, snoek, mackerel, yellowtail, angry steenbras, occasionally kingklip; and from the shallows a lobster that, with a shriek, turned bright pink in boiling water. 'A shriek that spoils the appetite and makes Beatrice cry,' wrote Mrs Hansen. 'That sort of scream can stay with you all your life.' But she was the only one to hurry away from the cooking lobsters. The others made gluttons of themselves, feasting amid empty carapaces and sucked-out legs, swilling it all down with melon wine until there were as many lobster shells on the beach as there were whalebones.

Then baby Beatrice took ill. Health, bounce, rosy cheeks, eager lips at the swollen nipple, all vanished like a ghost at daybreak. Knut was at sea, doctor carpenter with him. For three days and nights the baby cried, the more so when it should have been taking succour. In the church the congregation prayed. Down in the cottages the women shook their heads and crossed themselves alarmed that a baby should cry so much. The men stuffed their ears with cloth.

Alone, with the never ending cries shredding her heart, Mrs Hansen rocked her child through all the rooms, crooning lullabies, damping a dummy with melon wine, trying to squeeze milk between the lifeless lips. Day went into night, the perspiration dried, her hair turned lank. Rock-a-bye baby, rock-a-bye baby. For a moment the crying ceased and Mrs Hansen fell asleep to dream of lobsters with Beatrice's face screaming in a pot of hot water.

Night went into day. While the child withered its lungs seemed to grow stronger and stronger until her cries roused the wife of the goatherds. Packing herbs and a brandy from the bucchu plant into a pigskin bag she walked to the settlement and knocked on the Hansen door.

'Witch,' yelled Mrs Hansen. 'I'm not having any of your potions. Go back to the devil.'

Yet she herself must have looked like a witch, in a housecoat stained by leaky breasts and baby vomit, skull eyes and wild hair. Unperturbed, the woman put the medicines on the stoep, and went off to squat on a dune in a vigil of solidarity.

What happened during those three days and nights survives only as folklore. Mrs Hansen never relived the time in her diary. In fact it was some eighteen months to two years after the death of Beatrice before she again had the will or the courage to trust her thoughts to paper.

Who can tell what thoughts she must have had, what terrible thoughts, clutching the baby roughly to her as it shrivelled in her arms, smothering its face, wanting to drop it, to smash it, to beat it into health? Yet she didn't. She mothered her daughter right up until the moment the silence finally came.

When the crying stopped the wife of the goatherds went back to the cottage at the end of the lagoon. She passed the women coming out of their homes in the chill morning, gathering in hesitant groups, edging slowly towards the house until they all collected, pensive, half afraid. What to do? What to do? they whispered, until, in the evening drizzle, they sent Jong Jan's mother to knock on the door. Which she did, long and loudly to no avail, except that before the light failed mother and child appeared briefly at a window. So briefly that some, convinced they were both dead, said it was a ghost; while others, relieved that all was well, went home to cook their suppers.

Five days it was before Captain Hansen sailed in with as many southern rights in tow. He stepped off the boat and went home with the villagers' eyes hooked in his back. It was as quiet as the morning the cries stopped.

An hour later he came out carrying a spade and a small bundle wrapped in a blanket. Without a word he set off across the veld towards the koppie. On its landward side he dug a hole no jackal could open, placed his daughter gently on the bottom and, without resting, put the earth back where it had been. On the way back he passed a procession of mournful Filipinos, their heads covered, each carrying a candle.

Mrs Hansen wasn't seen for almost a year. Knut went about his whaling and his sexual forays as if nothing had happened but the house remained shuttered and curtained until the anniversary of Beatrice's death. By then tongues had been wagging furiously about what had become of Mrs Hansen. There was even one rumour that Knut had murdered her for letting their daughter die and buried her corpse beneath the floorboards. If her absence was a cause of well exercised tongues, then her Lazarus-like resurrection must have created much oral fatigue. By all accounts she was the colour of old spume, her blonde hair now white, her stoutness pared to the bone. Each day she would stand for three or four hours at the mouth of the lagoon, constantly watched by a wary sailor lest she choose to end it all. Such thoughts apparently were not in her mind. Instead there was this: 'It would kill me to have another child. I know it. For no logical reason I know it is the truth.'

After that, her diary entries resumed, now longer, less personal, more preoccupied with village life. There was a lot to keep her occupied.

For instance, Captain Beg-rip, that doughty old boozer and dagga smoker, had taken a shine to the most attractive of the unattached young ladies. The hoots of Norwegian derision that greeted his drunken declarations of love did not deter him, because, incomprehensibly perhaps, the object of his desire had an eye for him, too. No matter that he came four years short of being her great-grandfather's age, young Katrina had set her heart on the salty pirate.

Common sense, weeping mother, aunties, sisters; angry father, uncles, brothers; nothing short of death, she vowed, would change her mind. But he wasn't a Catholic, they protested. So Beg-rip converted. Or, more accurately, became religious, if that is measured by church attendance. In the end he, and no doubt his fortune and melon wine, won the hearts of father, mother, brothers, sisters, uncles, aunties and the marriage was grudgingly condoned. Four months later Katrina was well in the family way, ending all speculation on the old man's virility. When nature had taken its course she gave birth to a son, Marsdon.

There is one little detail in all this that escaped the villagers but not the caustic Mrs Hansen, namely, that Captain Marsdon Beg-rip was already married. For whatever reason, she kept the matter secret, confiding in her diary on the date of his marriage: 'Now we have a bigamist among us.'

However, life went on, although no one, except a despairing Mrs Hansen, actually realised it was getting worse. Not much worse, at least, not noticeably so, despite the bigamist the community was harbouring in its bosom. Yet in terms of the accumulation of real capital the coffers weren't growing any fuller. Not that the coffers of the likes of the Filipinos or even the Norwegian sailors had ever had much in them to start with. But now the box of dwindling coins had become a prison for Mrs Hansen.

'With money,' she wrote, 'at least we could leave this place.'

Of course the two captains weren't interested in doing that anyhow. Beg-rip had his son and his wife and his melon wine and his magic tobacco. Money was no use to him, and although Hansen paid him for the use of the ship, he personally hadn't seen a whale spout in years. As for Knut, while he probably wasn't quite as content, and may even have been a little jealous of Beg-rip's son, judging by the remarks his wife confided to her diary from time to time, in the main he had his whales, his business trips and his concubines, even if fewer and fewer of them were wearing whalebone corsets.

So while the good life seemed to continue, while lobster and galjoen were ever abundant, the number of whales in that wide ocean began to prove finite. Whereas in the early days Captain Hansen had sailed those waters alone, he now realised that years of loose talk in harbour taverns had filtered north, and his 'rights' were the subject of massive exploitation. Not an hour seemed to go by without sail or steam breaking the clean line of the horizon. If he found a small school, not even his countryman's amazing harpoon gun could help him claim them all before he had Yanks, Brits, Swedes, Danes and Russians calling the shots right alongside him. In the latter years he sometimes went home with only a calf to show for his troubles, but worse still, there was less and less to justify his business trips south.

'Perhaps,' wrote Mrs Hansen, 'a child would keep him at home.'

In the fifteen or thereabout years that separated the death of Beatrice from that of her mother, now and again the odd telling word or phrase crops up in the diaries about Knut's broodiness, his attitude to the young Marsdon Beg-rip, whom he spoiled silly with presents from town, and Mrs Hansen's very real belief that she would die giving birth.

On 4 March, a windless day, she notes: 'I think I must be pregnant.' A month later, with equinoctial tides sweeping up the beach to the door of their homes, she writes: 'I am pregnant.' Fatal words, ringing with pathos.

So, with the tides making an island of her house, she put down her pen, got up from the kitchen table and entered the room she'd not been in since the day Knut drew her gently out by hand and she gave him the three-day-dead body of their child. She opened the door on a mountain of pink and blue wool of every texture and thickness imaginable. Her eyes watered as she saw the immense longing of her husband, who had never said anything, merely stocked an entire room with enough wool to clothe a hundred babies against the day she might tell him his luck was in. Unravelling all the wool, and tying it alternate colours, first blue then pink, end to end, she led a thread through to her kitchen chair, took up needles she hadn't touched since the first child nestled within her, and began to knit.

That, presumably, is how Knut found her when he returned in the evening from flensing the smallest southern right he'd ever seen, a mere sardine of a whale that ten years before he'd not have bothered about. Without a word he ate his supper, never taking his eyes off the woman who sat quietly next to the stove knitting. That night he didn't drift off into his private world of borer beetles but began carving the history of his whaling life on an old sperm's tooth.

All winter a weak light guttered in the kitchen as bootees, leggings, jerseys, caps, gloves, shawls and blankets piled up beside her; while on the window sill as many teeth as there are in a sperm whale's jaw stacked up one alongside the other titanic battles between puny men and the world's largest mammals.

Although Mrs Hansen never looked into the room to see how much wool was left, she could feel the end coming closer, and she knew the sixtieth tooth was the last one. In the dark morning hours of 17 November, Knut sheathed his knife, polished the ivory against his trouser leg, and put the final chapter into place. Mrs Hansen looked down at the floor and saw a thin blue thread like a snake sliding backwards toward her. Then she must have known it was going to be a boy. And perhaps then she asked her husband to call him Baleen. The end came up and exactly laced the last bootee.

No sooner had the knot been tied than a contraction of alarming force hurled her to the floor, writhing like one possessed. Knut ran off for doctor carpenter and whatever team of midwives he could round up among the Filipinos. They battled until sunrise trying to get the good-natured Boatswain Baleen to leave the womb and cause the only grief he would be responsible for in his life. By all accounts, even that he tried to avoid, but it was as inevitable as sixty teeth in a sperm whale's lower jaw or the end of a room full of wool. When the excited doctor carpenter finally wrenched him free and Knut had cut the cord as quickly as he peeled back a skin of blubber, Mrs Hansen died.

The next day she was laid beside her daughter in a jackal-deep grave. Then came a rash of deaths, as if half the village had waited for her permission to die. First an old Kreef, next Katrina's mother, father, uncles, aunt, two brothers and a sister, Jong Jan's mother, a goatherd and their wife, septuagenarian Beg-rip, doctor carpenter, and after him one two three four five sailors. Disasters, too: Beg-rip's ship was wrecked, all hands drowned, a hyena got in among the pigs, half the melon crop was lost to a wily jackal, gales blew tiles off the nave roof, flood waters washed the body of an unknown man into the lagoon.

Little by little the village shrank, the way a beached fish shrivels and curls upon itself. Captain Hansen, proud, grieving, happy, sad father, put out to sea no more, his lusts diminished, his great whaler – stained by cormorants, black-backed gulls and oyster catchers, heavy with periwinkles and limpets – settled on the sand

and rotted. The great iron cauldrons toppled off their stands, rusted beneath the feet of terns and pipers. The settlement was lost to the world.

THREE

6

FUNERAL OF THE THREE VIRGINS

Of course what is begun cannot be ended. The pattern is a process and nothing can be lost to the world, even if for years and years nothing happens. And for years and years nothing happened.

Then at three o'clock one mild morning the family Jabaar sneaked out of the Harbour Hotel, hurried through the dockyard streets to the towering hulk of the *Heraklion*, boarded while the watch slept and snuggled down to stow away in a lifeboat. It was an ordinary enough event: no comets flashed across the heavens, the firmament wasn't filled with asteroid showers, no plague of crickets scratched in every bush, no portents horrendous signalled this beginning of all that was to come, except that on the high tide a tug hooter sounded and a tramp steamer lumbered out to sea.

As the Jabaars left, a rather depressed and insomniac Montague Planke was restlessly tossing in a cell at the end of a red-brick corridor which had been his home for the last four years, two hundred and forty-nine days. The building of which that cell and corridor are a part is the oldest jail in the city, inhabited by the ghosts of such famous prisoners as Gentleman Baroque, an architect of the last century who plastered the skeletons of street urchins, whores, drunk sailors, maids, madams, even, it was suspected, a young prince of the Dutch royal family, garnered on his nightly wanderings about the stinking town, into all the gracious homes and buildings he designed; or the modest John Sainsbury, gold-digger, pro-Boer sympathiser, who, enraged by the treacherous dealings of the governor at the Cape, travelled south for a month on horseback to level a shot at his head only to miss and be fallen upon by mounted police; or Agmat Ardeel, the mad Muslim, who in the month of Ramadan waged a jihad among the faithless, casting more souls into darkness than light; or Freeman Mdinga who returned to the vineyard of his ancestors' enslavement and forced the vintner to drink a barrel of pinotage to purge the family of the sins of the fathers; or Bishop Westerford who, at Ascension Day communion, used his piss in the sacraments because he'd drunk all the holy wine the night before; and a host of common criminals, horsethieves, pickpockets and scoundrels. All these have kept him company over the many days and nights. Of course he has kept other invisible company too, with the bitter memories of Charlie Goodboy Macaroni, Sidney Phoenix the Hump and, God rot his soul, Sir Maximilian Shroud, the double-crossing, double-dealing, treacherous, jumped up gentleman punter who put him up to it with his talk of a foolproof fortune.

'A truly foolproof fortune,' he told the intrigued Montague Planke, 'to be made, my good man, by inserting gentle alterations in the books of this most generous company from time to time. Are you with me, Montague? All you have to do is apply the standard procedure of double entry accounting with a little more enthusiasm than your average bookkeeper can muster even when he puts down his pen at half past four in the afternoon. One entry here, another there, a third posted to the journal and a fourth wherever you think most appropriate. Nothing wrong with all that, just lose bits and pieces in the system, are you with me? In Ledgers you will find Sidney Phoenix only too willing to oblige, and Goodboy Macaroni has been known to turn a blind eye at the yearly audit. As long as you're not too adventurous, too puffed with your own dexterity, you'll have a career for a lifetime, Mr Planke. Are you with me?'

Was he with him! Ever ready for the odd bit of fraud, an old hand at the game of petty larceny, schooled by some of the sharpest sharks in the business, Montague Planke was unquestioningly with him. So easy this was, flannelling here, laundering there, shooting the fast buck, sowing a bank balance of wild dreams until that fateful fourth company audit when Charlie Goodboy Macaroni came mincing into the office with not so much as a smile, plonked a ledger on Montague Planke's desk and said, 'Mr Planke, can you please explain what's going on here?'

'Come on Charlie,' laughed the unsuspecting Montague Planke, 'you know what happened.'

'No I don't, Montague,' replied Charlie Goodboy Macaroni. 'Money comes in, it's transferred here there and everywhere until whoops, it's gone, as if by the stroke of a magician's wand. Where to, I ask Sidney Phoenix, who searches among his ledgers but there's nothing there. Something that once existed has disappeared. That's fraud, Montague, stealing company money, a criminal offence for which we'd better see Sir Max.'

But even in the wood-panelled office of Sir Maximilian Shroud, Montague Planke could still not believe the note of high seriousness.

'Is this a joke, Charlie?' he insisted. 'Are you and the Hump pulling an April Fool?'

'I wish we were, Montague,' was Charlie Goodboy Macaroni's response. 'But the truth of it is we've had our eyes on you for some time, not so, Maximilian?'

'Quite so, Macaroni, quite so,' said Sir Maximilian, putting his fingertips together and resting his head on those praying hands. 'An awful disappointment, Planke, you of all people, with such a good record up to now and brilliant prospects. Did you know that, Charlie? Planke here was being groomed. Senior management I'd heard it mooted. In ten years' time a seat on the board. Such a shame, Planke, such a dreadful, dreadful shame. But take it like a man, Planke, do you follow me, and we'll be good for character references.'

For which Montague Planke had many bitter years to thank Sir Maximilian Shroud, Charlie Goodboy Macaroni, and Sidney Phoenix the Hump. Because, as the magistrate said in his summing up, 'You were so highly thought of by your colleagues, Planke, because this would seem to have been a temporary lapse in your otherwise flawless record, I shall suspend half your sentence but feel that no matter how contrite you have shown yourself to be it was a considerable sum of money you appropriated and spent in an excess of giddy living and for that you shall be taught restraint by putting in five years at the government's pleasure. Case dismissed.'

Which is how Montague Planke, who knew nothing of giddy living because he'd had less than a quarter share in whatever his wits had syphoned off the top, came to be lying awake on the hard bunk that had been his only comfort while the family Jabaar settled down on the equally hard boards of a lifeboat. What troubled the sleepless convict was not high remorse at his anti-social activities but the thought that when the sun rose over the mountains, the little metal door in the heavy metal gates would be thrown open and he would be set free in the world. Free, but penniless, destitute, poverty-stricken, with neither family nor friend to see him right.

Not many hours later, smelling faintly of mothballs from the suit that had been folded away those many years, his stomach loaded with disquiet, the taste of burnt porridge in his mouth, Montague Planke, no longer J69-11-26E, was signing for his valuables: one man's watch (broken), one fountain pen (dry), one wallet (empty), sundry clothes, and one dented cardboard suitcase.

'Well, there you go, Mr Planke, you've done your time, repaid your debt, the slate's been wiped clean. Have a good day,' said the commissioner, snapping shut his register and opening yet another file.

No ceremony here, no trumpets, no rowdy cheer from the inmates, just one old warden, the keeper of the gate, hobbling before him across the wet courtyard, inserting the dreaded key, opening the small metal door. Out he stepped into the drizzle, desolate and destitute, turned up his collar, braced himself against the slam of metal, never expecting the kind voice which said, 'I've seen many boys like you more frightened of this moment when I shut them out than when I shut them in. Strange thing that, there's never a sweeter word than freedom when stone and metal bars keep you from it, yet if you ask me there's none freer than those in here if you think about it because they've not got a worldly care about holding down a job, finding that extra bit so's the wife and kids have full bellies. I've seen it, the number of grown men I've had to push through this door you wouldn't believe. They take one look outside and they're looking straight in the smiling chops of freedom, gives them the horrors, believe me, especially those like you, Mr Planke, without family or what have you. So that's when I tell them what I've told so many over the years . . . Don't waste the time you've spent here, I says. You've met many interesting men, made plenty of contacts and could probably count one or two as friends. Go look them up. Have a glass of beer. Let me tell you there's more business done in some of the smokiest bars down there than in many a boardroom. And it gets done a great deal quicker and neater, so pay a little heed, Mr Planke, there's no telling how the world will look at four o'clock.'

Montague Planke mumbled his thanks (adding to himself, 'for nothing') and moved away into the smiling chops of freedom which veritably drooled in anticipation of his coming. But the voice behind him persisted.

'Here, wait a minute, Mr Planke, didn't you know Namaqua Drift? Surely you remember the captain, that big bloke with only five or six teeth and them as stained as old ivory and all the pictures of naked women tattooed over his body with the most special one done on his Jolly John Thomas? I know it was probably a year or two back now but wasn't it you I used to see him with at table or in the exercise yard, him waving his arms about in that dumb talk of his? I think he took a shine to you, because it's not everybody that Captain Drift leaves messages for. However and a day, he said to me, making all those strange signs but I got his meaning, he said, Mr Keeper, when you spring the key on that round little man called Montague Planke (although as I recall you're not as round as when you came in) you tell him to come look me up at the Tavern and if I'm not in port you tell him to stay there at my expense. He's got nobody, he said, has my friend, but let me tell you he's got one thing you and me hasn't and that's brains. So there you are, Mr Planke, that's the message and if I was you I'd pay some heed. I've heard he's bought himself a boat again and maybe he needs a deckhand or something. You never know, but either way the Tavern's as good a place as any for a man about to get another grip on his life.'

Montague Planke hadn't given Namaqua Drift a second thought since the day they parted, even though for eighteen months or so the captain had eased him through the middle and toughest part of his stretch: that time when the age it's taken to get half way still lies ahead, that time when even the strongest despair. Of all the good men who had passed through the lofty portals of that old jail, and of all those still incarcerated, Namaqua Drift had undoubtedly been the ugliest but the one Montague Planke had warmed to most. Truly an old reprobate, nothing better than a pirate, yet the man had in him a streak of humanity which was totally foreign to the likes of Shroud, Macaroni or Phoenix. And so, feeling that at least there was a prospect to the future, he went down into the misty city, through the streets of umbrellas and mackintoshes, passed the jewellers putting out their diamond rings, passed the merchants and the coffee shops, down to that quarter which had only just gone to bed, where the night's beer and blood still glistened in the gutters.

And so, as Montague Planke stood within the damp portals of the Tavern awaiting his second chance in life, many nautical miles out the family Jabaar, miserable, seasick and cramped after a mere nine hours on the ocean, contemplated theirs and found it wanting in practically all respects. Montague Planke was cold but at least he had reason for optimism and within an hour or two would be warm in body and soul; they, on the other hand, were cold, had no prospect of warmth and faced a future as bleak as the dismal sea and sky glimpsed through the holes of the tarpaulin that covered them. Yet such was their fortitude and strength that for three and a half more days, undoubtedly aided by the desperation of the hopeless, they stuck it out until, unable to bear it a moment longer, the beautiful Sheemina, wife of Fagmie Jabaar, burst through the thin canvas with a heart-rending, 'Captain, good sir, save us from all too certain death.'

To which Fagmie Jabaar, trying to pull her back into the boat, responded, 'Sheemina, what on earth you doing woman? You'll have us all thrown to the sharks like much too bad horse flesh.'

As Fagmie Jabaar, with wife and Little One, was marched to the captain's cabin, through his mind raced all the so recently read stories of some stowaways thrown overboard at the twitch of a bosun's finger, or others provided the dubious mercy of a week's rations and a small boat when land was as remote as the stars.

'Oh dear me, wife,' he lamented, 'what is now to become of ourselves?'

'It is better to die in a shark's quick jaws than to starve as a stowaway, husband Fagmie,' replied his woman, now calmer than a lagoon at sunset. 'Besides, it is time you showed more faith in mankind.'

Under the circumstances, this was a difficult thing to do, especially as he was faced with a raging Greek who banged the table, kicked the furniture, ranted until the spittle turned to foam in the corners of his mouth, then sat down, put his head in his hands and moaned, 'Why me? Why must you choose me? There are so many others who have spoilt records, for whom another stowaway is just like another breakfast. But me, a captain of thirty-five years with a record cleaner than marble, going home on his last voyage, doesn't want to have stowaways on his conscience. You have ruined my life. Oh what am I to do now?'

'Let me suggest, good captain,' said Sheemina, clutching the edge of a chair because she was weak with hunger, 'that you put out an advert on the radio.'

'Oh yes,' said Fagmie Jabaar, 'that is a very good idea, for we are most useful people.'

'Church of the Blessed Mother, Most holy Virgin of the most holy Son, All Saints and Almighty Father give me strength,' whispered the captain. Then he looked up and shouted, 'Get them out, away, such imbeciles, this is not a wireless station, I am not some record jockey with his request programme, I am the captain of the *Heraklion*, a respected man, a sailor, a father and a husband. Why now must the Lord try my patience?'

Even so, when the raki worked its way to his stomach and unknotted the fist of his intestines, the old sea dog took their advice.

'This is the captain of the *Heraklion*,' he announced to the shortwave universe, 'fed up to the back teeth with curry-munching slick talkers who he is going to consign to their fate unless some good Samaritan comes smartly to their rescue. So come on my Christian brothers, show tolerance and take in your Punjab brethren before Old Davy gets their bones, over.'

To which he had an immediate response. 'Come in, come in *Heraklion*. Shame on you to think of casting them away, this is Landed-Little Marsdon appalled at your turn of mind. Have mercy, sir, consider the sanctity of human life, rather suffer the inconvenience than have innocent deaths on your conscience for ever, over.'

'All very well, but stowaways are a captain's ruin whichever way you look at it,' came the weary reply.

Which is how it happened that, the next dawn, Jong Jan, Vygie Bond, the Brothers Kreef, and young Stevie stood in wonder on the jetty, amazed beyond belief that a ship so vast could put to sea and not sink as it surely by rights should, while the derricks winched down a lifeboat and the Fagmie Jabaars were rowed ashore.

Not a word was spoken, at least not one that could be heard, by child, man or woman gathered there as they'd gathered once before when a strange boat came in, only this time Mondling was among them. You could have heard an egg crack as they watched that boat rowing towards them faster even than the Brothers Kreef rowed a dinghy when racing a storm. And there was Fagmie Jabaar flashing his white teeth, waving from the back in such an enthusiastic semaphore of greeting it was a wonder he didn't pitch overboard.

When Mondling saw the colour of Fagmie Jabaar he started getting the mutters, but Landed-Little Marsdon did some quick talking which had the Jabaars accepted, especially when Fagmie Jabaar, in what looked like his pyjamas under a calf-length coat, followed by his missus swaddled in saris except for a bare roll across her stomach, stepped ashore to say, 'Thank you very much good sir for such kindness,' and clutched Mondling's alarmed hand, unfortunately the most inhospitable hand in the bunch. Such a rude hand that it shook itself free and began gesticulating to the accompaniment of language that singed the ears of even Jong Jan. 'Gott-in-hemel, coolieman, where is your respect? Donderwette, who is responsible for this outrage?'

At which Landed-Little Marsdon gallantly stepped forward and put the barbarian promptly in his place.

'Where is your compassion, Mondling?' he charged. 'Would you rather these poor unfortunates had died a miserable death at sea? Is that what you'd have preferred? How could you allow an innocent child – just look at him now, cowering in his mother's skirts because of your fuss – to die like that? How could you let them starve and thirst for days to an inevitable end unless the sharks got them first? Oh no, Mondling, such thoughts are wicked.'

That took Herr Mondling back a step or two. Like it or not (and nobody really seemed to mind once they'd got over the red dot on Sheemina's forehead and all the women had fingered her sari and Fagmie Jabaar had pumped the hand of everyone from Samuel to Stevie) the Jabaars were taken in as part of the community.

Fagmie Jabaar never really explained why he threw caution to the wind and did something as desperate as stow away, but he once told Montague Planke that it had something to do with people jeering at them, throwing bricks through their windows, even killing a pet cat and leaving its skinned body on the doorstep. Nasty stuff, enough to make anyone move neighbourhoods but not flee a city, but that was just the beginning of it. Afterwards came the police, waking them up at all hours of the morning, flashing torches into their bedroom, arrests, court cases, nights in jail. Their crime was that Sheemina wasn't Indian. She was Christian white, and before she met Fagmie her name was Rosalind Mills.

So much for the Jabaars, tucked up now in the safety of Lady Sarah's beds, with the sea breaking distantly on Whale Beach and the slippered feet of their hostess moving quietly along the corridor in her search for love and comfort.

Four hundred miles south, at the end of a desolate, thundering coast, is that quarter of the port beneath the mountain where sailors on the way back to their ships are so often accosted, where every doorway is a tramp's home, carpeted in cardboard, furnished in bottles of cheap wine, and where in a still, cobbled square surrounded by the black façades of hotels and gunshops a light burns and like a metronome a silhouette passes again and again before it. The silhouette is that of the insomniac Montague Planke, who during the last five days has been staying, on the account of Captain Namaqua Drift, in a room above the Tavern where the bed is the equal of any prison mattress and the chair engulfs you in its swollen maw. The five days have passed with agonising tedium, not to say mounting frustration, and although Montague Planke has been celebrated, wined (or rather beered) and dined after the enthusiastic manner of the locals (because it is not every day a man comes down from the slammer on the slopes, and the locals have many friends residing in the rooms of that state hotel), their hospitality has worn thin and his own dismal future is weighing greatly on his mind. However, although at this pre-dawn hour he is unaware of it, a saviour is at hand.

Well, almost. For at midday a bath-like packet rolls in and ties up at a secluded wharf. Apart from a motley crew, recruited in the effusion of alcohol and certainly never to be solicited again, who disembark and disappear quickly among the warehouses, it carries the large man with the pirate head and tattoos, leaping ashore with the agility of someone half his age, whom Montague Planke is soon to look on as a saviour. Watch him go, limping (because one leg is shorter than the other thanks to the polio that attacked him as a child), but moving with great zest, swivelling his hips in a gait that would have most normal people hard pressed to keep up, through those afternoon streets until tacking around Aziz's tailor shop (for all a gentleman's requirements with personal service guaranteed) he sails across the square into the Tavern and berths next to Long Martha's barrel of beer.

It was there that, not a minute later, his eyes danced a jig, a hole opened in his beard to reveal some brown stumps, a noise that in anyone else would have been taken for the pain of cracking ribs issued from that cavern and a hand came down across Montague Planke's shoulders with the force of a loose spar swinging in a gale. Apart from the ache in his back and the racking cough that consumed him for the first five minutes of his reunion with Namaqua Drift, Montague Planke knew a certain relief, a certain profound sense of well-being engendered by this man's solid presence and, later, by the bravado of beer.

Needless to say, the captain, who seemed to be vaguely involved in fishing and something in the export/import line, was full of good advice for the destitute Montague Planke. Where Montague Planke saw desolation, the captain predicted wealth; where failure loomed for Montague Planke, Namaqua Drift proclaimed opportunity. Despite his seadog appearance, he was more like a father encouraging a bankrupt son, or an author gently chiding a wayward character.

'No, Montague,' he said, with a flash of hands and fingers, 'where do you think all this self-pity, all this talk of running away, becoming a cook, caretaker or curator, is going to get you? Life's not like that. It may suddenly knife you in the ribs one dark night, but if you keep your feet you've got a chance of coming through; fall in the gutter and you'll be kicked to within a whistle of your last breath, because nobody likes a loser. So get up out of the piss and garbage and let's see some iron in the soul, some good old-fashioned spunk. But before you do that, a little advice from someone who's been about a bit, put in at hostile ports, weathered storms, never abandoned dinghy, boat or brig; and that is: be your own master, captain your vessel, life's too short to perfect a reef knot. Take a look at all these miserable sods sitting about you in the Tavern, Montague – that man leaning against the bar counter, drunk as you've seen him these past five nights, or Cynthia wearily plying her trade behind a come-on smile, or that group doing all the laughing, jailbirds every one and as likely to be back inside for stealing a jug of wine as a gent's watch this week or next, or that man, the one they call Lord George, a self-made millionaire who lost it all and can't get himself back on the road (it's a good day when he can order a poor gin) – how would you like to end up in such select company? Slaves every one. Many could be in hell for all the difference it would make. But now look at me, certainly not a picture of material wealth, holes at my elbows, frayed cuffs, a skin more pitted than rusty metal, but my own man for all that. Listen to me, Montague: trust not the high flyers, make your own way, be a freelance agent. Because that is where the money is. Imports and exports, buying and selling, you've got to have a penguin's brain not to see your chances, man. Listen. I met this peddler, Goldberg's Import/Export Agency, discreet sign, modest office, actually smaller than a trawler's craphouse, but he was coining it, buying this and that, pearls, stones, paintings, even the Old Masters, and selling them here there and everywhere, to the best of customers, cash only under the counter. Why not? I tell you, Montague, you get into that game and you're made. Come on, man, it's time to stop wallowing, to get off your backside, to show the world you're not a good-for-nothing gutless sponger. Get out there, get into the time-honoured pastime of trading.'

Which is how a modest brass plaque announcing Planke's Handling Agency, Foreign Trade Merchant, came to be screwed beneath the opaque glass of a door at the end of a dim linoleum passageway two floors up a building of anonymous tenants. In the two short years

Montague Planke did business there he never once passed a neighbour on the stairs, nor so much as caught a glimpse of a silhouette against the frosted glass of the doors that lined his hall. Yet he heard coughs and wheezes, steps on the stairs and in the corridors, the strains of a distant violin, voices raised in anger, sighs, and, once, a revolver shot that brought neither police nor ambulance yet sounded as fatal and tragic as any shot fired in the depths of a Sunday night.

Not that Montague Planke wanted to have poky neighbours sticking their noses out each time footsteps led to his door. Far from it. The less anybody knew of his business the better, even if he did sometimes long for the occasional company, the occasional shared pot of tea.

Aside from those oddities, Montague Planke could not have found more suitable premises (perhaps a little too far from the docks, being a good half-mile from the Tavern, the source of many deals), reached off a side alley, hidden among warehouses and garages, a street down from the Muslim quarter, inconspicuous, seemingly derelict yet filled with invisible lives. There Montague Planke not only negotiated some lucrative propositions, and some as disastrous as bad mussels, but also lived, sleeping on a loaned camp bed, cooking on a two-ring gas stove, sometimes happy with the way of things, sometimes living with the icy fear of a man sailing too close to the wind.

And then Customs and Excise, in the person of Captain Sylvester Nunes, put the finger on him for mere innocent and unsuspecting dealings, with one Phut Kittim, whom he'd met only twice and agreed to do business with against his better judgement, and the frantic signals of Namaqua Drift, because what he was asking appeared above board and good money. Of course, as things turned out, it was neither. In fact the merchandise, which Montague Planke was led to believe was ostrich eggs destined for European palates, turned out to be precious stones destined for Eastern dagger handles, crowns and studded belt buckles. Had it not been for a clumsy cold storage official, his hands numbed by too much overtime in the deep freeze, a crate would not have been dropped, eggs would not have smashed, and a Sheik's future jewels would not have been displayed before the disapproving but fascinated eyes of Captain Nunes. As the export agent, Montague Planke was Captain Nunes's first port of call. He wanted cash book, journal, ledger, invoices, consignment dockets, the whole lot.

'The supremo's got his eye on you,' warned Nunes, departing with what he thought was incriminating evidence. But the books were clean. After all, Montague Planke was a past master at posting entries here there and everywhere until they disappeared in a welter of journal figures. But there was still the matter of the ostrich eggs.

'Ah-man,' said Nunes, 'don't tell me you didn't know what was in them.'

'How could I have known?' protested Montague Planke. 'I was just the forwarding agent. I've got to put my trust in clients.'

That, however, was not the end of it. Captain Nunes did not take defeat lightly. So in heat, in rain, high winds, day or night, he had his lieutenants huddled in a doorway across the street to watch the comings and goings that he was sure would eventually land a big fish. Far from casting a subtle net, the lieutenants' unmistakable presence scared the fish. No one, not even Montague Planke's most honourable clients, wished to be doing business where the law was prying. And so Planke's Handling Agency fell on hard times, times that became so hard even Captain Nunes lost interest. Which, in the circumstances, was small consolation.

Montague Planke, once again, began to despair. Once again he was relying on Namaqua Drift's charity, although the latter never begrudged him a cent and indeed made every effort with his frantic hands to massage the life back into his charge. But this time the patient was not responding. Until, one mid-winter's morning, foul and cold, when any sensible man's thoughts are persuading him in favour of the Tavern, Captain Namaqua Drift came bounding in after more than a month out of port, shook the rain off like a terrier, and said in a flutter, 'Montague, your boat's come in.'

Behind him stood Fagmie Jabaar, who undid a piece of cloth to spill its contents in a glittering rush of amazement and fear on Montague Planke's table.

'Good Lord, man. Good Lord,' exclaimed the nervous proprietor of Planke's Handling Agency. 'Put them away, quick, put them away before somebody sees.'

Not that there was anybody to see through the dusty, rain-spotted windows of his first-floor office, but in those days he wasn't taking any chances.

'Oh hell, captain,' he sighed, 'what are you getting me into now?'

What he was getting Montague Planke into is known in the trade as IDB – illegal diamond buying – which carries a minimum sentence of life imprisonment, unless the big mining houses, who have their own judges, put you away on the spot. Muscling in on their turf is most unwise. So it is hardly surprising Montague Planke wanted those hefty sparklers out of sight almost as soon as they rolled on to the desktop, but not before he'd had a chance to gaze into their flawless depths where all kinds of temptations lurked. Mainly one called greed.

He looked up at the sharp, expectant face across the table.

'You can get more like these?'

'Oh yes indeed, sir. Heaps, sir. Where I'm owning a general trading, tick arranged, most lucrative business, sir, especially now, these are all of value.'

'I see. And where's that?'

'Up the coast, Mr Gentleman,' and Fagmie Jabaar grinned broadly.

And so Montague Planke heard how this settlement was 'being a forgotten village until Namaqua Drift put in one day, thank Mohammed in his mercy, and a supply line was established to keep the trading store in stocks because they were such a bunch of fast-asleeps with no concept of business an honest merchant couldn't earn his bread, would you believe it, sir, because they were sharing everything among themselves, not buying and selling, could you believe such a going on? You're not going to make your fortune here, Fagmie-fellow, I said to myself, but there's no need to live in stink and squalor either. Oh no, Mister Montague, it didn't take a sharp eye to see what could be done. You-all, I most modestly proposes, because they are humbles, sir, fisherpeople with no need of money, can pay me with pretty stones like the one on Mrs Beg-rip's finger. Deary, deary me but they are coming with stones big and small without a fleck, sir, Mister Montague, as you see for yourself. One stone for a tin of beans, two for black chocolate. Who is to complain? They are richer than they know. But, good sir, a man who cannot sell his stones is a poor man still, which is why myself, this poor Muslim, stands before you, Mr Gentleman.'

Needless to say, Fagmie Jabaar and Montague Planke came to a very simple but highly satisfactory agreement. He would continue to charge the good folk of the settlement a diamond for this, two diamonds for that, which was as good as dishing out charity because all they had to do was wander down to the beach, scratch around in the shale, and hey presto instant money. When stocks ran low he would have Landed-Little Marsdon call up the ubiquitous Captain Namaqua Drift and sail south with his hoard of gems so that Montague Planke, banker extraordinaire, could convert them into hard cash, thereby contributing to the general upliftment of a poor village.

As Montague Planke put it, who was he not to help a fellow mortal, in fact not one but a whole village of mortals who had never known an easy day nor the sweetness of sherbet? This was not just business, this was philanthropy, the highest feeling one man can express towards humanity.

But while Montague Planke was relaxing in the thought of great wealth to come, Mad Minnaar went tooth and nail at Fagmie Jabaar for bringing the curse of Mammon on their heads. She knew a thing or two and stormed along the jetty in full rage to collar him as he stepped all smiles from Namaqua Drift's tug.

'I tell you, Fagmie-devilman,' she raged, 'no good will come of this, no good will come of tinned peas, dark chocolate, sherbet, jams, tea that is not made of hard leaves, sour wine that has forgotten the sweetness of melons, you mark my words, I tell you, go back to sea and give this to the deep, for I have seen signs in the stars and on the land that point to the one thing which I have prophesied and will prophesy again, the coming of the goat. Beware the time when people's teeth will crumble into their sockets, when the sky is filled with strange omens, when birds are quiet and crickets sing, for maybe there will be angels come down from heaven but also the sea will give up its dead and for days and nights a bad wind will blow off the land stinking like goat's breath and we will know our time has come. I tell you, this very morning again, shush! shush! why don't the birds call? There is light at land's end, a hand in the darkness has fingers, yet not a peep, not a chirp because they know it is Satan's spit passing through heaven, showers of asteroids, globs of rock, the same death's stillness when Marsdon-father rowed out to die, you must be quiet, keep your head covered, face west. Oh Lord protect us, Fagmie what have you done? You have brought this plague among us: the land crawls with black crickets, the very air screeches with their noise, silence is banished, no one can sleep, dark clouds gather on the flats but it is not rain it is crickets and locusts which sweep over us destroying all we have planted; see how our gardens lie in ruins, not a sprig of green at water's edge or on distant bushes. This, Fagmie Jabaar, is what comes of money, and worse, worse by far when long stars traverse the night bringing comet's fever, the madness of dire straits, then we must be alert to all dangers. Watch out for the cloven hoof-print: always we have lived in the shadow of the goat's return, waiting generation to generation convinced of the inevitable, knowing only that when we were poor no more, no longer living the simple life, he would come bringing hardship, even death, and we would suffer his sojourn. Oh Fagmie, praise the Lord, we are poor sinners helpless before his ways, and it shall come to be as it is written in our history. First there was, I tell you, Baster Jan on a donkey, slave runaway with a bunch of rogues at his side and a taste for white flesh: white flesh, I tell you, and the first time he tasted that was in the same hour he shot his master through the head by chance and star's fortune because he had never pulled a trigger before in his life. There he was, suddenly face to face with the man he hated most at the end of a vineyard with the dark coming in and a horse-pistol in his hand, knowing nothing but evil thoughts. How else could he do anything but aim and fire? At such short range a baboon could have blown out the farmer's brain, and then leaving the corpse ran back to the house and in the kitchen grabbed the woman he saw every day, her stomach large with child, and took her backwards on the bed that his dead master had carved from vine-wood, biting all the time at her neck until he tore off a strip and chewed it the way he chewed tobacco, even spitting out the juice and a lump, I tell you, that was when he got his taste for white flesh and went on a rampage through the valley, freeing slaves, attacking women, and learning to shoot with an accuracy which showed his master may have had no chance at one or a hundred paces until a commando was formed and Baster Jan took to the mountains as if in the long line of nations and creatures that spawned him there was a goat, I tell you, a sign of the devil, the nimble horse of Satan prancing and dancing among the rocks of no more substance than a rising mist to emerge on the hot plains with his brigands, striking into the depths of the hinterland until there wasn't a white woman without a bandaged neck who didn't tremble when he passed even a hundred miles from her bed, remembering the gracious smile, oh yes, the bright teeth as sharp as a rat's nuzzling in, the cattle stampeding beyond the wagon and her husband knocked out somewhere or watching in fury the masticating jaws of a man-beast fallen from grace with God, chewing, chewing, I tell you, chewing. Even when a man in a rope collar and black cloak, his shoes in tatters from miles of hard walking, stumbles in tied at the neck like a dog but doesn't beg for mercy, merely holds up a black leather book with a gold cross and talks a hole in Baster Jan's head as big as the fatal one in the farmer's skull, I tell you, with Adam and Eve and Cain and Abel and David and Jonathan and Daniel and a host of others brought in from the wings, until the murdering carnivore repents with tears in his eyes, and pardon me Father for I have sinned, and won't you have a meal and teach us more of those wonderful Works, and convert us to the ways of the Faith because we have done dreadful things to appease our appetite? Holy Father, I tell you, the goat became a sheep, his knees grew callouses as big as tomatoes from all the prayers, prayers, prayers on a hard mat as many times a day as you think necessary, Baster Jan, and who would have thought such devotion to the Lord was possible after a long life of bloodletting? But every day he watched the church go up and his heart swelled with pride, bigger and bigger, as his cathedral got bigger, until he died, I tell you, in his sleep, quietly, without waking anyone, just like that, stopped breathing and was gone to heaven or hell, who knows, but to heaven as far as the priest was concerned, such is the power of God, Praise the Lord. But saving a man doesn't save a village, not a chance, flesh is flesh and as weak as a soft caress be it a hand brought up to clasp another in prayer or the feel of silk hair at communion, and as you saved us Father from the horrors of our other life won't you take this daughter to be your spouse because it's not right that a man like yourself, a man who can care for a woman, should not have a woman to care for him, and surely God has meant us to be man and wife and to bear fruit, to go forth and multiply, I tell you, by the sharp beak of an octopus, by the stink of a cormorant's shitnest, by the bloody incisors of a blessed neckluster, that's what he did, that priest, that man of God, that sworn celibate took none other than one of Baster Jan's many daughters as a wife. But his fornicating didn't start or end there, no sir, he'd been at it already sowing his seed whenever women needed comfort. It was a son here and a daughter there, I tell you. The daughters aren't numbered for who gives a damn about women, only the sons count and there were six of them, three inside, three outside the bonds of holy matrimony; it was the youngest of the legal trinity that looked like the grandfather he'd never known but was as sharp as a bad wind off the land, quick as a jackal, mamba-eyed just waiting for the day his father in mid-sentence, this is my body, eat this in remembrance of me, this is my blood, drink this in remembrance of me, sank to the floor letting melon wine stain his black robe. Women fainted, children screamed, men came forward to lift the poor Father but the pulse was down, he had expired, hardly was his body cold in the grave, hardly the last stone heaped over him than Wicked Jan was plotting and scheming and taking long walks late at night round the lagoon, doing what, I tell you, stirring up the evil of this place, calling forth the goat of his grandfather, the part which is forever Satan, and it came, too, where there hadn't been a goat spore in years they were suddenly everywhere eating the vegetables and the melons, chewing clothes because what is bad is bad and that cannot be changed until the right time comes. And Wicked Jan was scheming and plotting and sharpening his knife against moonstone with one thought in his mind, I must be captain, chief, I must be Baster Jan again, none of this God the Father nonsense, none of this God the Son business, or God the Holy Ghost worshipful heavens, but Baster Jan again with a taste for white meat that isn't fish or fowl, grate, grate of steel against stone until the edge was as keen as a bad wind and he got up to go and do his mischief before the sun rose. First it was in some of the lowliest huts of the village where his father had laid on more than his absolving hands, he crept in quieter than sea lice and slipped his great dagger between the sleeping ribs which collapsed with no more than a sigh, that could even have been a lobster's last sad breath hardly loud enough to hear unless you listened closely. Twice more he did it each time getting closer to the one large house where he should have been asleep. Is that you Wicked Jan? said his mother softly in the darkness. Yes, Mother, I've been fishing beyond the Head. Go quietly and don't wake your brothers, she said, turning over with the sore heart of the recently bereaved, thinking what has happened to this one since his father's death, and Wicked Jan went quietly and didn't wake his brothers, not even when he stuck the long blade between their ribs. No one breathed a word, how could they, without feeling a pain slide into their hearts, knowing that was the route traversed by steel; poor Mother, you've killed me too, she said, leaving Wicked Jan to grieve for the first time. Mother, I didn't mean to, come back; come back, stupid goat as if she'd walked off a little way instead of going beyond all hearing for ever. So once more there was carnage, even more terrible, if that is possible, than in the days of his grandfather, with major battles, towns besieged, the peaceful plundered without remorse, laid naked beneath a hot sky to rampant savages riding long-horn cattle, oh merciful heavens, blessed Creator, what a mess, I tell you, north and south and east the earth trembling beneath the hooves of his war cows, every dust storm had him at its centre, Lord help us what a time, deaths by the cartload, orphans everywhere, and all types streaming into our village until there wasn't a Godfearer left, the church in ruins, its roof full of holes, weeds among the pews, never a breath of air that wasn't heavy with dagga, not a sober morning or night from day to day. Now I've got everyone just where I want them, said Wicked Jan, none of this God stuff, none of this faint-heartedness at the thought of death, there's nothing beyond here anyhow. But there is, of course, why else would history repeat itself, I tell you, this is not coincidence, this is Grand Design just as finally this sinful corner will be purged, so watch God interfere when things are at their worst, when he's drinking the blood of young babies for breakfast, and supping off the kidneys of virgins, who should arrive but an angel of mercy from nowhere other than the distant heavens, because how do you explain this miraculous presence that didn't crawl out of the sea or across the land? Stake this man, shouted Wicked Jan, stretch him out for the jackals, but no one would touch him, instead they brought him food and water, you might be chief Wicked Jan, they said, but you can't fly, true enough, he replied, but without wings neither can he, and before they knew it he had a rope collar round the angel's neck. People came from further than anyone had ever heard to hear him talk about the wondrous world to come, world without end ah men, with none of this crawling in the dirt, here was forgiveness and light. Shut your face, said Wicked Jan, I won't have any witchcraft preached here, but the Word was out and see if you could stop it now Wicked Jan, hallelujah, hosanna to the Highest. Keep him from water and food and we'll see how much of an angel he is, said Wicked Jan with a grin from ear to ear as he rubbed his stomach swollen like a pregnant women's and threw the bones of his meal to the dogs, Lord help us, the barbarian, the miserable turd of a wily dogfish; as blind to the stars and what is written in the sky as a mole, listen, I tell you, and all is revealed to the willing ear, but not him, oh no, I am the chief, the heir of Baster Jan, when I speak others listen, all right, and this man is no angel. Before our eyes he wilted, withered, shrank, the flesh fell off him until he was a covered skeleton standing there too dry-throated for anyone to hear what the good Lord had to say, so the people stayed away, the human river from the interior became a trickle and dried up, who was interested in an angel who couldn't speak? No one, I tell you, no one, except Wicked Jan, now where have they all gone, he asked, get them back, hey you preacherman get them back, but the preacher had gone too, just a pile of bones in the front yard, so meatless even the dogs left them, and that's when Wicked Jan went mad, completely, absolutely, with the skull of that angel-preacher his only companion till the day he died ten years later, by which time no one could remember this place, it had been lost, thoroughly blotted from the minds of men, I tell you. Listen to the old woman, she knows, she saw it all, the decay, this lost settlement with fat Wicked Jan and his talking skull day after day after day sitting beside his hut door. Tell me skull how's my mother, why doesn't she come to see me anymore, I shouldn't be forsaken, clack, clack, clack, went the jaws he'd wired up and he never got an answer, until the syphilis had left his face as skull-like as his companion's, two grinning death-heads in the late afternoon sun, and then it went to work on his enormous stomach, so that was the end of Wicked Jan and probably then he got an answer but no one can tell if it was what he wanted to hear, I tell you, mark this well, ever since those fat bad men brought sin and disgrace to this forgotten corner of the good Lord's earth sinners have come here to die, unloved, unblessed going from the despair of the here and now to the fires of the hereafter, but it is written, everywhere there are signs, in the stars, in the tides that turn the sea blood-red, in the beaching of whales and the cry of penguins, believe me I tell you, these are signs that this place will be purged through pain and blood, trumpets and revelations, dancing in the streets and cleansing fires. I tell you, he will come in a cloud of dust from the land, the third time of Satan, an heir of Baster Jan from the loins of Lucifer because that's the way it is written, that's the way all stars tell it, I tell you, and it will happen in our time, you will be there. So rejoice I tell you, you privileged sinners at the glory of God and take up your trumpet in the universal fanfare, I tell you, we are saved, but first we must be punished, cleansed, of the wrongs we have committed and those committed by our fathers in this sorry land, amen.'

Just the sight of Mad Minnaar storming down to the jetty brought out the whole village, and each and every one of them stood open-mouthed at her dressing-down of the luckless Fagmie Jabaar. Even when that tirade came to an end, even when, wild-eyed, bosom-heaving, she elbowed her way through them and disappeared among the dunes, no one moved, over-awed by this flood of history with its visions of apocalypse, and frightened, without a doubt frightened, at what seemed so clearly to be their fate.

Yet the human heart is a fickle organ and Fagmie Jabaar had a tongue smoother than the healing balm he sold, so while the villagers were ready to push him and his family back out to sea in the nearest fishing boat one moment, the next he was tempting them with the very sherbet and chocolate Mad Minnaar had slandered, drawing them irretrievably into his net of demand and supply.

'How can these goodments bring down such thunders and furies?' he proclaimed, handing out sweet slabs to all and sundry. Of course, the fisherfolk were hooked from the first bite, all the awful prophecies of Mad Minnaar were as vague as last month's gale; they wanted more and more and more. But clever Fagmie Jabaar, always one jump ahead, held up his hand and said, 'Oh no, these things are costing much cash from my pocket, and if you desire more then you-all must be paying for what you want.'

And once they'd been told the currency and the rates of exchange they paid gladly.

Economically, life became much easier, and if there did seem to be a retribution in the form of all sorts of omens and portents, plagues and discomfort, which they should have been more concerned about, well, who listens to prophets in a time of ease and good fortune? Certainly a comet did traverse the night sky filling some with fear, others with wonder, and no doubt there were asteroid showers, and maybe birds did cease from their twitter as hot chunks of rock burnt up in the stratosphere; certainly there were crickets which kept everyone awake to a constant, maddening shrill, and from all accounts the countryside was devoured by locusts forcing bankrupt farmers to seek work in town as railway guards or bus drivers or printing press minders. And then a strange thing happened near the settlement: Augustin Shoote fell out of the sky.

Augustin Shoote fulfilled Mad Minnaar's ravings in the most unique of ways, and the villagers can be forgiven for temporarily confusing him with the recounted angel, although there were some among them, Stevie's mother, for one, who never thought he was anything other than a heavenly messenger.

Perhaps, knowing a little of the conflict within the man, one can understand why he was unhappy as a fighter pilot; why one morning at thirty thousand feet he peeled away from his squadron and, un-noticed, set a course westwards with nothing in mind except to escape, to forget the war, to find a place where he could once again come to terms with his God.

'At times like those one has no plan,' he once told Montague Planke. 'One acts irrationally, madly, trusting. No, hardly trusting, more led by blind faith into believing everything will be all right, because where could I have hoped to go? Where could I have hoped to find sanctuary? Clearly I didn't think about that – in fact, I didn't think about anything until I saw the vast blue of the sea filling the horizon; then suddenly I knew what to do, I saw an opportunity to vanish without trace, presumed dead.'

So it was that Augustin Shoote parachuted into the settlement while his abandoned craft described a graceful parabola into the distant sea.

To Augustin Shoote, the hand of God was everywhere: in the church with its nesting bats and cormorants; in the relics of Catholic worship; in the whalebone cross above the driftwood altar; and not least in the bowed heads of a clearly devout, clearly reverent congregation. 'Praise the Lord, our Father, for not forgetting us, his children, in these forsaken parts, who, after so many long years, sends a preacher for this pulpit answering our prayers that our lives and those of our fathers and mothers will not stay unblessed in the graves behind the koppie; hear our prayers against all evil, locusts and crickets, that we can once again live in the grace of your ways.'

And from what Fagmie Jabaar recounted to Montague Planke that is exactly what happened. One night the fisherfolk realised the shrill chorus had ended; the next morning the veld moved as the locusts went north. For hour on hour the villagers watched them passing down the side of the church, and even though the Brothers Kreef, Stevie and Vygie Bond set out to find an end to the swarm they returned just before dusk, struck with awe that there could be such miles and miles and miles of hoppers.

'The Lord is merciful,' said Augustin Shoote and ushered his congregation into the church to give thanks.

As the plagues ended and the comet disappeared from the sky, the people of the settlement could return to their new-found pleasures without guilt. If they did not get rich they at least ate better, although the incidence of toothache was possibly more frequent than it had been before. Even Mondling, who had scorned the Jabaars and vowed never to set foot in their store, suddenly began taking a morning coffee, first at an outside table, no matter how foul the weather, then at the table beside the door which became his and his alone. He paid with the very best of coins, which eventually ended up in the hands of Montague Planke and found a ready market in the antique shops.

While Augustin Shoote brought solace to most of the souls at the settlement, there was one, imbued, although definitely to a far lesser degree than his father and grandfather before him, with a romantic restlessness that kept him from sleep and made him sigh heavily at frequent intervals throughout the night and day. He had cast a discerning eye, another inherited facility, about the women of the village and found that there wasn't one among them who stirred any emotion in his heart. Boatswain Baleen began to pine for the mate he didn't have. Lady Sarah saw it, but for once was powerless to ease the ailment; Fagmie Jabaar saw it and immediately knew the solution. Whenever Boatswain Baleen came in for a pint of beer (the local melon wine now gathered dust on pantry shelves since Fagmie Jabaar had introduced the wonders of beer), the scheming proprietor would tell, mostly tall tales, of the hundreds of beautiful women on the streets of the city where he did business. Women, it sounded to the desperate Boatswain Baleen, who were just waiting for someone to kneel before them with an offer of marriage. The more beer he drank, the easier his chances sounded, but unlike his father and his grandfather before him, women terrified him and for months he procrastinated, finding every excuse not to head south on what Lady Sarah called a mission of love. So one night before Namaqua Drift's tug was due, Fagmie Jabaar plied beer on beer on the unsuspecting Boatswain Baleen until not even his hard head could cope and he fell beneath the bar. Next morning, Stevie and the Brothers Kreef stowed the still unconscious man in Namaqua Drift's small cabin, which had a sealed porthole, so there was no chance of the incumbent's escape.

Many hours later Montague Planke opened his door to the grinning Fagmie Jabaar and his bedraggled companion.

'This man's come to seek out a most beautiful bride, Mister Montague sir,' proclaimed Fagmie Jabaar.

Which, as it turned out, was easier said than done. First of all, the women of Montague Planke's acquaintance, all good women working hard to make a decent living for themselves and their offspring, although the more righteous would probably baulk at the use of the word decent, were hardly what Boatswain Baleen was looking for. In fact, even the most inhibited among them terrified him. So strange to think that his father and his grandfather would have revelled at the delights of the Tavern, even if the soft caress of the whalebone corsets was no longer a prelude to the delights of the flesh. Not so much as an ancestral glint fired his eyes when he was introduced to big-busted, big-hearted Rosa, soft-bummed, soft-headed Wanda, wide-thighed, wide-eyed Sandra, cute-nosed, cute-toed Cynthia, delicate Delene, splendid Sue, moaning Minnie, Jane-the-Jump and Perpetua. Girls at their best, girls who could coax life into the most flaccid member, yet who singularly failed to send Boatswain Baleen crashing to his knees with a spontaneous avowal of undying love and devotion.

'What are we to do, mister sir?' lamented Fagmie Jabaar two nights later. 'This man hasn't a clue when he's looking the most wondrous types in the boobies, types who stir you with a mere fluttered eyelash. Oh Sheemina, wife, forgive me.'

It was a problem. Three nights later – a failed bottle of brandy on the table between them, Montague Planke's meagre resources of eligible women depleted, Boatswain Baleen sunk in a depression deeper than a lobster hole, Fagmie Jabaar convinced that only an Imam's holy water could unlock the boatswain's timid heart – Montague Planke came across a notice in the classified advertisements: 'Dying grandmother urgently seeks caring husband for teenage bride orphaned since a baby, loving, friendly disposition, character reference supplied by priest.'

'Here's the answer, Fagmie,' he cried. 'Here's just what you're looking for. An untouched woman, pure in body, mind and soul who will be wife, companion, mother to his children; devotee until his dying day. And, most importantly, a woman young enough to train in his ways.'

Next morning, fighting through a thickness of brandy, the trio made their way to a dilapidated quarter of narrow streets and large women resting their massive breasts on stoep walls. It was a place where Montague Planke had not done business before, yet in the dim corridors of those small houses he sensed ready agents must lurk, layabouts and unemployables who would have their fingers smeared with the stuff of many pies.

The house they sought seemed smaller and grimmer than the rest, a mushroom among toadstools, walls flaking and blistered, the front covered in a mass of weeds and cat mess with the stench of a hundred years of boiled shanks and marrow breathing from the crack beneath the door. Which to their knock opened as if of its own accord, and a faint voice summoned them down the passageway, old dog bones cracking underfoot, to a room of grey light, grey sheets, grey face upon the pillow.

As it turned out, although the old lady was on her death bed she had lost none of her shrewdness when it came to dealing with men.

'Don't think you can score a fast one here, my buckos,' she croaked. 'This old duck's had the measure of you-lot all her life long so there's not a man living or dead who's pulled the wool over my eyes and I'm not inclined to let it happen now. It's a happy death I'm keen on, not an eternity of playing ghost. So, Sonny Jims, cast your sparklers on my granddaughter, and if you're then of a mind to seek her hand we'll discuss further.'

'No, no, grandmother,' Montague Planke hastily had to inform her, 'it's only our friend, the good Boatswain Baleen here, who's searching for a soul mate. Him' – Montague Planke indicated Fagmie Jabaar – 'and I are already bespoke or otherwise engaged so to speak.'

'Well then get, gents,' retorted the old lady. 'If your good Boatswain's got a tongue in his head and can take his eyes off my charge for half a minute we might get down to a more serious business before the Lord in his mercy sees fit to snatch me away.'

So Fagmie Jabaar and Montague Planke abandoned the love-struck Boatswain Baleen to his fortunes and left that house of old bones for the fresh outside air. Yet they had hardly got that musty air from their lungs when Baleen, agitated, flushed scarlet, buttoning up his flies and yet incongruously smiling, called them back. Clearly the old lady had taken him in hand: he had been weighed and not found wanting.

'This is a good man,' she said when they were all once more grouped round her bed. 'He will treat my granddaughter as a woman should be. Please go now, but stop in at the church and tell the priest I have finally made my choice and died.'

And that, bar the shouting (and wailing, of which there was quite a bit from the young Finella when she realised her grandmother was no longer of this world), was that. On the next tide Captain Namaqua Drift took the by now mutually devoted couple and Fagmie Jabaar back to the settlement and a magnificent wedding.

How much living went on between the magnificent marriage and the awful events that befell the settlement towards the end of a bitter winter no one could tell. Some, Boatswain Baleen, Lady Sarah, Augustin Shoote among them, said it was months. No, argued Jong Jan, Stevie, Landed-Little Marsdon and Fagmie Jabaar, it was no more than a week or two because hadn't the whales washed ashore after a savage spring tide, such as only happened between the equinoxes? But whether it was months or weeks didn't really matter because Mad Minnaar's dire predictions seemed to be coming horribly true.

This time of suffering and misery started when Mad Minnaar's man, the bottleman, came running up from Whale Beach, his eyes wild with alarm, frothing at the mouth, babbling incoherently, so that every one thought he'd taken to smoking dagga on a head of wine. There he was, on his knees, shouting away and pleading with everyone to come and see for themselves until Mad Minnaar broke in and slapped his face with the strength she used to beat a live snoek to death against a rock, one two three. The shouts became whimpers and she was down beside him pressing his face to her bosom, stroking his crusty hair. 'There there my sweet, my cherub, quietly, there there.'

'Drunken sot,' breathed Mondling but got no further.

'No. No,' screamed Mad Minnaar. 'Oh no, Lord, not that, not now. Have mercy, we beseech you, on humble types. Bodies!' she shrieked. 'There are corpses on the beach!'

Vygie Bond, Stevie, Fagmie Jabaar, the Brothers Kreef, Boatswain Baleen, Finella, even the children were off at a sprint, and the rest, too, as best they could manage for five miles along the exhausting beach until they came to them: three bodies, two men, one woman, still young, naked, eyeless, tied by the ankles with thin wire, bloated, grotesque, long drowned, or, perish the thought, murdered before they were dumped in the sea.

'Lord have mercy on their souls,' gasped Augustin Shoote. 'Lord have mercy, dear God, amen.'

Regaining their breath, disconsolate, troubled, the villagers sat on the sand, not looking at the corpses, thinking their own thoughts until the sea birds began to gather: for some death is always a feast. What else to do but drag the bodies back for proper blessing and a decent grave, poor nameless wretches.

'Prisoners of some sort,' conjectured Mondling at Fagmie Jabaar's that night. 'Without a doubt evil-doers, why else tie them with wire?'

'Never, Mondling,' spoke up Boatswain Baleen, 'why not stowaways? There's not many a captain who'll treat the likes of them with anything less than a whipping. Although it's beyond imagining to be punished so brutally for so small a crime.'

'Or victims,' said Augustin Shoote without further elaboration.

'Or political prisoners,' said Vygie Bond quietly.

'Oh no,' chided Mondling. 'Political prisoners aren't allowed to swim off just like that. Oh no. They'd be chained and handcuffed, not looped together with a bit of wire.'

'Someone put out their eyes,' persisted Vygie Bond.

'Their eyes were put out by fish and birds – don't go getting any notions, boy,' snapped Mondling, getting up to leave.

'More drinks, gentlemen?' offered Fagmie Jabaar, bringing round his bottomless jug.

With hindsight, Vygie Bond was probably right. Especially when, just two days later, another eyeless victim, this time chewed up so badly by the sea and sharks there was no telling how he'd died, was rolled into the tide-line.

'Another political prisoner?' scoffed Mondling. 'This one's not even tied up.'

But Vygie Bond ignored the jibe and went on digging a pit in the hard earth near the grave of a drowned man, over which Augustin Shoote intoned, 'May the Lord have mercy on this poor man's soul, and grant him peace in the hereafter for ever and ever, amen.'

Just a fortnight later, under skies as grey as the skin of the dead, the whole village stood bare-headed before ten shallow graves:

> Oh God our help in ages past,
> Our hope for years to come,
> Our shelter from the stormy blast
> And our eternal home.

'Our Father, which art in heaven, hear the words of Your children in this troubled world, grant us the peace to live far from the evil doings of wicked men, and the grace to honour and love Thy name, to pray for the poor and oppressed even as they labour against injustice and to be grateful for our lot which is humble but without trouble and thankful for Your goodness. Unto Thy eternal care we commit these men and women, mere mortals, victims of their time, to rejoice in Thy name, world without end, amen.'

And so, spade for spade, they were covered up, the naked, eyeless, wounded remains of men old and young, women, girls, boys who had been tortured, witness: whipped soles, mutilated genitals, lacerations, bruises, burns that weren't the doings of the sea. Even Mondling was silent when the men sat later around Fagmie Jabaar's tables, nursing glasses, too sick at heart to drink, wondering inwardly and out loud with Boatswain Baleen, 'How could any human being do that to another?'

'Where's your God now, padre?' Vygie Bond wanted to know.

'You must have faith, Vygie Bond. Only faith can help us in adversity,' responded Augustin Shoote.

'Faith! What's faith against those poor remains. For God's sake, padre.'

'Yes, for God's sake, Vygie Bond.'

These victims had been found not half a mile from Lady Sarah's house. Mangled, misshapen, human flotsam and jetsam washed up like kelp and sea jelly to be sucked and nibbled by snails, lice, even a mooching shaggy hyena hoping for nothing better than baby seal carcasses.

'Get out of it, beast. Violate not the dead,' screamed Augustin Shoote to put him to flight. 'Dear Lord, what is happening that the oceans no longer run with fish but with the bodies of the slain, that we should bear witness to such atrocities as these committed on children who must be innocent, on the old who cannot be guilty, on men and women perhaps asking for nothing more than a decent life? What currents sweep them up from the cruel south to disturb our peace, our hard, calm existence? Why should ten manacled and chained find their desperate way here to make a last statement? And pick us?'

'What rubbish,' argued Mondling. 'It is nothing but coincidence and unseasonal tides. Don't read anything further into these corpses. Certainly they're not a fulfilment of the witch's mad prophecies. And political deaths or not, who cares, they're nothing to do with us.'

But the sea wouldn't rest from its morbid revelations: each few days it washed another small group ashore. And what it gave with one hand, the sea withheld with the other: while there were corpses there were no fish. The fuller the graveyard the emptier the villagers' stomachs.

'Pray God we don't starve before there's fish again,' said Stevie's mother. 'Just look how thin the children have become, and ill with colds and fever.'

'We're being punished I tell you, and I've told you all along, for the sins of our fathers and our fathers' fathers. It's always been said when there are no fish left in the sea, the drowned will appear. Mark my words, there's worse to come,' shouted Mad Minnaar at the lamenting women.

And the boats came in night after night with empty baskets until the evening the fishermen tied up saying, 'That's it. We are not going back. The dead have become fishes: we look down and see schools of the drowned passing through the depths, we pull in our nets and bodies like these appear where there should be a mackerel.'

And they took from the boats three young women, by their looks not long dead, not bloated, discoloured or sea-ravaged like the others, still beautiful, still soft-skinned, imaginably warm. Lady Sarah brought a canvas to cover the violated: although who would have said, seeing only their faces, that they had not died young virgins in their sleep, or perhaps death was a mother's hand to soothe away anguish and suffering. Whatever, Fagmie Jabaar's was empty that night: people went to church or stayed home with heavy hearts.

That was the saddest funeral, the funeral of the three virgins. Such beautiful young girls to be treated so badly, the least that could be done was to give them proper blessing and mourn their passing. All that night women kept a vigil by candlelight, praying for their souls, reciting psalms out loud to keep themselves awake and warm. What else could be done to right the wrongs of a cruel world? All night Augustin Shoote led the most devout in worship, while Lady Sarah brought steaming mussel soup, and Fagmie Jabaar offered hot samoosas at the first sign of dawn. Poor girls; although Mother Bond sewed through the dark hours she could make no more than the roughest of winding sheets with a crude crucifix embroidered over the heart.

Out at the cemetery from early light the men who dug the graves dug with liquid eyes – how else? Despite all the horrors that had washed up on the shores the girls' deaths touched the fisherfolk most deeply. A man must be without compassion if he cannot shed tears on the hard earth where the innocent lie. Poor procession, leaving the church, gaunt-eyed, in black, carrying the corpses on driftwood planks to a special corner set aside for the massacred where everyone stood as the bodies went into their pits and Boatswain Baleen, Stevie, and Vygie Bond shovelled the soil in gently, because after all those girls had been through no one wanted to hurt them any more.

With bowed heads they waited for the prayers of Augustin Shoote, waited for his wonderful voice to ease the ache in their hearts, to remind them of the glory of God, of the world hereafter where everyone will sit on His right hand radiant in His love, but Augustin Shoote said nothing. Not even when people shuffled their bare feet, not even when Mondling walked off muttering, 'What's he think he's doing staring into space when he should be laying souls to rest?' or

Mother Bond sat down, or the children whined to be picked up, not even then did he utter a blessing. After what seemed like hours, one by one they left, sprinkling daisy petals on to the mounds, casting curious glances at the dumb-struck preacher, waiting until they were behind the koppie before the surprise loosened their tongues and for a while they forgot to mourn.

'I don't know how long I stood there,' Augustin Shoote told Montague Planke on that curfew night in Fagmie Jabaar's, 'maybe six hours. Certainly we went to bury them early in the morning and the sun was well into afternoon when suddenly I realised where I was. Can a man stand for that long in a trance? Who knows? I looked down at the three graves which seemed to belong to a time long ago, a simpler time, when the Bible I carried, had carried since a boy, was so much more than a book, it was the Word of God, whose voice was gone now. No matter how hard I listened I had become deaf. I can hear you, yet I am deaf to the Voice that has been my mentor and conscience. No matter what hours I spend on my knees I can hear nothing, not even an echo. Although sometimes I think I do catch the faintest of sounds, wind over stones, and it reminds me of the Voice I last heard in that cemetery. Ah Montague, there are times I want so much to believe again.'

Outside rain was still lashing down, Stevie was about and so was Captain Nunes. But Augustin Shoote was in a tormented world of his own.

'Think of Thomas, think of all the great doubters, Montague, and consider, none of them was as wretched as I. For all they did was doubt whereas I do not even have the benefit of doubt. Can a man lose his faith so completely, so quickly, Montague? Is it possible? Can it be like falling out of love, a loss so sudden that between one moment and the next the world is altered, fundamentally changed, never to be the same again?'

'I don't know, Augustin,' replied Montague Planke. 'We are each alone.'

After the funeral of the three virgins the settlement suffered: Jong Jan wouldn't put to sea and rarely left his cottage; Stevie, Vygie Bond and the Brothers Kreef sat on the jetty flipping stones into the water or else, desultory, restless, played dominoes with a hard smack on the tables at Fagmie Jabaar's.

Day on day, night on night, Augustin Shoote bent his knees. 'Please God, hear thy humble servant.'

Even Mondling, the cynic, kept to himself and his house, shunning all contact with the disease that gripped the settlement.

'It's no good,' said Boatswain Baleen. 'The joy of living has gone out of us, only the children are still carefree. But for how long, when Finella is moody all day and I have the temper of an adder? This thing is killing the village.'

Which Lady Sarah knew and did her best to overcome by baking scones, cakes, doughnuts, custard slices, meringues, and taking them round to each house herself (because Samuel refused to leave his room where he watched each daylight hour through a powerful telescope the long sand horizon, expecting at any time to see the dark figure of a man break the line) with words of comfort as if the village were suffering the bereavement of a long standing member. 'Come on, Fagmie, why don't you whistle any more, we haven't heard your tunes for days, and why doesn't Sheemina sing in the kitchen? All the taste is going out of your food.'

It was not that easy. Especially when one morning the bottleman came stumbling into their horrified midst yelling, 'Dreadful news, dreadful news' so that children dropped eggs in the chicken run, women tipped over buckets of fresh prawns from the lagoon and men left their coffee at Fagmie Jabaar's as they came running with loud hearts.

'What is it? What is it?' they shrieked. 'Speak bottleman, speak.'

But all he did was throw a bottle on the sand, an old bottle covered with barnacles, and hold up a slip of paper like a tiny flag.

'What use is a note in a bottle?' scoffed Mondling. 'You drunken sot.'

And the fisherfolk would have laughed, relieved that it was nothing more, had not Mad Minnaar grabbed at the piece of paper, screaming, 'Give me that. I know what it is. It's about him, isn't it. It's my prophecy come true.'

Then others snatched it from her, until in the tussle the paper tore and came away in half a dozen hands. Ashamed, the culprits let the pieces drop like stolen crumbs.

'It's not a good idea to tear up the Devil's name,' said Mad Minnaar. 'Now there's no saving us.'

But quietly Finella picked up the pieces and arranged the most fateful jigsaw of her life to spell the name, Nunes. 'So what,' some shrugged. 'Huh,' grunted Mondling in derision – after all, what's in a name that no one, not even Namaqua Drift, had heard of. But the mark was on them and they turned away without a word.

The first time the fisherfolk forgot their depression was when the monthly tug put in and everyone rushed to the jetty with one question. 'What's happening out there? For God's sake tell us.'

'You won't believe it,' snapped Namaqua Drift's hands and fingers, 'but it's true, on my word, you've got to have the devil's imagination to make up what's been going on all over the country. Cows, sheep, pigs, goats butchered for no rhyme or reason and left to bleed a long death till morning. Whole flocks, whole herds lost to the blunt axes of who could it be, no one knows, but my Lord it's terrible. Yet that's not the worst, not by a far stretch, oh no. With my own eyes I've seen men stoned to death, family men with children like yours, Mrs Baleen, and with my own ears I've heard the most atrocious tales. Nor is stoning the worst, heaven help us. Mayors chopped to pieces, their little sons burnt while the demons danced, wives and daughters raped and battered, that's what's been going on in these days and nights. Inconceivable savageness, everyone in fear and trembling. So many people shot, so many people swallowed up never to be seen again.'

And the villagers nodded, thinking of those in the graveyard behind the hill.

Usually when they unloaded the tug everyone went to it with a will and laughter, but not then: they took out the sugar, flour, coffee, tea, sacks of seeds and fertiliser, the chocolates and bon bons with the heaviness they had felt when digging the graves, and poor Namaqua Drift had to put back to sea without even a thank you or a decent cup of tea.

How awful the way of things, how deeply depressing, how morbid to live day by day waiting for the bottleman to say there were more bodies on Whale Beach. Yet as the days became weeks, the weeks a month, without any corpses except seal pups and old cormorants being washed ashore, the settlement began to breathe again. Stevie noticed gannets diving out at sea; from the Head the Brothers Kreef saw the dark shadows of mackerel shoals passing through the bay. Eventually Jong Jan was persuaded to leave his cottage and go fishing.

Once more the fish were biting. Fagmie Jabaar put out clean tablecloths and new candles, gave sweets to the children and a free glass of wine to whoever stopped by for a curry stew. Little by little the fish returned. The children grew fat; the smell of boiled galjoen hung over the settlement as a faint reminder of the days when the stench of blubber could be smelled as far inland as the goatherds' hut. Samuel abandoned his lookout, Boatswain Baleen regained his easy temper, Finella smiled about the house and streets, Fagmie Jabaar whistled, Sheemina sang the flavour back into her cooking, Mondling took his evening walk along the lagoon shores, stopping off for a drink and coffee at Jabaar's Goodtime Trading Store, Lady Sarah heaved a sigh of relief, vowing never to bake another meringue again, only Augustin Shoote was left in a shattered world, forsaken, godless, haunting the empty church night and day in hope of a miracle.

Outside everyone knew there had been a miracle: how else were the cruelties and deaths stopped? The bottleman could come and go all he wished, he could no longer do anyone harm. Once more the fisherfolk got used to their life, grumbling at the late frost, threatening to put in new jackal traps, wondering when to plant the seedlings. Perhaps deep down they still feared the moment when someone would raise the alarm, but with each passing day the fear became as remote as a ship sailing over the horizon. Like cripples they learnt to accommodate their disorder. If they paused while digging out the stubborn potatoes, or looked up from preparing the evening meal to the koppie silhouetted against the sunset and let their thoughts conjure up the massacred dead in the graveyard beyond, then those were moments of weakness they had to learn to overcome. Just as they had to learn to put flowers on the other graves when they put flowers on the graves of their own dead.

7

THE BOOT

Early on the morning of a new June moon, the end of Ramadan, not ten hours after Montague Planke had seen Fagmie Jabaar out on the rising tide, Captain Nunes, working overtime, for it was gone three o'clock, kicked at the door of Planke's Handling Agency with all the force that authority can muster.

'Customs and Excise,' he shouted. 'Open up.'

Holy Jesus, thought Montague Planke stumbling up through sleep, heart pounding as loudly as the hammering on the door. Holy Jesus! But then he remembered there wasn't a diamond in the place; he was as clean as an Imam's shirt at Eid.

Even so, Captain Nunes worked him over. 'Ah-man, Planke, just tell us where they are. We know what you're up to.'

Nunes pushed Montague Planke on to the bed. 'Tell us, Planke. Ah-man, it'll be so much easier.' He held up three fingers, folding them back into a fist as he counted: 'One, two, three.' Planke took the fist against his unsuspecting head. It knocked him off the bed, for a few seconds it blacked out the world, it made him nauseous, it opened a cut which started to bleed in three streams that ran out of his dark hair, collected at the line of his jaw and dropped in gaudy splashes on to his pyjamas. Montague Planke sat on the floor, one hand clasped to his bleeding head, face down, looking at the boots of Captain Nunes.

'For six months we've been tracking down all your falsehoods, Planke,' said Nunes. 'That's a lot of wasted money, Planke. Government money. Government time.'

Two open-handed slaps banged against the sides of Montague Planke's head. He cringed. Once again Nunes held up three fingers. 'One, two, three.' Two blows in quick succession knocked the bleeding proprietor head-first to the left then to the right: the rest was oblivion.

When Montague Planke regained consciousness, his face encrusted with blood, every muscle and bone in his body stiff with pain, he was lying on the floor in the midst of a devastated room. Clearly Nunes and his lieutenants knew how to search for diamonds: the obvious places had been slashed open, mattress, pillows, chair cushion; drawers ransacked; floorboards pulled up; pelmet pulled down; toothpaste and shaving tubes emptied; even half a stale loaf of bread decimated. His only triumph was that they had not found the diamonds because the diamonds were safely closeted in a small leather pouch between the enormous breasts of the Tavern's Long Martha. Ten years back that was one of the most public places in the city, but since menopause she had shunned all men and rampant youths on the theory that if a lake doesn't get flushed out every now and then it goes stagnant, and she was not having her insides silted up by every Tom and Harry's dick.

Great consolation, in the circumstances, great consolation. Had he not obeyed a whim, the diamonds would most surely have been found and he would now be languishing in some damp cell.

Needless to say it was a difficult month, this month between one visit of Fagmie Jabaar's and the next. A month of intense physical discomfort which even Long Martha's supple hands couldn't relieve.

'Oh my, now here's a sorry case if ever I've seen one,' she said when Montague Planke finally (about a week later) crawled into the Tavern. 'They beat you up well and truly, didn't they, son. Just as well you've got someone like Long Martha to trust with these little beauties,' and she shook her breasts into massive motion. 'Just as well.'

It was also a bad month in the market place. Those with the ready for a diamond, even those he'd not sold a bad egg to in all his years of business, took one look at his bruised and battered face and saw all the IDB victims who'd ever been, personified in one man, Montague Planke.

Everyone was terribly polite, however. 'Good day, Mr Planke, sorry to see you looking poorly, Mr Planke,' and then hands up in horror at his proposition. 'No, no, business is down, Mr Planke, business is bad.' But even then trade went on: stone by stone Montague Planke slunk around to all his more mendacious merchants – 'My my, Mr Planke, are you having an accident mit a bus?' 'Goodness gracious me, Mr Planke, but that is a nasty shiner.' 'Oh my, Mr Planke, have you been mixing with Izzy the Pot?' – and put up with their weak jokes, cracking a lip each time the price turned down. Those sharks could smell dead meat: no matter how vigorously he protested life.

'How about next month, Myneer Gunst?' he asked, hoping against the odds for a quick deal when Fagmie Jabaar landed again.

'Next munds ist next munds Myneer Planke, who can tell wat it is right to buy next munds?'

Who indeed? Could they all somehow see the lurking figure of Captain Nunes about to clamp his hand on Montague Planke's shoulder with a triumphant, 'Ah-man, Planke, I'm arresting you'?

But the hand of Nunes was nowhere apparent that month. Nor, for that matter, did the lurking lieutenants haunt the opposite doorway or clumsily open a newspaper whenever Montague Planke suddenly turned to see who dogged his footsteps. Nobody did, and that is exactly what worried him.

'There's no need to be so nervy, Montague,' was Long Martha's advice as she buried the last warm stone in his hand. 'There's not been a new face in here without the radiance of the innocent, so believe me all they wanted was to sow the fear of the damned in you.'

But that was too easy an explanation, and perhaps even Long Martha knew it because she'd seen them work on her regulars many a time. The way Montague Planke looked at it, it was better to be hounded morning, noon and night because at least then you had the cold comfort of harassment. All he had was the frightening memory of a vicious encounter and the unspoken promise of more to come. That Captain Nunes for one moment doubted he was on to an IDB racket was inconceivable: he was just biding his time, waiting for the next boat and with it the unsuspecting Fagmie Jabaar.

Night after night as that dismal month whittled away Montague Planke tossed and dreaded the coming of Fagmie Jabaar, or else lay in a funk convinced that Nunes and his lieutenants, annoyed at the length of their wait, were coming up through the town to get him. And so he heard the old church round the corner strike the hours, each stroke before three tightening the fear, each stroke after pealing with the relief of morphine, until from the mosque tower the moulana called the faithful to prayer and he was released to sleep.

So his fearful life continued: hour by day, hour by night, willy-nilly into Nunes's clutches. But how to escape those eager fingers? How to be one over the odds when Fagmie Jabaar was even now somewhere below the line and steaming up faster than a stung coot? Sure, he had neither the captain nor his lieutenants breathing down his neck, but who needed them in a battle against the very laws of inevitability?

Which was why, in those grey minutes it takes the moulana to climb his tower, an old adage came to mind: if the powder's wet, tears won't dry it, run. Sound advice for any frontiersman faced with a charging rhinoceros; sound advice, too, for lesser mortals faced with the charge office.

Come first light Montague Planke took off for the lanes where the wanted, the hounded, the desperate have so often gone to ground, where the search warrant is as useless as a dry mop on cleaning day, stopping only long enough to whisper Beinkinstadt off Hanover in Long Martha's ear.

'You take care now, Montague, and don't settle too much curry on a weak stomach or you'll be paying your way in bog-rolls,' was all she said as he left through the kitchen.

Where else was there? Where else such a confusion of lives to hide a confused life? Where else a chance to duck out of the main stream, bag in hand, hurrying now, glancing back every few quick steps to make sure it wasn't the dreaded Nunes leading his lieutenants that turned the corner, arm raised, gun drawn, shouting, 'Stop or I'll shoot,' perish the thought, thank God for the normality of women and children, snot-nosed brats, and out-of-work men squatting over cards, ah the sanctity of small streets and hard cobbles, the hundred-year ruin of hundred-year buildings: mildew, rising damp, woodrot, up the Seven Steps beneath the mountain, winding, winding, past grandmothers in forgotten courtyards, through the stench of fruit, vegetables, spices, pepper, samoosas, flowers, marijuana, gas, everywhere and overpowering gas, goodday to rabbi, imam, priest jostling for souls, beware the sting of the Scorpions, the skollies' quick flick-knives, the layabout queues at the British, with each safe step nearer my saviour to thee and the ask-no-questions-bearded-face of Mrs Beinkinstadt board and lodging, hot bath second landing, Tuesdays, Thursdays and Sundays only, pay one week now into the horny outstretched hand for a room at the back without sun and view above a yard of washing, goats and chickens, pigeons against the panes, palms rustling, rustling. Where else could he possibly go?

But even there, where he had never been before, where no one, least of all Nunes, had cause to look for him, Montague Planke was as restless, as afraid as the Montague Planke who had cowered beneath the blankets until each Muslim dawn. And maybe this was worse. How foolish to think he could hide when their eyes and ears were everywhere, when even now Nunes's heavy boots could be striking sparks from the cobbles. What use then was a back room when the first warning would be his spectral presence in the doorway?

'Mrs Beinkinstadt, I need a room facing the harbour,' he requested.

'No rooms, all full,' was the only answer he got as she folded thick arms in disapproval.

So, holed up for a week and a day by fear and a grenadier guardswoman, he watched the goat in the yard below, pigeons in the palms, went weak in the bowels every time the hallboards creaked, became increasingly convinced that they knew, that Nunes stood gloating at his window, smoothing moustache with thumb and index finger, knowing that in the sprawling ghetto on the lower slopes he would find his quarry any time he chose in a room without a view at the back of Mrs Beinkinstadt's board and lodging. How could they not know? Such is the power of the state, nothing is hidden, nothing is sacred. And almost, like the crazy hunted, he went begging to Nunes for arrest.

For a week and a day the fear possessed him: neither drink, which brought first a bravado then a maudlin self-pity, nor sleep, which unleashed a dark film of terror, offered any escape from a deep dungeon, until, dreaded moment, in the hall he heard the tread of Mrs Beinkinstadt and another lightly following . . . knock, knock.

'Kum kum man! Vake up there is here a boy.'

A boy, indeed, one of those Long Martha kept about her skirts until their own lusts arose, with a message.

'Aunty Martha says, Uncle, to tell you Mr Fagmie' – God help us, whispered Montague Planke – 'is waiting' – heaven forbid, he prayed – 'in your office' – for Christ's sake, Montague Planke almost shouted.

Of all the dumb, stupid, thoughtless, dim-witted, confounded, foolish, irritating and thoroughly pig-headed things to have done. He could have spat, screamed, beaten the boy, poor cowering messenger of bad tidings, hurled plates, raged, cried tears of frustration. Didn't the man have any sense? Damn it all, it wasn't as if they hadn't been through just this sort of problem before, decided that when the chips were down the last place of sanctuary was Planke's Handling Agency. Fagmie Jabaar you idiot. But to the boy he spoke gently – after all, Mrs Beinkinstadt stood arms folded beside him and she didn't look the sort to tolerate child abuse.

'Go to Mr Fagmie, there's a good boy, and tell him that Mr Planke doesn't work there any longer so he must come and see me here.'

And not being an ungenerous man, he slipped a big coin into the boy's hand which, at least, elicited an approving nod from Mrs Beinkinstadt.

In what torment he passed the hours of that fateful afternoon, a highly agitated man pacing in classic fashion his small and squalid room, pausing now and then to stare from the window at the goats below, smoking, crushing out the butt, lighting another, his hands, with a life of their own, now knotting and twisting, now thrusting into his trouser pockets, but always on the move, as he is, hardly still for a moment, pacing, sitting on the bed, springing up, briefly mesmerised at the window, then up and down again, pausing to listen, even opening the door a crack on to the empty landing, looking at his watch as if in disbelief that time can move so ponderously.

Until. Eventually. At long last the tread of Mrs Beinkinstadt and another lightly following . . . no need this time to knock, they meet in the passageway. 'And where is bloody Fagmie?' shouts Montague Planke.

'Forbidden shouting,' shouts Mrs Beinkinstadt. 'This house is respectable.'

Blood in his face, the hammer of it in his ears, the all consuming knock of it in his chest.

'Where is Mr Fagmie, son? Don't be frightened, you can tell me.'

In faltering voice comes the reply. 'He says, Uncle, that he can't come here because of all the bad men who don't like him.'

'What rubbish!'

'Forbidden shouting, forbidden shouting,' stamps Mrs Beinkinstadt waving her arms. 'No one is to shout.'

But Montague Planke is finished with them. Hours of pent up dread, days of fear, a month of panic burst in the need to act heedless of consequences. Without pausing for jacket or tie he flings past them, takes the stairs two and three at a time, shoots into the road and keeps going over cobbles that almost tilt the world from under him, round the snoekman's horse and cart, dodging barrows, cars and children down the crumbling Georgian streets into town, Nunes territory, but not even that warning could stop his mission. Only crowded streets and the leisurely gardens where nothing is more suspicious than a running man slowed his headstrong plummet, until the sight of the lieutenants eating fish and chips around the corner from his block had him ducking for cover.

With night and a sea mist Montague Planke returned, making his way shadow by shadow up the street, listening for any sound in the thickness: the scuff of a man shifting his weight, the rasp of a suppressed cough, straining to see yet thankful for the blindness, weak to the pit of his stomach. Oh, he raged, how Captain Nunes must be rejoicing at this unexpected bonus, better than any trap he could have devised. And how he hated the thought of the captain's smirking lips peeled back in glee, waiting, waiting, for the ripe moment.

So he slipped without a squeak through the street door into the gloom of the forty-watt hallway; then up the stairs, back to the wall, arms at twenty past eight. Nothing moved in the dimness. From the landing he measured the fifteen paces down the passageway to the only door with a streak of light at the bottom. His key went in, the door opened and closed. Inside, his back to the door, Montague Planke faced, in all the splendour and innocence of a De Beers counting house, the biggest mound of unpolished glories he'd ever seen. And Fagmie Jabaar grinning at him in triumph.

'You fool, you dumb, unthinking, blundering idiot,' burst out Montague Planke. 'Why here? Why bring it here, when we agreed, when Long Martha must have warned you, Fagmie, he's in hiding, something's up, when the young boy told you where to find me, but most of all when we agreed, we actually agreed here in this very room with you nodding your head nineteen to the dozen that this was the last place on earth we should be seen together and especially with an enormous heap of diamonds? For crying out loud Fagmie Jabaar, what's possessed you, man? Huh! Do you know what they'll do if they find us with that lot? Do you? Let me tell you: with this lot there doesn't even have to be a trial. With this lot in one pan and us in the other even a squint-eyed judge with a brandy head, and lord knows there's enough of them, wouldn't feel any pain in sending us up for a long stretch. IDB is bad news, dear Fagmie the Innocent. In these courts IDB isn't just theft, it's rape, murder and treason all in one, and for what we've got here there's many a justice who would think a dawn drop too good for the likes of us. And that's just the good side. Rather death than life up the hill, oh rather, rather. What d'you say, Fagmie, to piss-wet floors and crap-holes filled with more blueflies than a corpse in summer? Not much, heh? Because there's not much for a dumb, blundering, idiotic, unthinking fool to say.'

Which was when, pausing for breath, he heard what could only be a lieutenant stepping on a loose floorboard. The creak went through the collaborators like a blasphemy on Sunday. Beloved Mary Mother of Jesus, this was it. And Fagmie Jabaar was now whiter than a circuit judge. 'Gee whiz, Montague, gee whiz,' was all he could say.

'Shh, man! Shh!' hissed Montague Planke.

Since time immemorial the forces of Draco have massed in such stillnesses, and they were massing again behind the door. Then came the knock. A knock that was no knock at all but fists and boots enraged.

'Quick, Fagmie, quick, the table, the diamonds.'

The table went against the door; the diamonds into their pockets.

'Oh goodness gracious, oh goodness gracious –'

'Don't whine, Fagmie, just don't whine, dammit.'

Now that this most dreaded of moments was upon him, Montague Planke knew exactly what to do – after all, hadn't he spent a month of mornings anticipating this terror, planning such escapes? And wasn't there one obvious, albeit rather alarming, way out of Captain Nunes's trap, namely, via the window? To a desperate man a single-storey drop is no drop at all. Except that Fagmie Jabaar didn't agree. Even as Montague Planke forced him on to the ledge he was protesting, 'Oh no, Mister Montague, sir, this is too far to the ground.'

But the splintering of wood and Captain Nunes's shouts soon convinced him it was no time for argument.

'Out, Fagmie, out,' screamed Montague Planke as the lock snapped and captain and lieutenants launched themselves across the table into the room. That did it. Fagmie jumped. Montague Planke followed. Behind him there was an explosion, then the pavement came up and he rolled and rolled, fighting for air.

'This way, this way, mister sir,' called Fagmie Jabaar, and they were off into the mist.

Streets of fire, streets of searing pain. They ran and ran. His blood too loud to hear if they were chased, his life in Fagmie Jabaar's hands, Montague Planke followed his business partner up into the Muslim quarter. There wasn't enough air in the world to soothe the fire in his lungs, not ever enough salve to soothe the wound in his flesh, but it took some time for him to realise it was also blood that wet his pants. The reality penetrated like a bullet.

'I'm hit, Fagmie,' he gasped, and went down in the gutter.

Montague Planke came round some hours later on a bed, in a sweat, with his trousers at his ankles and a family of eight staring at his punctured bum.

'Please lie still,' said an Oxford voice in a white smock, 'and we'll have this little beauty out in a jiffy.'

A woman near his face smiled to reveal a set of nutmeg teeth. One by one a row of children with fingers in their mouths passed before his eyes.

'Fagmie,' he whispered, 'Fagmie, where are you?'

'Right here, Mister Montague, sir,' came the quick response, 'doing very nicely, thank you.'

'Can't you get these women out of here? Goddammit, man, I'm naked,' he croaked.

'Oh, not to worry about that,' replied Fagmie. 'No one is in the least embarrassed, in fact all these women most interested to see such a white bottom.'

Then a needle, which felt the size of an eight-inch nail, injected insult into Montague Planke's injury.

'Is this man some voodoo quack, Fagmie?' he screamed.

'Please, not to be concerned, Mister Montague, this man is Dr Taj, most excellent doctor, and these are his families.'

'Is this painful?' enquired the Oxford voice. A hurt, acute, hot, frightful, tore through Montague Planke's bowels. 'Yes, I rather suspected it might be,' he said, 'that's the trouble with a ricochet, when a bullet tumbles it makes a bit of a mess. But you're a lucky chap to have such a fatty bum. Hold still please.'

How Montague Planke longed for oblivion. How he sweated, bit the pillow, even prayed for the good Lord not to forsake him. But he wasn't forsaken, he had the full attention of Dr Taj, his fishing forceps, and fascinated families, although they were more concerned with the two hemispheres of white flesh than the shapeless wad of lead their husband and father was tearing from one of the buttocks to a drooling commentary, barely managing to contain his saliva in an ecstasy of professional absorption. 'Just hold still one more moment, Mr Planke, almost there now. Oh my, Mr Planke, just look at that, a real beaut,' as if drawing a bullet was little more than common dentistry. And then, in belated answer to Montague Planke's prayers, came the oblivion he sought.

It was some time the next day before he awoke, stiff and sore, in a room empty but for a pencil of grey light penetrating the curtains and the prone figure of Fagmie Jabaar on a *chaise-longue*. On a stool beside the bed was a glass of liquid and in it a lump of lead, freed from human bondage. The sight was enough to turn his stomach, to recall in instant reply the horrors of Dr Taj and his families, and make him call out, 'Fagmie, Fagmie, wake up, dammit. I'm in pain, I've been shot, I've got to get to hospital.'

But no amount of pleading was going to wake Fagmie Jabaar. And as Montague Planke hurt too much to get up there was only one alternative. Carefully he poured the liquid out of the glass on to the floor, rolled the spent bullet on to the side table, picked it up and with a superhuman side-arm fling caught his sleeping companion a glancing blow to the temple. Fagmie Jabaar was awake in an instant.

'Eina, mister,' he lamented. 'That was not funny.'

'You're damn right,' Montague Planke replied. 'You're just bloody lucky you didn't get it where I did. Now help me up, I've got to see a doctor.'

'But Mister Montague, Dr Taj is the most excellent doctor who has done all he can to mend your rump. All you must do now is rest.'

'Rest! Rest, Fagmie! How can I rest when the captain and his lieutenants are out there looking for my blood? Blood which I must have left all over the streets. Blood which must lead right to this door.'

With a wave of his hand, Fagmie Jabaar dismissed Montague Planke's fears, turned over, disappeared under the blankets, and went back to sleep.

For five days Montague Planke stayed in the house of Dr Taj, lonely, frightened and in pain, dreaming both awake and asleep of Customs and Excise. And those five agitated days brought on a fever that turned the wound septic.

'Very interesting,' said Dr Taj, stripping off the stinking bandage. 'This is the way it sometimes occurs,' and all his families gathered round to see Montague Planke's suppurating injury. 'It is a known medical fact,' explained Dr Taj, 'that if one is to be shot at all it is better to be shot naked. Because when the bullet passes through cloth, you see, it embeds minute threads of fabric deep in the wound which can turn very nasty indeed. As yours has done, Mr Planke, as yours has done.'

Then, into the quiet contemplation of the pus-exuding wound, came pounding and panting Fagmie Jabaar, who had been missing most of the day, to say that Namaqua Drift had arranged to meet them off the Point in three hours.

'Ridiculous, Fagmie, that'll be in the middle of the afternoon, broad daylight,' exclaimed Montague Planke. 'What are we to do, swim out to him?'

'No, no, Mister Montague,' explained Fagmie Jabaar, 'another man, Abdul Abdurman, he is standing by to row us.'

'To row us! I am badly wounded, Fagmie.'

'And he now has a fever,' chimed in Dr Taj, 'so there is no chance of him leaving the bed,' and his families all sighed in agreement.

Fagmie shrugged. 'Consider, Mister Planke, it is a month before Namaqua Drift returns and I am most sadly missing Sheemina and Little One.'

Three hours later, having contemplated a naked month beneath the curious eyes of Dr Taj and his families, abandonment by Fagmie Jabaar and all he knew in the world, confident that in a last desperate attempt to save face Captain Nunes would demand a house to house search of the town, Montague Planke was being transferred from a rowing boat that would have sunk in a swimming pool into Namaqua Drift's tugboat which should have been scuttled a decade or more back. But the pain, damp and cold notwithstanding, he was glad to see the skipper.

But oh what a voyage! For a man not used to the oceans, for a man who gets seasick just wallowing on his belly in the shallows, such crests, such troughs are enough to cause a flutter in the stoutest heart. And when that man is in fierce pain with neither proper bedding nor a mattress to lie on, the tortures of Captain Nunes suddenly seem like paradise compared to his living hell. And when he has a companion who squats beside him and utters such platitudes as, 'This is a fine life, I'm thinking, to be sailing on the ocean waves,' or, 'Come topside, Mister Montague, quick sir, to see the leaping dolphins,' he can be forgiven for harbouring malicious thoughts not far removed from murder.

So it was that Montague Planke, a portly man, too short for his weight, lying like a foetus on some sacks in the hold, arrived at the settlement in Namaqua Drift's boat on a Thursday morning to be met by all and everyone. Even before the engines had died, the fisherfolk were clambering aboard to view the sick man. Montague Planke opened his eyes. Through small pupils not unlike a pig's, he stared up at Lady Sarah bent over him in nursely concern, and groaned loudly.

It took a month of Lady Sarah's nursing to put Montague Planke back on his feet. Once he was well enough to leave her house, he moved into the old whaler's cottage and began baking bread. He'd be up in the early morning hours, firing the oven, kneading the dough with his feet the way the ancients did, and on perfect summer mornings

the fishermen would put to sea with the warm smell of baking bread
in their nostrils. A good inducement, Montague Planke used to tell
Fagmie Jabaar, to speed their safe return. By mid-morning the women
would come for their loaves, at first standing to one side and darting
forward, like meerkats, only when he moved back from the counter, but
later, used now to his presence, laughing their shrill quick greetings,
fending off children who danced for fresh bread. Even Mondling,
who initially refused to acknowledge the newcomer although he took
his bread, came to nod cursorily at him and eventually would cough
a 'Gut morgen, Mister Planke' as he picked up a loaf and went home,
stooped like a vulture.

But baking was by no means Montague Planke's only occupation:
he was also devoted to the pursuit of diamonds. In the long, after-
customer hours, he and Fagmie Jabaar used to plan elaborate schemes,
which always came to nothing because neither of them could afford
to be freebooting merchants when their only market was protected by
Captain Sylvester Nunes.

'It's no good, Fagmie,' conceded Montague Planke, 'we're stymied,
we're sitting on millions, and we can't do a damn thing about it.'

'Oh no, Mister Montague, sir, that is taking too poor a view of life,'
Fagmie Jabaar would counter. 'In my life the goods come up when
the time is right.'

And a week later the time was right. Which caused Montague
Planke to wonder if a person's frame of mind doesn't determine what
happens to him. After all, hadn't he always been obsessed with the
diamonds of that place and, more particularly, how to market them?
Surely all the energy he put into his useless schemes wasn't just
dissipated in a glass of beer, in an evening of dreams. Surely an
arbitrary decision one day to break a habit, not to stop at Fagmie
Jabaar's for a cup of coffee before heading down to the beach, but to
go to the lagoon where he'd done no prospecting and have the coffee
on his return, a decision made on the spur of the moment as he closed
the back door, surely that was not coincidence.

To get to the lagoon he had to pass Landed-Little Marsdon's house
where Mrs Beg-rip lay lamenting her lot and her son sat at the window
of his radio shack eating jam sandwiches with tea. Montague Planke
stopped and was about to praise the brilliance of the spring weather
when the radio crackled a foreign language.

Landed-Little Marsdon jumped up with an 'Ah-ha, he's back,
that's Captain Lubentsova.'

Montague Planke walked on, wanting to sing, wanting to shout, but hardly daring to think the thought that was racing his heart with excitement. Surely, he thought, there was some higher order in the realms of chaos. Surely those random twists and turns of his life had an order of their own, an order that says the world is filled with wonderful harmonies and coincidences which are not the effects of menial causes, not the doings of hidden powers, but his own will creating himself moment by moment, event by event.

'That's the answer,' said Montague Planke, staring out across the pink lagoon sifted by flamingos, patrolled by kingfishers. As Fagmie Jabaar put it: eventually life does produce the goods.

The rest is a five-year rags to riches fairy tale of how a breathless Montague Planke run-splashed, stumbled and fell back to the village almost unable to get his words out fast enough to a soon delighted Fagmie Jabaar, of how a surprised Captain Lubentsova agreed to do a deal, of how that evening Montague Planke wheeled and dealed with two strange men, exchanged a heap of big ones for a pile of tattered notes, and agreed same time and place six weeks hence for another round of business.

So the settlement prospered. Fagmie Jabaar could once again pay Namaqua Drift to buy provisions, there was chocolate, sherbet and marmalade jam, and although Jong Jan once had to take an oar to the Brothers Kreef because they said they'd rather look for diamonds than go fishing, life didn't really change too much. It was a summer of content, of early mornings in the smell of bread, of evenings in the late light when everyone sat about the square eating mussels with cold wine and told stories of their other lives, glad now that those troubles were over. Each day was a mirror of the next; fish dried on the fences, lobsters screamed in the pots, they were happy, managing their affairs, even acquiring a little wealth in a box beneath the bed. Of everyone, Montague Planke should have known it was too good to last; he should have known that somehow the boot would be put in once again. And it was, by a thin man in a Bedford lorry who arrived with his beautiful, gentle daughter, who was to break Stevie's heart and her own into the bargain, on the day the goats mysteriously got out of the camp and went rampaging through the yards.

On a Thursday, before dawn to be exact, when Samuel, from Lady Sarah's high window, saw dust on the horizon, and Mad Minnaar, from her doorway, saw the goats had got out of their camp and were eating the last of the season's vegetables – cabbages, melons, tomatoes, just weeks from picking – the villagers woke with two cries of alarm running into their dreams. Then, and only when their shattered sleep was thrown off with the bedclothes, did the thought occur: Is this what has haunted us all along?

The first cry was Mad Minnaar's who, at the sight of the animals among her herbs and medicines, recalled the prophecies and vented a wail that stopped everyone's hearts but did nothing to stop the goats. The second, Samuel's, as he saw all he had dreaded, all everyone feared, appear as dust on the horizon wearing dark sunglasses, dressed in a captain's uniform, and the alarm broke in his throat, rather a groan than a cry, yet one people felt more deeply and caused the fishermen beyond the Head to pull up their traps still empty and row back.

Yet everyone went chasing goats because at least something could be done about them. And so they were driven from the vegetable patch, but no one could herd those stubborn, biting animals back into the camp. No, they scattered in all directions as if the devil himself now possessed them: breaking into Lady Sarah's yard to chew her peignoir, her cotton frocks, silk stockings; snatching the checked covers from Fagmie Jabaar's outside tables; taking hot bread and honey from Mondling's hand as he enjoyed an autumn breakfast in the sun; running through the houses butting children, leaving hard, black turds where women had just swept; even ransacking the church to finish off the work moths had begun in the altar cloth, then lapping up that most sacred of bread and communion wine, heads bowed in supplication, until Augustin Shoote, with biblical fury, beat them out. Still they could not be caught, and goats that just yesterday had been known as Meisie, Sonny, Lang Piel, Gruff, Billy, Blikkies and Bliksem, pets that had taken peanuts from everyone's hands, were suddenly wilder than jackals and laughing at people's fear of being kicked by a cloven hoof.

All this time the distant danger thickened, clearly, more than the whirlwinds and dust-devils that play across the flatlands in March, but no one heeded either Samuel at the high window, his face set in foreboding, or the darkening sun.

Instead, as Jong Jan, Vygie Bond, the Brothers Kreef, and Stevie-them-all, red-faced from hard rowing, splashed out of the shallows, not bothering to run up the boats, which were left to swing in the eddies, the rest shouted for ropes and nets, laughing as if this was some sort of game, a festive goat chase through the streets and yards to celebrate the equinox. Then the children, braver now at the sides of brothers and fathers, picked up the spirit and took after the goats with a vengeance, waving sticks and brooms, laughing as fathers and brothers were dodged, butted, bitten in the clumsy net-ripping maelstrom that kicked up a good dust of its own but never once, in all that fracas, diverted Samuel's eyes from the horizon.

What a time everyone had of it: a wild dance on the square that has seen other wild dances, yet nothing to equal the quick, frenzied foxtrot cha-cha of them-all and those devils. But in the end they had them back among the thornwood and cactus, hobbled and glaring with a look in their eyes that was not animal.

'See,' yelled Mad Minnaar, 'what I told you each and everyone about too much sherbet, jams and chocolate is coming true, not a word of it a lie, and believe me this is just the beginning.'

'Go tell it to the cormorants, Mad Minnaar,' Vygie Bond laughed as everyone flopped down on the beach in the shade of the boats to drink long draughts of Fagmie Jabaar's best beer, although it was still before ten. Only then, with not a heaving chest among them, did Landed-Little Marsdon remark, 'Funny how there wasn't a hole in the camp a mouse could have squeezed through, let alone a goat.'

And Vygie Bond's son said, 'No, the gate was wide open, that was how they got out, Uncle.'

Which made all of them stop and think: Who could have done it? Not one of them, and the children wouldn't dare; and then they noticed a pillar of dust had risen across the sun.

One by one they drifted back to their lives, their brief hour of happiness over, and took up where each had left off: peeling potatoes in the kitchen, darning socks on the stoep, the children listlessly playing house in the hen coop while the fishermen looked to the nets ruined by the goats and cleaned out stinking bait from the lobster traps. Although everyone was busy no one was doing anything. Fagmie Jabaar stood in the shadow of his doorway looking down the long road the captain would come; behind him at the counter Sheemina wiped the glasses that were clean already; outside Mondling still sat over his ravaged breakfast, picked his teeth, and watched Boatswain Baleen doing roof repairs for the winter.

'Dear God,' prayed Augustin Shoote at his bare altar, 'deliver us from this hour,' and in the vestibule, like a crow, Mad Minnaar breathed, 'Amen.' Through all this Montague Planke circled, having just left Lady Sarah's house where even the clocks had stopped in reverence to the silence: she in the downstairs drawing room, her best china ready for a tea she couldn't relish, Samuel upstairs at the high window, his eye become the telescope he'd kept in oiled cloths for just this day. This day, which to him could have been any day before, but became the Thursday when the goats got out, when not a breath misted the glass of lagoon or sea, and the only defect was dust inching off the horizon as the lorry got nearer.

Closer came the Bedford truck, winding its way through a desert that had no road with the sun glinting on the windscreen until, in that orange light, the potato-peeler stood anxiously at the window, the woman on the stoep left off her darning and the children, brown and snotty, gathered about their mothers' skirts. Only then did Augustin Shoote rise from his knees and in the belfry pull once, twice, a hundred times on the long rope until the bell that had sounded the watch on Beg-rip's whaler set up a cacophony that sent Mad Minnaar flapping across the scrub and brought the men up from the beach to squat in the square the way people do before an announcement. So everyone waited, as the engine strained nearer, pulled free of the desert on to the hard salt pans, accelerated to a pitch, climbed the sand dunes and rolled down, like a beetle, slowly towards them.

FOUR

8

DUST AND STINK

It is like this, my life is full of hate. Sometimes it is so hot within me I stink of it, worse than hyenas. Then beware, Captain Nunes wants arse. Try me, go on, break a curfew, see if I won't shoot. But know this, if I must I will kill. For what is a life? When you're dead no one talks about you. You are nothing. I've seen men come and go, good men who wouldn't squash snails, scum who've never had a woman straight on; and when they're gone, what's left, nothing, at least nothing that makes a difference. Ask the marabous, the saint tastes the same as the sinner. Not that I believe in saints. No life is all good, especially not that slimeball fisherboy. So why all the tears when he dies, and him a murderer, a strangler who hooks out his victim's guts? What evil is that, what devil was he breeding in my girl? Do you blame me for saying, enough, take a walk, get rid of that evil tadpole? Wouldn't any father who loved his daughter do it?

Ah-man, I loved her. Such a beautiful girl, soft, always so soft. Okay, I went further than other fathers, but all fathers think what I did. They all want to squash those new breasts under their hands, they all want to stroke the silky fur. Don't fool me, I've seen the lust in men's eyes for their girls. And why not? The ram takes his kid, so much the better for father to cover daughter than to leave her for some stinking fisherlout behind the boatshed. I could love her the way I couldn't love other women, especially her mother. Jealous bitch, first shaving the child like a nun, then burning her with cigarettes, as if that could bribe me to give her back my love. Crazy. Crazy woman. It gives me the sweats just to think of her. No, dammit. She was my girl. Always my girl. Those were my eyes, my flesh and blood, mine. She didn't need anyone else, especially a mother like you. Damn woman to come back now, gloating at me. So I am ill, so the hate has become hot rocks in my stomach. So I sweat like a roadgang. So what, bitch, the girl is mine. It is me she has loved. Oh my Frieda! Come back from that witch. You can't leave me, not now when there are fires in my stomach and such pain I could cry. Dammit, come back.

Not a sound. When I go calling for her, not a sound. Just a shack of frightened mice whimpering until I go away. Let her out, Mad Minnaar, I know she's in there. Bang bang with the gun butt on the door. Ah-man, I could bring that tin down with one kick. Thump thump with the boot.

It is like this, I hate women. They spurn me. My mother, even my own daughter, spurns me. So what! What do I care? I have been alone before. And where are those women? Huh, mother? Huh, wife? Dead. Gone. Except in my head. They always come back in my head. So, Mother, welcome again. What do you think? A nice place in this little fishing village by the sea, not a mine for a hundred miles, not a slag heap, no tuberculosis, plenty of clean air for healthy lungs. See how well your son has done to escape. Take a seat, please, don't mind the guest, if he so much as opens his mouth I'll knock every tooth out. Won't I, jackal. And enjoy it. You and that mongoose Jabaar. I fixed him. Did you see how I fixed him? Ah-man, that was good. Bruises, blood and teeth, bursting skin. I feel no pain for that coolie crying beneath my fist. It's the only way to treat your sort, not so, Planke? Hey, scumball, hey, hey, look up when your betters talk, you subversive, traitor, I'll have your balls for this, my God I'll have your balls. Yes, Mother, where was I, sorry, where were we? Ignore him, he cries for nothing, ignore him. Oh yes, how is Uncle? Still screwing the maids? Good old Uncle Hard-on. Game for anything, even a sheep. The bastard. You bastards. Good old Uncle Hard-on. What a man he was, scumball, not a snivelling heap like you. A man who scratched gold from the rock with his bare hands, a man with enough rot in his lungs to drop a horse. Not so, Mother, a man. Not a useless prick of a child. But he died. Ah, shame, he died. Don't cry, Mother, there's plenty other uncles out there. Jesus, you had them all. More uncles in a week than days in a month. What a mother. Just another shaft to mine. I tell you, sleazeball, it's all there is to women. It's all there ever was to this one here, it's all there ever was to my wife, maybe that mackerel will tell you it's all there ever was to Frieda. Ah-man, this heat.

Frieda could stop it. Her hands could put out these fires better than a jug of water. She could take away the hate with one caress. Blot out this place, this stinking hole, these people, these frights soaked in melon wine, give me peace, give me a cool valley among high mountains, rivers cold as snow, deep shadows where I could sleep. So a man dreams, a man who has known no pleasures but dreams. A man with such fires in his gut he could spew lava. And who must he thank for it? This scumball here, the snivelling Montague Planke, swamp rat, lizard, weasel. Look at him, what a polecat. Hey, dog-turd, who needs a magistrate for a skunk like you? Who needs a trial? Guilty as charged. Guilty of wasting government money, guilty of wasting government time, not to say guilty of cheating people out of their rightful property, lying, defrauding, embezzling, smuggling. You think I wouldn't do it, fruitbat, you think I wouldn't play his honour chief magistrate right here and now and sentence you to life imprisonment or death whichever's cheaper? If you think I got to take you back like it says in the book, think again, sandflea. Nobody'd give a tear to see you dead. File closed. Well done, Nunes, what a shame he didn't live to stand trial. In the city, I still have some authority you know. I have my jurisdiction. Nunes isn't all washed up at Custom's House, much as you might like to think he is. There's men in those offices who remember when I filled the jails with your sort. My name carries weight, gecko. You think I lie, you think you put the spot on me. Forget it, vole, you were small-time on my beat. You were lucky, that's all, I had a heart for you, I wanted to hear the magistrate put you away for so long you'd forget the colour of flowers. I'm all heart, fellow, I could've shot you dead, what a pleasure, but no, what do I do, all good Samaritan, all weeping Jesus, I put lead in your bum. That's the soft option, pig-face. With me it doesn't come softer. And what thanks do I get? Huh! Huh! You tell me, what thanks do I get? Ah shut-up, skink. You know nothing, let me tell you. First there's my own shame, know what I mean, at letting a barbel like you get away. Then the ridicule of my so-called friends: Hey, Nunes, whats-a matter, man, you in love with the cockroach? What a paw-paw, ever seen such a fumblefingers? Not to mention sniggers from the rank and file. That's more than anyone should get, caterpillar, but that's just the beginning. What about the supremo's tongue-lashing? You incompetent son of a mother-smelling amoeba, get your useless arse into the street before I kick it there and don't come back without that dune-rat's balls stuck in his cheeks. What about that, hey? That's a long carpet to be hauled over. But you wouldn't know about long carpets, tapeworm. You wouldn't know how a man shrinks before the supremo, how his balls get as tight as an acorn, how his rod, the very thing that makes him a man, shrivels up no bigger than a jube-jube. Oh no, you're too high and mighty for a boss's talk, too cocksure for an honest day's sweat, you'd rather go stealing good men blind than mix your hands in the pigswill work. Mister bloody smart pants. So you wouldn't know about demotion, what it does here in a man's heart, how he cringes like a beaten dog. Ah-man, earwig, what I have suffered for you, for letting you go, for not putting your brains all over the pavement.

Suffered, insect, suffered like I'm suffering now with all the coals of hell in my guts. Do you know what it took to look for you? Do you know what sort of a road that is I had to travel, seaslug? Hey, gerbil? Hey, hey, horsefly, stay awake, man, it's going to be a long night. Here, have some water. Go on, dung beetle, don't say I wouldn't share my little pleasures with a ratel. Ah-man, what's the use? You don't need water. There's no sweat on you. But I smell fear, animal, and that's good. Fear keeps you breathing, keeps me happy, when I don't smell fear, termite, I get angry. So have some water, fear dries the mouth, gives you bad breath. Like mine – hey, centipede, smell this, whoooo, perfume, huh, eau de sulphur. That's what it's like to burn, Planke, to burn with hate.

Let me tell you about this hate. Let me tell you about this long road that kindles the intestines. Know where it starts, serval, in the corridor outside the supremo's door. If you're lucky, hornbill, you're going to see that corridor, that cold, cold corridor with its echoes of typewriters and telephones, because that's where you're going to die, weevil, half in, half out the supremo's office with your brains on his carpet. Know what I mean, mothball, it was not a good place to start hunting down a cricket.

From there it's a long road, dammit, an oxwagon track through places no one's heard of, scattered here and there, so far apart a man could die from dust. You know what it's like? Don't nod your head, you can-of-worms, there's others in this room besides you. Ignore him, just listen to me. You know what they're like, these places, heat, dust, fowls, pigs, broken tractors, a kaffir digging? No hotels, empty houses and the only white man is mad. Ah-man, it's desperate out there. And killer country, macchia and stones, adders and scorpions, not a bite that won't kill you as slowly as it can. But who needs a bite, you can go crazy just being under that sky, day or night, it's too big for any man. Believe me, you can see cities out there, cities that don't look like those around here, not a chance, these are strange places with turrets and domes that melt as you look at them. Ordinary people like you and me don't live there, that's a country for lunatics, plagues and whores. Rinderpest, blackwater, syphilis, green monkey, your skin bursts in sores from them all: if you're lucky you die, otherwise you go mad or get the fires. I got the fires. I got them bad out there. I got them from hate. That's how it is, and that first hate was for my mother. Before I was even ten years old there was fires in my stomach that made me curl with the pain. When she brought in that uncle I got the fires so hot my piss steamed. Know what I mean, hate. Every woman I've had turned to hate. First they cool the fires, all lovey-dovey, real little Florence Nightingales, darling this, darling that, then, when you think it's gone out for good, whoosh they've stoked up a blaze that would melt steel. Bitches. Women bitches. I hate them. Out there in the backlands I got the fires so bad they never went out. Nor when I got here. Not once. Not even when I was all joy and light to these scumballs, not even then did the fires go out. Know why, because of that stinkbug sitting there. Yes you, frogface. You're to blame. What a weasel. Just look at him, cringing meerkat, not worth shoeleather, yet he gave me the fires so bad I thought I'd fry. Burn up. Char to a crisp. Just thinking about him was enough to make me spit lava. Now look at him. What a specimen. What a toad to get all excited about. Ah-man, aardvark, you've caused me more trouble than a life's worth. No man should do that to another, least of all an eel like you. Dammit, I said we must ignore him. That's you, tsetse fly, we can't let an otter like him distract us. Ignore him. Listen, each day I used to think about what I was going to do to him. Stuffing his balls in his cheeks was the least of it, there's a whole lot more you can do to a scumball before you cut loose his balls. Like what? Like panel-beating or the shitbath, ah-man, any cop'll tell you there's a hundred things. But that's not important. What's important is that I found him. In that whole world of broken axles and blown gaskets, I found him. The dungheap. To even think he could get away from me, Captain Nunes. Hey, civet, you should know Captain Nunes always gets his man. But what does he owe me? I'll tell you, eight years of life. Three in this guano bed; and five out there eating stones. Jesus, that's a slice of life. Measure it anyway, in towns, farms or miles of dirt, and it comes to the same thing, a goddammed big slice of life. No wonder the girl's turned a screw. Searching for a gerbil like this isn't easy. Hey, suckerfish! Hey, hey, tapeworm, you get pleasure out of giving others the run around. You miserable pangolin, just you wait till I'm through.

And look where I find him, at the ends of the earth, in a stinking cormorant's nest of a place that doesn't even have a name, that isn't even officially there. Not even a spot on the map, I mean, you tell me, who knows about this place, who's ever heard of it, who'd ever believe it existed? A cesspool, a morass, a carcass of lice. Let me tell you about this place, let me explain about a carcass of lice. It's all dust and stink, rotten as a dead seal. Know what I mean, okay on the surface but crawling with maggots under the skin. Maybe you've seen a dead seal? No? Up here you trip over them. But no matter, take it from me, it hums. But the smell's one thing, the lice're another. A whole army of them burrowing through the flesh. Put your foot on a dead seal, it crumbles in a heap of dust and stink, just like this place. One kick from my boot and look what maggots come crawling out, maggots like this slimeball. Just ask me why I don't squash him underfoot, rub him out, rub this whole place out. Go on, ask me. Ah-man, I don't know. There's not one that deserves to live. I mean, look at them: a preacher with enough booze on his breath to get you drunk at a yard, a bunch of fisherpeople so interscrewed not one of them has a hand of five fingers let alone a straight eye, that lady bitch in her négligé, taunting me with tits and bum as if I would go where her dog has been, a crone listening to voices in the sky, a stunted dwarf tuned into the dead, and this jelly fish and his salaaming sidekick up to more mischief than Lucifer. Jesus Christ, what a chickenrun. If they deserve life then I'm an angel.

Listen, I'll tell you one thing, he nearly got away with it. Oh, so nearly it gives me the shivers to think how close I was to going off on a wild goose chase through all these jackalpits. Sometimes a man doesn't know when he's staring destiny in the face. Ha, you might even say when it's just a hair's breadth away. Ha, ha. That's good, hey? That's funny. Laugh, suricate, it's the last chance you'll get. Laugh, scorpion. Louder. Louder. Let's all hear you laugh. The supremo likes playing jokes. He thinks it's very funny I'm wasting my life on this horsefly. He thinks I'm never going to escape these crowlands. But I'm coming back, supremo, with this leguaan tied over the lorry's bonnet. Then we'll see who laughs.

When I first drove in here this rabbit thought he was safe behind his beard. Beards are as good a mask as a man's got, but they're no mask to me. I knew you, Planke. I wasn't fooled. Me, I've never had a beard, even out here in these deserts I've never seen the need to stop shaving. It's the one luxury a man has who has a daughter. Dammit, man, dammit. Where's she now to shave her father's beard? Bitch. Young whore of a fisherman, spreading her thighs in the dunes, it's no wonder the house stinks of mackerel. I'll get her. It's no good hiding behind that devilwoman, Frieda. I'll get you. I'll get that crone, I'll get them all when I've finished with this snail.

You want to know when I stumbled on this squid here. Okay, it's like this. Wait, I must have water. The fires are bad, ah-man, bad. I'm burning. I've got hell inside my stomach. Let me tell you, don't ever get the fires, it's enough to make you want to go out there and drown in a cold sea. Know what I mean, it drives you crazy, so mad you can't hold your thoughts together, you want to go berserk, smash, kill. This centipede doesn't know how lucky he's been, all of them don't know how lucky they've been.

There, it's easier, now I can talk. Yes, this snake, this agama. Well, I watched everyone in the early days, to pick out the troublemakers, especially those whispering together, and there was lots of that but some, like this squirrel and his fellow traveller, did it more than others. Oh he thinks I knew nothing, but I knew everything. I knew what hours he came out of Jabaar's after hatching all his plots and schemes and conspiracies. The bedbug, the more I left the two of them alone, the more reckless they became, as if I couldn't see what poison they were spreading. Ah-man, I should've just snapped the cuffs on them and driven out, left this place to rot in its own stink. Who'd have known the difference? Nobody knew they were here in the first place. Today I'd be back in easy street with one on the supremo, I'd have my girl innocent and pure. But no it's not that simple for Captain Nunes, he's got a social conscience. You aren't going anywhere, captain, it says, until this lot's cleaned up. I ask you, what self-respecting officer can turn his back on a great crime, greater by far than these two reptiles? You got to sort it out, captain, bring some law and order to this vicetrough. Which I did. Left and right I pinned regulations on them: don't do this, don't do that, don't go here, don't go there. Stands to reason, doesn't it? People got to have regulations, laws. Only with laws do they behave right. Otherwise there's no morals. People, like this vulture here, just do what they want and that's not right.

It worked, I tell you. That stink got so faint sometimes you couldn't smell it. Just a whiff on the breeze, like a bad drain, you think you smell it then it's gone, and you're not sure. Know what I mean, maybe it's there, maybe not. Ah-man, that made me feel good. So good I smiled. Let me tell you, for a man like me smiling's a mistake. First time I smiled, Uncle walks in. I should have learned from that. I should have learned, captain, don't smile if you want to keep the fires away. But no, I smiled. The world was a beautiful place again. Okay, I thought, the holy work done, now what about these crabs? Dammit, I should have put the finger on them and gone in a cloud of dust before anyone knew better. Instead, what happens, that bitch woman, that bitch lady, temptress, wife of Satan, starts coming on stronger than a preacher at Lent.

Bitch. Woman bitch. I should have heard the figs in her voice. All sweetness one moment, sour as spleen the next. Ah-man, such evil from a woman's mouth, such honey turned to gall, such guano on a daisy. I spit on women. But who gets taken in?

So what goes on here, millipede? What black magic dances in your hearts? Ah-man, why bother to ask, there is only one thing for this scum: fire, flames to burn them all, to scorch their cancer from the earth. And I should start with this weasel, this snivelling dogfish. One gust of my dragon's breath would melt him like a candle. Whoosh. Feel that, porcupine, enough to singe the beard from your cheeks. Why should I suffer alone? Why should I burn in my guts while these jackals, these ants, run free? Huh, you! Answer me that. Where's justice, where's God's good eye turned that lets these scorpions live? I tell you there's only man's justice, only man's law and order to keep things right – are you with me? – only the gun and the rope that keeps human slime in check.

Already I've notched up the score, know what I mean, brought in law and order with the gun. Watch me, I'll teach them. Captain Nunes means business. Don't I, you miserable pangolin, whining like a beaten dog when the guns are out. What a wetneck. Never heard the bullets sing before, bushbuck?

Ah-man, that's songs, that's songs to set a man's blood rushing. And what does he do? What does this mouse-foetus do? He curls up on the jetty, hands over his head, whimpering stop it, stop it. Stop it, stop it. You skunk, you stinking polecat. Any man worth his sweat would get up and dance to a tune like that. Where's your spunk, chicken? I'll tell you where, pissed out in your pants, that's where. Ah-man, you're not worth bad breath. Like the supremo said, Nunes, he said, bring back that aardvark with his balls in his cheeks. Ha, ha, now there's a thing. Aaargh. Aaarghaeeeeeo.

Jesus. Bitch. Son of a bitch. Water, give me water. These fires. Aaargh. Aaargh. Aaeeeee-oy oh oh. Hah. Hah. Hah. I'm not going to burn, I'm not going to burn. These fires are my life, my hate. Aeeeee-oy. Huh. Huh. Hoooo, hoooo, hoooo, haaaa. You . . . you see, insect, haaa, I'm not going to burn. Captain Nunes will keep law and order. Aaargh. Law and order. Captain Nunes will keep it. Hoooo. Hoo. There, there. Now. Don't worry, my friend, Captain Nunes has a long way to go yet. He has his duty. He has to do his duty. He is doing his duty. The conspiracy is broken. There are no more secrets. This horsefly is going back to face the magistrate. Aargh. Huh huh. And this place, this place can go to hell. Hell. Tomorrow is hell. I shall burn them to the ground. All of them – the fishershacks, the church, that coven of witches, Jabaar's whorestore, this francolin's bakery, that bitch-woman's mansion, the whole lot, burn them to a heap of ashes, a black spot on the sand. Get rid of them for ever.

You think I've gone mad, huh. Hey you, my friend, and you, sheepface, you think I've gone mad, you think the fires have burnt a hole in my brain. Huh, huh, is that what you think? Forget it, I tell you. This is not madness, this is cold logic, the reasoning of a sane man. See this, my hand doesn't shake, not a tremor, not a twitch of a muscle, rock steady, the rock of law and order. No my friend and foxturd, this is not a dying man, this is aaargh, this is Captain Nunes, policeman, upholder of law and order, defender of Christian ways and God's word aaargh. Hoooo. Hoo. You laugh, creature, you laugh at my pain. Go on laugh, wet your pants, piss yourself aaeeee-oy huh huh. I will get you. With this gun I will get you. Put your brains on the carpet, the supremo's white carpet, your brains matted in the long hair of his flokati. You like that? I like that. Ah-man, life's a bitch, life's a bitch for us men. Fucked by women. Interfered with. Our business interfered with. So it comes down to this one thing, hate. Always I must hate. Hate where I am. The mine, this stinking hole, these arselands. My daughter. Hate you, my friend, I shit on you for seeing me like this. This burning, this fire in my guts. And that moth. Get out moth. Run aargh aargh aaaargh fly aeeeeeee-oy so I can huh huh hooooo swatyou aaaargh. Let me stand up. Let me

9

A TASTE OF SHERBET

I was the only person to witness the strange death of Captain Sylvester Nunes.

It happened in the early hours of the morning after the funerals of Stevie and Mondling. Only Nunes and I were in his house. He hadn't seen Frieda since she had shaved him on the stoep the previous day and, with the deaths and grief, no one could blame her for curling up in a corner of Mad Minnaar's hut. But it galled Nunes: I could see the pain and hate twisting across the muscles of his face.

The light that shone from his kitchen window was the only light in the settlement; everywhere else was as dark as the curfew. In their cottages the fisherfolk lay terrified, far too disturbed to sleep, because earlier there had been much shooting. Fagmie Jabaar, bless him, beaten as black and blue as he was, made Sheemina light a candle and say prayers for the dead, so convinced was he that I had died in the crossfire. But I hadn't. I was sitting handcuffed and manacled to a chair in Nunes's kitchen. Facing me across the table was the captain. We'd been like that for five hours, with him raging, sometimes sighing, sometimes groaning, drinking jugs of water, sweating although it was mid-winter. Never before had I seen Nunes so wild, a madman stinking of sulphur, his eyes glazed and red. Often he shouted, made to hit me, stuck the revolver barrel into my throat until I choked with fear, but most of the time I don't think he even realised I was there.

Why he wasn't elated, cock-of-the-walk, I can't say. Certainly he should have been. Hadn't he just cracked the case that had given him such a run around? Hadn't he caught the main culprit red-handed? And, to boot, hadn't he killed or at least seriously wounded some of the smugglers? The file, which he'd had to keep open for so many years, would soon be closed. All he had to do was tidy up the loose ends in the morning. But no, Captain Nunes looked like a man with nothing left to live for. And I saw my death horrible and cold on the kitchen floor.

How Nunes knew that at midnight I would be standing in the wind at the end of the jetty will forever remain a mystery. Certainly, it was too dark for him to make out any activity from his house and I was careful about shielding the light against chance eyes. Much later, Fagmie Jabaar swore blind he never told Nunes a thing, claiming that although he was tortured frightfully the captain didn't ask him a single question. Which leaves only pure coincidence. Perhaps, needled by the absence of his daughter, not to mention the absence of his chief suspect, he decided to prowl through the streets on the off-chance that I might be up to something. Maybe, too, it was a policeman's intuition.

Nothing could have been a clearer sign of the times than Nunes arresting Fagmie Jabaar at Stevie's funeral. Of course, he couldn't have chosen a worse day to do it, but such is the way of the world, one has to adapt to circumstances. So as we left the cemetery, I joined the mourners who were marching in protest at Fagmie's arrest, but skipped ranks when the crowd passed the bakery. In no time I was out again and on the path, the same one Stevie and I had taken the night before, that winds through the sand dunes down to Whale Beach. Bulging the deep pockets of my coat were the bag of diamonds, a torch and a loaf of bread for supper. Behind me I could hear the fisherfolk's slogans of protest until Nunes, using a megaphone, gave them three minutes to clear the street or he would shoot. Before the three minutes were up the curfew siren sounded although it was still two hours to sunset. After that there was an eerie silence.

Barefoot, trousers rolled up, shoes in my hand, I walked through the shallows for some three miles to a rocky outcrop. In the early days of Nunes's regime, many of the transactions had been made in the lee of those rocks with their clear vista to the settlement. If the captain set out to track me down, I would know before he'd gone a hundred yards.

It wasn't until well after nightfall that I felt safe enough to leave the rocks, a supper of fresh bread sitting heavily in my stomach, and found another refuge in the scrub near Stevie and Frieda's love nest. From there I could watch the village, although it was such a dark night that an army could have hidden in the blackness. All the same, I got the impression the streets were deserted. So, too, might have been the houses for most were in darkness: here and there a light burned, at Boatswain Baleen's, Jong Jan's, the church nave. Only Lady Sarah's house was flooded with light, and I could hear music as she, feverish, wild-eyed, held up by Samuel, waltzed among the shattered ornaments and broken furniture. Then the music stopped; one by one the huge chandeliers went out.

Not long afterwards Nunes threw Fagmie Jabaar into the street. I could see him lying there on the edge of the light that leaked from Boatswain Baleen's window. He lay without moving for what seemed like ages. Even when it began to drizzle he didn't stir. Reluctantly – after all, hadn't we pledged ourselves to a cause? – I decided to sacrifice everything and go to his help. But just as I moved, so did he, and with singing heart I watched him stagger and crawl his way to the store.

My eyes couldn't have been the only ones watching Fagmie Jabaar's progress, because the door had hardly shut on his battered body when Nunes appeared, heading towards Mad Minnaar's shack. I saw his torch flicker on the corrugated iron, heard him shout and kick at the door, threatening all kinds of dire punishments if he was not let in. No one responded. He pounded on the tin again, then moved off, passed Mondling's house down to the fisherhuts. I could see his torchlight swinging from one cottage to another, pausing at Landed-Little Marsdon's, then moving on to my bakery. He peered though every window, occasionally knocking on the glass. When he was satisfied I was either not there or hiding, he quietly let himself in. The dull glow of his torch appeared in room after room as he searched the house, not very thoroughly I later discovered. Was he expecting to find me hiding in a cupboard or under the bed? He must have known his bird couldn't have flown far, which made me decide that the time had definitely come to leave the settlement. No one expects honour among illegal diamond traders: I would flee with the smugglers. Seeing Nunes's dark shape leave the bakery and cross the road only confirmed my intentions.

With fifteen minutes left to the rendezvous, I slipped down the path behind Nunes's house, pausing, as Stevie had done, to look in at the kitchen window. Despite the cold, the captain sat in vest and shorts cleaning his revolver. Bullets lay scattered on the table, various parts were wrapped in oiled rags. He worked methodically, the way men who have a mission do. The sight filled me with apprehension; I hurried on. At Landed-Little Marsdon's window I knocked softly: two quick, two quick, pause, one.

'No change, Montague,' came the whispered reply through the closed shutters.

On the jetty, in the teeth of wind and squalls, I took the last gamble and signalled out to sea. For five minutes nothing happened. I flashed the torch briefly once more. From out of the darkness a voice said, 'Is that you, Mr Planke? Can we have another light please?'

'It's too dangerous,' I hissed back. 'The captain's still up.'

'So is the swell,' said the voice. 'We could smash against the jetty.'

'Well, this is the way you wanted it,' I reminded them irritably, 'so come on, hurry, man, hurry.'

Chancing all, I switched on the light, and there, not ten feet away, was the dinghy with the man I had come to know as Tamas standing up, money bag in hand, already reaching out for the diamonds. In they came on a swell, only to be sucked out in the trough. Again and again it happened until Tamas, in exasperation, yelled 'Throw the bag' and threw his. I watched the wind snatch it back into the darkness.

'Throw the bag,' he shouted again, 'the money will wash ashore.'

'No, no,' I replied, 'I'm coming with you.'

They were less than an arm's length away when Nunes, who must have been watching the whole fiasco from behind one of the fishing boats on the shore, came pounding up the jetty towards us.

'Give me the diamonds,' yelled the now desperate Tamas, as Nunes and I wrestled on the very edge of the boards.

I have often wondered what would have happened if Tamas, one of the swashbuckling breed who keeps a gun tucked into his belt, had not begun shooting, whether to save me from Nunes or to kill us both is an open question. Would Nunes still have done what he did?

In that rocking tide Tamas's shots went wide, but the effect on Nunes was electric. He threw me to one side and, at what was almost point-blank range, fired at the men in the boat. I saw Tamas fall and the man at the tiller clutch his head. The four oarsmen who had miraculously escaped injury bent their backs against the oars and headed for the darkness. Nunes put another clip into the magazine, and, using my torch as a spotlight, fired at the disappearing dinghy. In return came a defiant salvo of four or five shots which passed harmlessly overhead. Perhaps Tamas wasn't that badly wounded after all. Above the wind, we heard an engine wheeze into life as my last chance of escape headed out to safety. For some time Nunes stood straining into the night, until all sounds of the engine had died, then he picked up the bag of diamonds, and with a flick of the revolver, waved me before him.

Four hours later, before my eyes, Captain Nunes burst into flames and burnt fiercely for about five minutes until all that was left of him was a patch of ash from which the remains of his right leg and boot protruded.

As I remember it, Nunes had poured out a drink from a jug he had just refilled. As he put the glass down he groaned deeply and belched. From where I was sitting, a good five feet away, I could feel the heat on his breath. Then, abruptly, he stood up, toppling over the chair, and burst into a pillar of flame that reached the ceiling. Strangely, his clothes – once again he was wearing vest and shorts – caught fire only shortly before he collapsed. The fire came from within him, exploding first from his stomach, then chest, melting his head with its intensity. For perhaps a minute he stood in the middle of that inferno, one hand raised in a gesture of despair, the other uselessly clasped to his stomach, as if, when the fires had first ignited, he had tried to beat them out. Slowly he sank to the floor behind the table, his left leg buckling under him, his right sliding out to where I could see it. Within five minutes the fire was out, leaving a heap of greasy ashes, some blackened fingerbones, the leg that I could see, and an asphyxiating stench.

I screamed, as much from the horror of the burning as from the fear that the house would catch fire and I, too, would be burnt alive. Screamed and screamed. But the gale snatched away my calls for help, as earlier it had snatched the bag of money. And I should have realised that, gale or no gale, nothing, especially cries of terror, would have brought any villager out on that night. But what good is reason when someone has gone up in smoke before your eyes? Then hysteria takes charge, as it did, tipping over the chair to which I was so securely fastened and giving me a clear view across the floor to Nunes's smouldering remains.

I had many, many hours to look at those remains because it was not until late in the afternoon that Boatswain Baleen, Augustin Shoote and poor Fagmie Jabaar plucked up enough courage to find out what was going on in Nunes's house. By that time I was delirious from the horror, the stench, the exhaustion.

But as I lay there, what struck me first, with great relief, was that neither the table, nor the chair he had knocked over, nor even the floorboards, had caught fire, although they looked a little charred. And then it occurred to me that I had not felt the heat of his fire, despite being only five feet away. It was such a personal death that, apart from the scorched ceiling and floor, nothing else had been touched. Yet his fire had been hot enough to melt his bones, which, as Augustin Shoote pointed out some weeks later while he waited for Namaqua Drift's tug, was more than they could do in a crematorium.

As he finished his wine, and Fagmie Jabaar, still bandaged and aching, poured him another, he said, 'It just goes to show – you never know what the good Lord's got lined up for you.' He raised his eyes to the ceiling, then looked at me. 'One thing though, Montague, he's got a kindly eye for you and so has Fagmie here because if he hadn't persuaded us to go in I wouldn't have set foot near the captain's house for eternity.'

We laughed, but at the time it had been no laughing matter. By midday, when there was no sign that anyone was coming to my rescue and I was hoarse from shouting, despair began to weigh in heavily.

Then a strange thing happened: I heard the front door open, soft feet came down the passage and stopped in the kitchen doorway. Being partly under the table, I couldn't see who it was, but the legs were those of a woman, slender, covered in fine down, streaked with what could have been mud. Frieda's.

'Help me,' I begged hoarsely. 'Help me.'

But the legs didn't move. Frieda stood there looking at the burnt heap of her father; I lay crying tears of helplessness under the table. Softly she hummed the song she had sung in the early days when she shaved her father on the verandah. She had stopped singing ever since her love affair with Stevie, but now she hummed the tune again, or, rather, one phrase repeated over and over.

'Frieda,' I whispered. 'Please help me.'

The humming stopped.

'It's me, Montague Planke.'

The legs turned, she started humming again, then suddenly ran out of the house.

Perhaps I fainted, perhaps I fell asleep, but I next remember sunlight in the room, a shaft of late afternoon sunlight filled with Nunes's dust. With each breath I imagined those motes rushing up my nose, until all the captain's charred remains lay heavy and yellow in my lungs. The thought was enough to drive anyone delirious. Which was how Boatswain Baleen, Augustin Shoote and Fagmie Jabaar found me, hawking and coughing fit to choke.

'Ja,' said Boatswain Baleen, 'you were lucky, Montague. Though I've never heard a man talk such nonsense before or spit and spit as if he'd eaten bad fish.'

'Not a pretty sight,' agreed Augustin Shoote, and I hoped he was thinking more of the gruesome spectacle of Nunes than of me hawking and spitting.

By that time the whole village was gathered in the passageway or peering through the kitchen window. Then, much to my immense relief, Baleen bent down to see what was going on underneath the table. I spat in gobless protest but neither he, nor Augustin Shoote, nor Vygie Bond would step over Nunes's ashes; instead they broke down the kitchen door to free me. Never has brack water tasted sweeter than that I was given to rinse Nunes from my mouth.

Hours later, when I'd regained my voice, Augustin Shoote asked the question that was on everyone's lips.

'It was Frieda, wasn't it? Did she throw a lamp at him, is that how the fire started? It must have been, we all saw her come running out of the house like a woman possessed.'

'No,' I said. 'No, it was all over long before she came in.' And I told them what happened.

When I'd finished they were silent for a long time until Augustin Shoote said, 'Yes, we all make our own deaths.' And Vygie Bond, probably thinking of Stevie and the small damp parcel Mad Minnaar had given him, muttered that some shouldn't have to die. 'Nor go on living,' added Boatswain Baleen quietly, and I wondered if he meant Frieda.

From the day Frieda the Husk, as she became known, shaved her father for the last time and embroidered a tropical jungle in Mad Minnaar's quilt, she never again uttered another word. The only sound she made was to hum a tune from a nursery rhyme, which was usually a prelude to her going off to sit among the grasses on the dunes for days at a time.

Frieda the Husk never once visited the grave of her child or the man who, in happier times, would have become her husband. It was as if his death had not occurred, as if, for her, he still waited in their love nest the way he'd done every night of that brief summer. Not even when Stevie was disinterred and buried among his kinsfolk did she join the rest of the village, at last able properly to mourn the death of their son. No matter how Mad Minnaar tried to coax her to the cemetery, by offering sweet tea, the embroidered cloth, a dress of calico, Frieda the Husk would not budge from the shack. Only when she was finally left alone, when Augustin Shoote could delay the funeral no longer, did she come out and run into the dunes. As Namaqua Drift put it, she had her own service to attend.

Stevie's second funeral finally broke Jong Jan. As he hammered into the ground the new cross, on which Augustin Shoote had inscribed, 'Stevie, fisherman and father', he broke into a fit of weeping that wouldn't stop even when his heart gave up less than two hours later. The next day, when the Brothers Kreef, Vygie Bond and Boatswain Baleen placed him in a grave alongside his nephew, there were still tears in the old fisherman's eyes. And no matter how often Augustin Shoote tried to brush them dry with the hem of his gown, the tears welled up again. It is because we have never cried before, said Mad Minnaar, now we will cry for ever.

Captain Nunes wasn't buried in the cemetery, nor even on the outskirts. As Vygie Bond said, 'There mustn't be a sign that he ever lived here. We're going to drink sherbet again as if he'd never been.' So what happened to his ashes or the leg that escaped the flames is known only to the Brothers Kreef, who cleared him up.

Captain Sylvester Nunes disappeared from the minds of the fisher-folk as quickly as he'd disappeared from their world. There were no celebrations, at most perhaps some quiet prayers of thanks, but otherwise no one ever spoke of him again, or the three years of his tyranny. The nightmare was over. Captain Nunes's house, like mine and Mondling's, began succumbing, day by day, to drifting sand, his old lorry a permanent roost now for hens and geese.

Even before I left, the sand and fowls were taking over, quickly moving in where brooms had once defeated them. Sand scoured under the doors and piled in corners, windows blew in, hens nested in the cupboards. Boatswain Baleen grew morose and talked of Norway; Fagmie Jabaar looked at his empty shelves and shook his head.

'I'm telling you, Mister Montague,' he said, 'this place has had it. I'm getting out.'

But who knows if he ever did? On the day I packed my bags, all he said was, 'Where to, Mister Montague? Please tell me where to,' and went on wiping the glasses, which were clean already.

'So you're really going, Planke,' said Augustin Shoote, joining us at the café tables.

I nodded.

'Well,' he said, 'I suppose there'll be those of us who'll be following you soon enough.'

'I suppose,' said Boatswain Baleen.

Fagmie Jabaar poured another round of drinks and we drank glumly until Vygie Bond came in to say Namaqua Drift's boat had just rounded the Head.

After I left the settlement on that sad afternoon with everyone lining the jetty to wave goodbye, tears in Fagmie Jabaar's eyes, I never heard of them again. Perhaps there is still a place on that bay, blown by high winds, lost in mist; perhaps Vygie Bond and the Brothers Kreef still row out to fish beyond the Head, and each year new melons swell in the difficult gardens. No doubt sometimes there is fish and sometimes there isn't. When there isn't, life is hard, the children cry and suck seaweed for comfort. Maybe sometimes there is a faint sweetness in the air to torture Vygie Bond, and maybe sometimes Mrs Beg-rip, gone to a restless death, forces her hand out of the shallow grave in complaint. Perhaps through Lady Sarah's magnificent rooms the wind still sighs, the brocade curtains now shredded, the furniture in skeletons, where she, wearing nothing but her chewed up peignoir, dances each evening.

I still long for the settlement, for the excitement when the boats return at midday, for the nights in Jabaar's with dominoes and melon wine. But mostly I have an urge to bake bread, to knead dough, to slide into the oven my famous French loaves that the children would eat with bokoms under the screaming gulls. One day I shall go back with tinned food, pasta, tea from China, blue cheese, chocolate, nuts. Once more they will line the jetty to welcome Namaqua Drift's tug. Once more Fagmie Jabaar's shelves will groan beneath the miracles of the modern age. I can see faces pressed to the store window, waiting, the way fishermen wait on empty days, eager to know again the wonderful taste of sherbet.

A NOTE ON THE TYPE

This book was typeset using Ehrhardt, a typeface based on a design
by the Hungarian Nicholas Kis (1650–1702) who worked as a
punchcutter in Amsterdam from 1680 to 1689 at the height of the
Dutch Republic. A set of his matrices was acquired by the Ehrhardt
foundry in Leipzig, hence the name adopted when the modern face
was cut.
The type has all the sturdy Dutch character of the *Gôut Hollandais*,
the characteristic type-style of the latter part of the seventeenth
century. The relatively narrow, densely black letters also show the
influence of German Black Letter type.